*Advance Praise* for Whiskey Snow:

"I just ordered Apology Accepted, and can't wait for Whiskey Snow! Faith Wood, I love your books, and I'm simply riveted by every paragraph and page—I actually don't enjoy ANY other fiction books, or authors!!!"

—RONI-LIL SHAPKA

"Love, love, love this book! Wood is a master of dialogue!"

—KATHY JACKSON

"Whiskey Snow is a fantastic read from cover to cover! Each book in the Colbie Colleen series doesn't leave readers feeling disappointed. There's a new mystery writer in town, and her name is Faith Wood! Good stuff!"

—TANYA MARSHALL

"I'm pretty picky about my mysteries, so when I find a new author who checks all of my boxes for a good read, I'm a happy camper. Wood checks all of the boxes! I'm a happy camper!"

—MARTIN ASHFORD

"What can I say? I absolutely love Wood's new book—couldn't put it down!"

—BETSY DAVIS

# BOOKS BY FAITH WOOD

*Life Under the Limbo Bar*

*Fundraising on a Shoestring*

*Taking the Bully by the Horns*

*The Graduating Bully*

*the Accidental Audience*
*a Colbie Colleen suspense fiction novel—Mystery 1*

*Chasing Rhinos*
*a Colbie Colleen suspense fiction novel—Mystery 2*

*Apology Accepted*
*a Colbie Colleen suspense fiction novel—Mystery 3*

# WHISKEY SNOW

# WHISKEY SNOW

FAITH WOOD

Double Your Faith Productions
Vernon, British Columbia, Canada

# DEDICATION

*For our grandmothers, and the trails they blazed for us.*
*They suffered. Sacrificed. Succeeded.*

*I will always be grateful.*

# CHAPTER ONE

**66** How long are we going to be gone?" It wasn't that Brian really cared, but he preferred to put a time frame on things, so he would know what to expect—it was an idiosyncrasy he displayed for years.

Colbie stopped loading the dishwasher, stripped off her rubber gloves, then leaned against the counter. "Does it make a difference?"

"Not really—just thought I'd ask . . ."

"Well, I wish I knew, but I can't imagine we'll be gone more than a couple of weeks. Besides, this trip isn't a normal gig—it's for family, so who knows?"

"Did your mom give you any idea of what to expect?"

"No—all I know is Uncle Harry got himself into a spec of

trouble, and she asked me to help. From what I understand, he's feuding with some of the ranchers in the area, and tempers are running hot . . ."

Brian's expression said it all. "I still don't see how you can help—you're a profiler, not a lawyer. From what you told me right after your mom called, it sounds as if this is one for the authorities . . ."

"I agree—that's what I think. But—how could I turn her down? She adores Harry and Evelyn, and for her to think he needs to notch his temper down to a simmer, well . . ."

"Those were good cookies . . ." Brian commented as he crammed his milk glass on the top rack. "I get it . . . there's not much you can do until you get there. Speaking of which—when do we leave?"

"Tomorrow afternoon—we should get into Gillette no later than seven." After one final glance at the counter and table, Colbie closed the dishwasher, ramping it up for a full wash. "My aunt is going to meet us at the airport . . ."

The truth was she wasn't looking forward to the trip. It had been years since she even breathed her family's names, and the last time she saw her aunt Evelyn? She couldn't have been older than fifteen or sixteen. Harry? Not since her early twenties. Even so, her family probably knew less about her than she knew of them—and, she preferred to keep it that way. From what her mom told her, ranch life in and around Sundance, Wyoming, was a far cry from her life in the city. People took care of themselves and, if someone got in the way?

They took care of that, too.

\*\*\*\*

Brian grinned at Colbie as he shoved his carry-on in the overhead compartment. "You didn't tell me we had to take a puddle jumper!"

Colbie laughed as she slid into her seat by the window. "You have to remember—this is Wyoming we're talking about. Gillette isn't exactly the urban capital of the state . . ."

"True—I'm assuming we can rent a car there . . ."

"We can—it's not that tiny!"

By the time they taxied the runway, Brian was well on his way to a quick snooze. Colbie, however, wasn't so lucky—all she could think about was meeting a family she barely knew. Growing up, conversations with those outside of her immediate nest were saved for birthdays and holidays—and, the occasional funeral. But, from the time she turned eighteen, familial conversations plummeted to zero, and she never gave keeping up with Aunt Evelyn and Uncle Harry a second thought. *What will they think of me—what I do for a living?* It seemed to Colbie an intuitive behavioral profiler might not be something they could take seriously. After all, from what her mom told her over the years about her aunt and uncle, they didn't seem to be the types who would welcome such a career with open arms.

Colbie glanced at Brian, his head propped against the airplane's window. *What about you, Brian? Do they know about your kidnapping?* Recounting their lives for the past several years didn't appeal to her, and she hoped the subject wouldn't come up.

But, she knew it would.

The flight was quick—time zones shifted and, an hour and fifteen minutes later, they were on the ground, Colbie thinking she recognized her aunt standing at the gate. The only thing she really remembered about Evelyn was her curly, red hair, and the person waving at the plane filled that bill. She was slender and petite like Colbie, and Colbie could have sworn she saw a bit of her mother in her.

"Hey! Wake up! We're here . . ."

Brian opened one eye. "Already?"

Colbie grinned as she stepped into the aisle. "Yep!" She glanced out the window. "We should hurry—it looks like snow . . ."

"Do we ever go anywhere in the summer? No. Always winter . . ."

"Or, the threshold of winter . . ."

They laughed as they grabbed their bags, and headed for the exit. "If we play our cards right," Colbie added, "we can be back on the coast by Thanksgiving . . ."

Minutes later, Aunt Evelyn wrapped her arms around her niece, exclaiming how much she looked like Colbie's mother. "You're the spittin' image!"

By the time they made it to baggage claim, introductions were complete, and Brian was already starting to feel at home. "I've always had a bit of cowboy in me," he told Evelyn as they split up so Colbie and he could rent a car. After promising it wouldn't take long, they agreed to meet her in the parking lot so she could lead the way to the ranch. "If you don't know where you're going," she told them, "it's easy to get lost . . ."

She was right. Brian was pretty good at directions, but he had to admit he was glad Evelyn was in the lead—within the half hour, their two cars pulled through the ranch gate, Evelyn honking as she pulled up to the house.

"Holy cow! Look at this place!" Brian's jaw dropped as he scanned the ranch house, and several, well-lit, nearby outbuildings. "I didn't picture this!"

As he parked, a salt and pepper haired man stood on the porch, waving. "That's Uncle Harry!" Colbie waved back and, when she and Brian reached the porch, he scooped her up in a big, western-welcoming bear hug.

"If I didn't know better, I'd think you were your mother!"

Colbie laughed, allowing him to enjoy the moment. "Really, Uncle Harry? I'll take that as a compliment!"

"It was meant to be one." He greeted and shook hands with Brian, then led them up the steps. "Now, we need to get something in your bellies . . ." He looked Colbie up and down. "You're as scrawny as your mother when she was your age!"

"Show them the kitchen, Harry—they can raid the fridge to their heart's content . . ." Evelyn motioned for Colbie and Brian to follow her husband.

Brian slid his arm around her shoulder, giving her a quick, one-armed hug. "Sounds good to me! I'm famished!"

Harry's and Evelyn's house was the epitome of a western lodge. Yes, they had modern conveniences, but much of their lifestyle included the old ways—a vintage wood-burning stove still served to prepare meals for ranch hands, and a massive fireplace in the kitchen was it's main heat source. A great room included a moss-rock fireplace, as well as well-worn leather chairs placed just so for day dreaming.

"This place is magnificent!" Brian squeezed Colbie's hand as Evelyn took them on the grand tour, then ended up back in the kitchen. "You can pull up your chairs in front of the fireplace," she suggested as she rummaged through a full refrigerator. "I told Harry earlier this afternoon I think we're in for a winter storm . . ." She paused as she unwrapped a package of sliced roasted beef, placing it on the counter. "He doesn't agree, but I think it's going to turn out to be a whiskey snow . . ." Again, she paused. "It's chilly out—hot chocolate?"

Colbie and Brian nodded in unison. "Sounds great!"

"What's a whiskey snow," Brian asked.

Evelyn chuckled, placing all condiments necessary for the perfect sandwich next to the package of beef, then tackled the homemade hot chocolate. "I forget you don't see much snow in your neck of the woods! A 'whiskey snow' is when we lose our electricity during a blizzard, and we have to make do until the boys from Gillette get out here to fix it—that can take days!"

"I still don't get why it's called 'whiskey snow' . . ." Brian glanced at Colbie for confirmation of confusion.

"Because my grandfather said in order to make it through, you need a jug of whiskey at the ready. So, every time there was a blizzard or heavy snow, he called it a 'whiskey snow' . . ."

Brian grinned at Colbie, as though thrilled by Evelyn's story. "We'd never have enough snow to warrant a full jug," he laughed as Evelyn handed him a steaming cup of creamy hot chocolate.

"What makes you think this will be a whiskey snow?" Colbie accepted her mug as Evelyn took a seat beside Brian.

"I can feel it—snow clouds are different from rain clouds, and I noticed today the livestock is drifting with the storm. They only do that whenever there's going to be one hell of a blizzard . . ."

As Colbie listened to her aunt, symbols formed at the forefront of her intuitive mind. Nothing major, with the exception of her vision of a young girl pitching hay in a ramshackle barn. Red-haired with freckles peppering her face, the girl stopped as if listening to something—or, someone.

Then, it was gone.

She rejoined the conversation just as Brian noticed an old-fashioned telephone mounted on the wall—of course, it didn't work, but he was sure it did long ago. "Nice phone . . ."

Evelyn glanced at it, then focused on her new house guest. "Believe it or not, that phone has been on the ranch for decades—my great-grandfather Hedwin didn't want anything to do with it, but my his wife insisted. 'New fangled doesn't get the job done,' he said, fully aware he was going to lose his argument. A few weeks later, the phone claimed its rightful spot on the wall by the kitchen door leading to the great room!"

Colbie watched Brian carefully as he listened to Evelyn tell stories about times long passed, knowing she was witnessing something she hadn't seen before. There was a spark—a fire—that played on his face like a kid at Christmas.

\*\*\*\*

Colbie lay in bed, rewinding the day's events. Earlier, Harry popped his head in the kitchen to say goodnight, backing up his wife's prognostication for a blizzard. "Get ready," he warned. "We're in for a big one!" He briefly explained he and the ranch hands would be up before dawn to start on chores, then disappeared to the west wing of the house. Shortly after, everyone drifted toward their respective bedrooms, ready for a well-deserved night's rest.

Except Colbie couldn't sleep.

She tried tapping into her intuitive senses, but there was nothing except a fleeting memory of a young girl with red hair. Colbie had no idea who she was, but she had a strong feeling she should know. The red hair alone indicated she may be a relative, but there was no way to know for sure unless Evelyn could fill in the gaps. *I'll ask her about it in the morning . . .*

Just before midnight, her thoughts drifted as a slicing, sideways snow slapped at the window, backed by gusts of forceful, wailing wind. *Evelyn was right,* she thought as she listened to nature's fury, considering whether she possessed the wherewithal to live such a back-to-the-roots lifestyle. She doubted it. Even though she spent her summers camping with her parents when she was growing up, she never truly experienced anything like Evelyn's and Harry's way of life. And, although it was dark when they arrived, she imagined the expanse of the Wyoming high prairie. Evelyn mentioned their ranch was more than fifteen thousand acres, and that fact alone was enough to make Colbie crave a quick return to the city. *Tomorrow,* she planned, *I'll get the low down on why I'm here—and why, exactly, Harry needs me . . .*

Finally, a restless sleep.

****

Shortly after eight the following morning, they arrived in the kitchen as Evelyn was finishing breakfast dishes. Harry and the ranch hands left long before sunup in an effort to make as much progress as possible before whipping winds and stinging snow made visbility impossible.

"In case you didn't notice, we're on 'natural light'—oil lamps and fireplaces, too."

"No problem—we're the hearty types!" Colbie watched as her aunt glanced out the window, a look of concern on her face.

"I worry when there's weather like this," Evelyn confessed. "Of course, we plan for it, but, once it's here, it's always worse than we thought . . ." She handed her guests mugs of coffee, and gestured toward the fireplace. "Make yourselves at home . . ."

"I take it this is a whiskey snow," Brian commented as he stared out the window, looking toward the barely visible barns.

"Indeed, it is!"

"How long will they be out?" Colbie noticed Evelyn's concern wedge itself a little deeper as she and Brian chose two chairs directly in front of the fire.

"The lights? No telling . . ." Evelyn hesitated. "But, we have other things to talk about! I suppose you're wondering how you managed to get yourselves into a mess like this . . ." She gestured toward the window, then joined them.

"Well, I confess I'm not sure why we're here—all Mom

told me was Harry was in a troubling situation, and he might be able to use my expertise."

"And," Brian interjected, "Colbie would never consider leaving family to fend for themselves if there's some way she can help . . ."

Colbie shot him an appreciative glance. "That's true—so here we are!" She paused, noticing Evelyn's expression shift from worry to a slight sadness. "So—why don't you start at the beginning . . ."

Evelyn sighed deeply, collecting her thoughts. "About three weeks ago, the sheriff showed up to talk to Harry . . ."

Colbie straightened a little in her chair. "What did he want? Talk about what?"

Evelyn paused, as if trying to find her words. "He thinks Harry knows something about a murder . . ."

"A murder? Whose?"

"Do you have a pen and paper," Brian interrupted as he realized the seriousness of the conversation.

"Over there . . ." Evelyn pointed to a small desk tucked in a corner by the window, then waited until he was again comfortably situated in his chair. "Ready?"

Brian nodded. "Shoot—I'll try to keep up!"

Colbie took the lead. "Okay—who was murdered, and why on earth does the sheriff think Harry knows something about it?"

Evelyn placed her cup on a side table. "I'm surprised you didn't hear about it—it made national news."

Brian scribbled something on his pad. "How long ago?"

"A couple of months—two young men were found murdered, their bodies miles apart."

"Two? That's kind of unusual—were the bodies found at the same time?" Colbie began to think things were more convoluted than she previously thought. Never did she consider a trip to Wyoming may place her squarely in the middle of a murder, let alone two.

"Within a day or two of each other—the sheriff thinks the murders are related."

"Why does he think that?"

"Because the boys were brothers . . ."

Again, Brian scribbled something, then focused on Evelyn. "How old were they?"

"Mid-thirties . . . rumor has it there was a family disagreement about who should get their ranch. The patriarch passed last year and, from what I hear, several family members want to sell. The boys, however, wanted to explore the ranch's natural resources."

"Such as?"

"The usual—oil, gas, or anything else they can find."

Colbie detected a shift in Evelyn's tone as she thought about the situation. "I take it you don't approve of the boys' idea . . ."

"No—and, neither does Harry. When he heard about it, he went ballistic!"

"Why? If the family goes the natural resources route, why do you care?"

"Because of the disruption it would cause to our land—

Harry says they don't have any right to impact our livelihood like that. But, due to the brothers' murders, that idea is probably dead in the water . . ."

Colbie sat for a moment, considering possibilities of Harry's involvment. "Even if it is, I still don't understand why the authorities think Harry might know something . . ."

Evelyn looked at Colbie, her eyes filling with tears. "Because Harry threatened to kill them . . ."

Colbie refused to show her surprise. "When? What did he say?"

"Oh, good heavens! It was nothing more than Harry running off at the mouth . . ."

Colbie shook her head. "That may be, but the sheriff appears to be taking him seriously . . . do you know what he said, exactly?"

Evelyn nodded. "I was there—he said if they moved ahead with their plan, he'd make sure it would be the last thing they do."

"That doesn't mean he'd kill them . . ."

"Perhaps—but, that's what he meant, and it was pretty clear. At least to me . . ."

"Did anyone other than you hear Harry threaten them?"

"No—it was just me, Harry, and the brothers."

Colbie sat silently for a moment. "If there were only the four of you involved in the conversation, how did the sheriff find out Harry threatened them?"

"Well, now, that's the question, isn't it? I imagine the brothers told someone—probably their family—and, they told the sheriff."

Again, Colbie sat quietly, thinking. "You're probably right about that . . ." She turned to Brian. "First, we need to research everything written or reported about the murders. Second, as soon as we can get into Gillette, I want to check out the courthouse for everything in public records."

"Check . . ."

She returned her attention to Evelyn. "I don't know what it is, but there's something about this that doesn't seem right . . ."

The three of them sat in silence until Colbie figured it was time. "Evelyn—do you know what I do for a living?"

"Not really—your mom just said you might be able to help. I figured she said that because you used to be a cop . . ."

Colbie nodded. "That's true—but, what I do now is different . . ."

"And, what is that?"

Colbie took the last sip of her coffee. "I'm a psychic, behavioral profiler . . ."

Silence.

# CHAPTER TWO

Four days after the blizzard, county roads were finally plowed, and life on the ranch returned to normal. By midmorning on Friday, armed with Evelyn's directions, Colbie and Brian set off for the county library and courthouse in Gillette—but, what should have been a thirty-minute trip turned into an hour as they found themselves behind a snowplow.

"I'd hate that job," Brian commented as he watched the driver attempt to maneuver the plow against a massive snow drift. "It's only twenty-eight degrees . . . if the heater goes out, he's sunk!"

Colbie laughed, playfully slapping him on the arm with her glove. "I don't think it's that dire!"

"Still—anyway, what do you think about Harry's involvement with the two murders? Does he strike you as that type of guy?"

"No! That's the thing—Harry might have threatened them, but . . ."

"If you believe Evelyn, he did threaten them . . ."

"Okay—even though Uncle Harry threatened them, I don't believe for a second he had anything to do with it."

"It makes me wonder who else is on the suspect list, if anyone."

"Same here—are they looking at others, or is the sheriff honing in on Harry?"

Both were silent for the next several miles. When Colbie accepted the invitation to visit Wyoming, neither she nor Brian thought the situation would involve the law. "Harry could be in serious trouble," Colbie commented. "It's up to us to find out as much as we can . . ."

Brian nodded as he turned in the direction of the center of town. "Let's stick together—where do you want to go first?"

Colbie thought for a moment as she pulled on her gloves. "Let's see what we can find out at the library—they'll have a comprehensive history of the area, and we should be able to trace the history of the murdered boys' land. My family's land, too . . ."

"How about if I research the ranch adjacent to Harry's and Evelyn's while you find out what you can about your family?"

"Perfect!"

****

There wasn't a person in the county who didn't know the Beeman's lived their lives according to their own rules. Set foot on their property? A shotgun ruled the conversation. So, when both brothers turned up dead, the family promised whoever did it shouldn't live to see another day.

They'd see to it.

That was right after they heard about the boys' untimely demise. A few days later, however, remaining family members began to wonder if their passing were a blessing. "Now," their mother whispered to her husband at the wake, "we can sell this God-forsaken place, and be done with it!" The problem was Grandma Hattie overheard, quickly promising she'd never disgrace the name of her ancestors by selling. Besides, her great-grandsons wanted to keep the ranch in the family, as did her husband. The conflict, though, was turning out to be a fight she might not win—with three funerals in a year's time, she was losing her desire to wage battle with those younger than she. But, why should she sell? She was sitting on one of the most prime pieces of property in eastern Wyoming. Slightly larger than Harry's ranch, there was little doubt as to the land's viability when it came to natural resources—a situation she always considered money in the bank.

No, Hattie Beeman—so named after her grandmother—wasn't about to sell.

Ever.

\*\*\*\*

"Call my attorney—and, Colbie!"

"Watch it," the sheriff warned as he protected Harry's head with his hand, then closed the car door.

Evelyn stood at the base of the porch steps, tears streaming. She waved and nodded emphatically, letting Harry know she heard him. "I'll call right now!"

He didn't hear.

Within moments he was gone, the sheriff's SUV plowing through remnants of deep snow. Evelyn hightailed it to the landline in the kitchen, quickly leafing through their address book for Andy Herlein's number—he represented Harry for the last thirty years, but not for something so serious. A murder charge? It seemed impossible—until Evelyn realized she was standing in their kitchen alone, and she didn't know if Harry would ever be home for dinner.

She dialed. "Andy—it's Evelyn . . ."

Twenty minutes later she hung up with the assurance Andy would bail Harry out as soon as he could. Unfortunately, it was late on Friday afternoon, and Andy couldn't make any promises—chances were good Harry would enjoy the hospitality of the county jail at least until Monday morning.

Next—Colbie.

Evelyn lucked out—Colbie had just turned her cell back on as she and Brian left the library. "Colbie?"

Instantly, Colbie was aware something was wrong.

"Evelyn? What happened?"

A soft sob. "The sheriff arrested Harry!"

"Arrested? When?" She glanced at Brian.

"About thirty minutes ago—I called his lawyer as soon as they pulled away . . ."

"Good! You did the right thing . . . did the sheriff tell him the charge?"

Colbie waited while Evelyn blew her nose. "First degree murder!"

"What? Are you sure?" Colbie couldn't believe what she was hearing! If the Beeman brothers' murders were only two months ago, was that enough time to bring a case against Harry? Colbie doubted it.

"I'm sure . . . Andy said he'll get Harry out on bail as soon as he can, but that might not be until Monday morning!" Another sob caught in Evelyn's throat.

Colbie thought for a minute, certain there was nothing she could do. "It's late—I can't do anything until there's an arraignment hearing. That's when Harry will be formally charged, and his attorney may be able to post bond."

"What do you mean 'may?'"

"The judge may decide because of the seriousness of the charge, there will be no bail . . ."

"What?"

Colbie hated hearing the anguish in her aunt's voice. "I know—the situation sucks. Let's hope the judge grants Harry bail, and he can be out at the beginning of the week . . ."

"What if he doesn't?"

"Well . . . we'll deal with it." Colbie glanced at Brian, motioning for him to start the car. "We'll be back within the hour . . ."

"Hurry, Colbie. Please, hurry . . ."

\*\*\*\*

Amanda Beeman could care less what her sons wanted. The fact her greatest opposition—her grandfather and the boys—croaked within months of each other placed her in a strong position, and there was only one person standing in her way. *I know I can convince Gram to sell*, she thought as she stood on the veranda's porch, coffee and cigarette in hand.

But, she also realized it wasn't going to be that easy. Hattie Pearl Beeman possessed a fierce loyalty to her ancestors, and her mother—Hattie Mildrid Beeman—told her land was the only thing of any value. "Hattie Pearl," she said when her daughter was fifteen years old, "if you have land, you'll always have a place to hang your hat—and, it will be your home . . ."

It was a story Hattie Pearl didn't hesitate to tell every time she got a chance, and Amanda tired of it by the time she reached eighteen. Land meant nothing to her—it didn't translate into cash on a daily basis and, unless the ranch were sold to a development company, she'd never see a dime until she was too old to enjoy it.

It also meant nothing to her that she grew up there— seventeen thousand acres to explore when she was ten was great. But, now? Not so much. She couldn't remember the last time she traveled the perimeter of their property— maybe thirty years ago in the back of her granddaddy's truck as he checked the fence line. The way Amanda saw it, she had no reason to take part in any of the ranch chores, and she didn't hesitate to let her grandmother and grandfather know it. Incorrigible since she could walk, Hattie Pearl and her husband tried their best to make her mind, but Amanda would have no part of it. She defied them at every turn, certain she would eventually get her way.

She did.

\*\*\*\*

"So, let's compare notes—what did you find out about the Beeman ranch? Anything we can use?" Colbie plucked off her gloves, placing her hands in front of the heater vents on the dashboard.

"Well—I want to go over my notes, but I couldn't put my finger on anything that would be an eventual cause for murder . . ."

"Neither did I—although I got caught up in my family's story, so I wasn't making the best use of my research time."

Brian glanced at her, and smiled. "Was that weird? Reading about your family, I mean . . ."

"In a way, it really was—there wasn't much information before Hedwin."

"He's your great-grandfather—right?"

"Yep—from what I read he was in trouble with the law from the time he was old enough to drink. Not only that, I gathered from old newspaper clippings he wasn't the nicest guy around . . ."

"In what way?"

"You're never going to believe this—it seems great-grandpa Hedwin threatened to kill anyone who set foot on his property. He did, too, but the judge considered it trespassing, and Hedwin was as free as a bird. Nothing came of it except a tiny piece in a two-bit paper . . ."

For the next half hour, Colbie and Brian discussed their library research, making plans to visit the courthouse the following day. Their main concern, however, was her aunt—Colbie wondered if Evelyn were more fragile than originally thought. By her call, the thought of her husband's being in jail seemed more than she could tolerate.

It was something she never thought possible.

\*\*\*\*

"I don't know, Harry—after a quick glance at the paperwork, I think you deserve an experienced defense attorney. You know that's not me—I'm strictly a real estate guy with a few additional skills thrown in . . ."

Harry sat silently, listening to his lawyer cough up reasons why he couldn't represent him—all of it bull in his mind. "But, you know me better than anyone," he rebutted. "That's gotta count for something . . ."

"Unfortunately, knowing you is a detriment. Do I know you're innocent? Of course, I do—but, I think that's based on blind allegiance. You need someone who doesn't know you— someone who can view your case with unbiased eyes." Andy Herlein paused, eyeing his friend. "Think about it, Harry— you know I'm right . . ."

"If not you, then who?"

"Well—I've been thinking about that. I took the liberty of contacting an old friend of mine—he's the best in the business."

Harry nodded. "Okay—I get it. And, you're right—as much as I hate to admit it, I'm in a crapload of trouble. I assume your friend said he'd take a look at my case?"

"He did—his name is Jeremiah Hastings . . ."

Harry's right eyebrow arched as it always did when something caught him by surprise. "Hastings? From Laramie?"

"One and the same—I take it his reputation precedes

him?"

"Not really—I just remember hearing about a case he defended about five years ago. He won, if I recall correctly."

"Anyway," Andy continued, "I told him I'd make certain you were represented at the arraignment hearing—and, I told Evelyn I'd work on getting you out."

Harry glanced around the barren visitors' room. "This place sucks . . . when will Hastings get in touch with me?"

"I'm not sure, but it will probably be within the next couple of days. I know he's wrapping up a case . . ."

Harry fell silent for a few moments as he thought about the enormity of his situation. "I appreciate your help, Andy— now get me the hell out of here!"

\*\*\*\*

Evelyn saw headlights in the driveway shortly after six. "Thank God! They're here!"

Colbie and Brian sat at the kitchen table, quickly glancing at each other. "Do you want us to make ourselves scarce," Colbie asked, watching Evelyn wipe her hands on her apron.

"Good heavens, no! Don't be silly! Besides, I'm guessing Harry will want to have a bite to eat, then sink into bed. He probably didn't get much sleep over the weekend . . ." Then she was off to greet her husband at the front door.

"I don't want to press him," Colbie commented to Brian, "but, in order for us to do the best job for her, we need to talk to him as soon as possible."

Brian nodded. "Agreed—I think, though, Harry knows we're here to help, and I get the feeling he'll want to fill you in quickly."

"I hope so . . ."

Before Colbie could finish her thought, Harry strode through the kitchen door. "Glad you're here," he commented as he kissed Colbie on top of her head. "I'm going to need all the help I can get . . ."

Colbie stood to give her uncle a hug. "We wouldn't be anywhere else!"

"I second that," Brian added as he extended his hand.

"Well, that's good—I suppose, too, we need to have a serious talk about what happened . . ."

Colbie nodded. "Indeed, we do—Evelyn told us a little, including your threatening the Beeman boys, but there has to be a lot more to it . . ."

Harry sighed, taking a seat at the table across from Brian. "There is—and, I gotta tell you . . ." He paused, his voice catching slightly. It was clear he wasn't comfortable with something and, until he was, Colbie and Brian would remain in the dark.

"Tell us what," Colbie prompted.

Her uncle took Evelyn's hand in his. "It scares the hell out of me . . ."

# CHAPTER THREE

"That's it?" Jeremiah Hastings picked up the manila folder, leafing through the few notes his paralegal took when speaking to Andy Herlein about Harry's case. "It doesn't give us much to go on . . ."

"True—Andy didn't have a lot of information to give, but he was insistent his friend and client is innocent." She paused, then pointed to her notes. "He mentioned his niece and her partner are visiting from the West Coast, and they're available to give us any help, if needed."

Hastings tapped the sticky note with his index finger as he muttered Colbie's name. "Colbie Colleen—where have I heard that name before?" His forehead scrunched as he tried to recall.

His assistant grinned, handing him an eight by ten copied picture of the stunning redhead. "She's only one of the top behavioral profilers worldwide . . ."

"That's it! She was profiled in a trade magazine—something about her cracking an art theft case in London."

"And, Cape Town—it was quite the story of intrigue!" Liz Carpenter recognized the look on her boss's face. "You're going to take the case, aren't you?"

"Well—I can't very well say no. Andy and I have been friends for years, and he's never come to me with a client before. That tells me . . ." he paused as he looked at Liz's notes. " . . . Harry Fenamore must be in a heap of trouble." He took a seat in front of Liz's desk. "So—what else do you know?"

"Like I said—not much. The charge is first-degree murder, and I already requested the paperwork. When I spoke with the county clerk in Gillette this morning, she told me who's prosecuting . . ."

"Anyone we know?"

"Nope—she said he's a new guy. A young gun . . ."

Hastings grinned. "That could be good for us! Name?"

"Marshall Sage . . ."

Hastings turned the name on his tongue a few times. "Alright, Mr. Marshall Sage—game on!" He checked Liz's notes one more time. "Schedule me as out of the office for the rest of the week—I haven't been to Gillette for a few years. I think it's about time, don't you?"

"Since you just settled the Griffin case, I knew you'd say that—I put a copy of the file on your desk. Good thing you settled—you're free until next Monday."

Hastings stood, and headed for the door. "You know

where I'll be—let's keep in touch . . ."

\*\*\*\*

In the firelight, Harry's face showed crevices of worry, each line deepening as the realization of his murder one charge hit home. Until recently, the Beeman boys had little impact on his life, and he preferred it that way. *Nothing but ungrateful punks*, he thought as he recounted every moment with them. Every argument. Every time they defied him to his face. He considered them insufferable, but was that reason enough to kill them? As nice as the thought was, he wasn't so off the beam that he would risk his life for one moment of pure gratification. *They weren't worth it . . .*

He looked up as Colbie and Brian made themselves comfortable in front of the great room's moss-rock fireplace. "Where's Evelyn? I know she'll want to be in on this . . ."

Colbie nodded. "She's feeding the dogs—she said she'd be here in a minute . . ."

"Good . . ." Harry grew quiet again, as though he were trying to figure out what he was going to say.

Within a few minutes, the Fenamore's and their guests settled in for Harry's side of the story. Colbie knew better than to take everything Harry would say for gospel truth, but she didn't doubt he would believe every word. "So," she began, "let's take it from the beginning." She focused on Harry. "How far back does your dislike of the Beemans go?"

Harry mustered a faint smile. "From the day I set foot on this property, forty years ago. I'll never forget it—I needed help with one of my balers, and I heard Old Man Beeman was one of the best mechanics around . . ."

"And?"

"So, I headed over his way . . ."

Colbie glanced at Brian, then at Evelyn. "What happened?"

"Beeman slammed his way out of the ranch house screen door, shotgun pointed right at me. 'Get off my property,' he screamed as I got out of my truck." Harry paused, focusing on that day. "You remember that, don't you, Honey?"

Evelyn nodded. "You were as white as a sheet when you got home . . ."

"I don't mind tellin' you—that man was a stark-raving nut!"

Colbie again focused on Harry. "He died recently, didn't he?"

"About a year ago—and, there was some suspicion around his death, but it didn't last for long. As neighbors, Evelyn and I attended his funeral, but we weren't particularly welcomed."

"What were the suspicions surrounding his passing?"

"Well, it's no secret his great-grandsons had a screw loose—they took after the old man, and I can't think of anyone who considered them friends. Rumors circulated among the ranchers that the boys decided they didn't want to wait for their inheritance, and they took matters into their own hands. And, it's no secret they wanted to drill on their property. Now, whether it's true or not, I don't know—but, I wouldn't put it past them . . ."

"Even if it is true, that situation doesn't have anything to do with you. I need to know why the sheriff thinks you're the murderer—he has to have something on you."

Harry glanced at Evelyn. "He does—he heard me threaten the Beeman boys at the Roundup."

"What's the Roundup?

Evelyn answered immediately. "It's a cowboy bar in Gillette." Then she focused on her husband. "You threatened them more than once?" Evelyn's voice shook on a shrill edge as she began to realize getting Harry out of the current mess wouldn't be that easy. "How many times, Harry? How many damned times did you open your mouth against the Beemans?"

Colbie wondered the same thing. It was one thing to threaten someone once—but, more than that? *No wonder the sheriff has him on his radar,* she thought as she listened to Evelyn reach the edge of losing her cool. "What did you tell the sheriff when he picked you up last Friday?"

"Nothing—not a damned thing. I lawyered up as fast as the words could come out of my mouth . . ."

Colbie nodded. "Good—and, while we're talking about it, is your lawyer the one who arranged your bail?"

"Andy Herlein? Unfortunately, no—I asked him, but he thinks he's not qualified . . ."

"Did he refer anyone?"

"Yep—Jeremiah Hastings out of Laramie. He's supposed to be one of the best in the country . . ."

"I've heard of him—has he contacted you yet?"

"Nope . . ."

"He will . . ." Colbie's confidence in Harry's attorney was sparked not only from Hastings' reputation—her intuitive mind was in overdrive from the time Harry arrived home the previous evening. The young red-haired girl made her appearance, but Colbie realized she didn't have anything to do with the present. Dressed in a dirty, white dress, her shoes tattered, Colbie got the impression she was sad, hurt, and abandoned. As she listened to Harry, the girl appeared again, holding out a beckoning hand. Colbie watched as the girl faded through a porch screen door, allowing it to slam and resonate in Colbie's mind's eye.

Then, a body.

Her intuitive mind watched as authorities loaded a corpse onto a gurney—but, from her vantage point, Colbie couldn't tell if the body were male or female. As she watched, suddenly the young red-haired girl reappeared, pointing to the body, then at herself. *What the hell does that mean?* It was then Colbie felt the strangest sensation—taking her hand, the girl led her to the body with a sorrow that coursed through Colbie, allowing her to feel the emotions the little girl felt. There was a—familiarity—Colbie couldn't explain, and she had the feeling the girl was trying desperately to tell her something.

In the next moment and with a soft breeze, she was gone.

On the periphery of her conscious mind, Colbie heard Harry trying to explain things to Evelyn as Colbie struggled to hold onto the vision playing as a video in her subconscious. *Is the body representative of the Beeman boys' murders? Or, is it an event that hasn't happened yet?*

She just didn't know.

The truth was her intuition was iffy over the last several months. Ever since the Remington case in Switzerland, her self-confidence wavered, and she seriously considered discontinuing her profiling career. Brian, of course, tried to talk her out of it, but Colbie maintained if her intuition were no longer reliable, what would she have to offer her clients? She had to accept the fact she was wrong more than once during the Switzerland case, and she found herself relying on Brian for confirmation.

It was a completely unacceptable situation.

As she surfaced to reality, it became clear Harry and Evelyn needed time to themselves to iron out their misunderstandings. Colbie stood, holding her hand out to Brian. "I'm exhausted—how about if we pick this up in the morning?"

Brian got the message. "Good idea—I didn't realize how pooped I am!"

Both bade goodnight to their hosts, soon relieved to be back in the comfort of their own room. "There's something Harry's not telling us," Colbie commented as she prepared to brush her teeth.

"I know—we didn't learn much tonight, did we?"

"No—I think we need to head for the courthouse tomorrow. I have a feeling there have been more than one or two run-ins with the Beemans—if that's true, there's probably something on record." Colbie paused, thinking what no one wanted to voice. "What if we're wrong? What if Harry really did murder the Beemans? You and I know stranger things have happened . . ."

Brian reached to turn out the light on his nightstand. "I don't know about you, but I think we don't have much more information than when we arrived . . ."

"I know—it's pretty clear we'll have to find out things on our own. I don't trust Harry to be forthcoming with us . . ."

It was the first time Brian heard Colbie express doubt regarding her uncle's honesty. "Where do we go from here?"

Colbie clicked off her light after checking her cell one last time. "I think it's time we pay a little visit . . ."

Brian rolled over in bed so he could see her face. "To whom?"

"The Beemans—who else?"

\*\*\*\*

The luck of the Irish? It's true. It turned out Colbie didn't need to pay that little visit to Amanda Beeman—they met at a local restaurant standing in line to get seated. "I don't know why I come here," Amanda complained. "There's always a wait . . ."

Colbie scanned the restaurant for empty tables. "Well, I don't know about that—I'm new to Gillette!"

"Really? Where are you from?"

"The West Coast—I got tired of the rain and, Brian here, figured a complete change was in order. We picked a state, closed our eyes, and pointed to a city on the map—Gillette was it!

Amanda stared in disbelief. "You really did that?"

Colbie laughed, and Brian nodded. "We did! I know, it's nuts—but, we're having a great time getting used to things here. By the way, I'm Colbie . . ." She pointed at her better half. "He's Brian . . ."

The tall woman with flame-colored hair extended her hand. "Amanda Beeman. . ."

Colbie couldn't believe her luck! There couldn't be two Amanda Beemans in Gillette, could there? She pointed to the table a busser was cleaning. "Oh—there's a table, but it looks like only one. Would you like to join us?"

Amanda glanced at her watch. "You know, I'd love to—I have an appointment in an hour . . ."

"Good!"

Within a few minutes they were seated, menus in hand. "What do you recommend," Colbie asked as she surveyed their choices.

"The prime rib sandwich is killer . . ."

"Prime rib! My favorite! There's a hole-in-the-wall steak house where we're from, and I forced Brian to eat there once a month so I could get my prime rib fix!"

"Prime rib, it is!" Amanda looked up at Brian. "Three of them?"

"Yep—I'm not passing that up in cattle country, that's for sure!"

Forty-five minutes of casual conversation passed quickly and, soon, Amanda had to leave for her appointment. "How about if you come to the ranch? I'd like to show you some true Wyoming hospitality . . ."

"We'd love to—name the day and time!"

Although scratching out the address and her phone number probably made her late to her appointment, Amanda didn't care. Colbie and Brian seemed like a nice couple, and it felt good to meet someone new in town. Randy, her husband, would certainly feel the same way—he often complained of being tired of the same old, same old.

As Amanda strode through the restaurant's front door, Colbie and Brian watched her go. "Can you believe it?"

Brian chuckled as he noticed the glint in her eyes. "Well—that couldn't have gone any better. There's no reason to let her know you're related to their current nemesis—it's the perfect opportunity to get another take on the case."

"It is perfect!" Colbie checked the day, time, and directions of their visit to the Beeman ranch. "If she has no idea we have anything to do with Harry and Evelyn, maybe we can get her to open up . . ."

"When do we see her next?"

Colbie flipped the piece of paper over in her hand. "This coming Thursday—two days from now."

"Good—that gives us time to get our stories straight!"

Brian thought for a moment, then grinned. "That gal sure has some red hair!"

# CHAPTER FOUR

It wasn't until the middle of week that Harry heard from Jeremiah Hastings and, from what he told Evelyn, Colbie, and Brian at dinner that evening, he had a good feeling about his chances with the renowned attorney. "He didn't beat around the bush," Harry commented as he reached for another serving of mashed potatoes. "I like that—I'm supposed to meet him tomorrow in Gillette . . ."

Colbie glanced at Brian, shooting him the 'don't mention we're going to see Amanda Beeman on Thursday' look. "That's good—I'm eager to know what he thinks. Although, he hasn't had time to get a defense together, so I imagine your meeting will be a fact-finding mission . . ."

Harry nodded. "Exactly what he said . . . I'm supposed to have a chronology of my run-ins with the Beemans."

"That's a good idea. Did he mention anything else?"

"Only that he wants to meet with you and Brian, too . . ."

Colbie reached for her water as she nearly choked on that bit of news. "Us? How does he know about us?"

"That's what I wanted to know—apparently, Andy Herlein mentioned you're staying with us for a spell . . ."

"Will he get in touch with me?"

"Well, he's hoping you can attend our meeting tomorrow, if possible . . ."

"What time?"

Harry sat back in his chair, pushing his plate slightly away from him. "Four-thirty . . ."

Brian answered before Colbie had the chance. "That works, don't you think?" He glanced at her for confirmation.

"It does—we're planning on doing some research tomorrow, but I think we'll be winding up by then. Where does he want to meet?"

"The Roundup—it's in downtown Gillette."

Colbie smiled at Evelyn as she removed plates from the table. "We were just there a couple of days ago for lunch— nice place!"

"Okay, then—it's settled. I'll meet you there at four-thirty. It shouldn't be too crowded . . ."

Colbie stood, signaling Brian they should retire for the evening—they had a lot of planning to do, and the last thing they needed was prying eyes. "Evelyn, thank you for such a delicious meal!"

"What? No dessert?"

"Not tonight, I'm afraid—I'll never fit into my clothes if I keep eating your fabulous home cooking!"

Evelyn smiled at the compliment. "Well, alright—we'll see you in the morning . . ."

Minutes later, Colbie closed their bedroom door. "Okay—let's get started. We should have a game plan before meeting with Amanda tomorrow . . ."

Brian flopped onto the bed, plumping the pillows behind his head. "I've been thinking about that . . . I'd really like to find out more about the contentious relationship between Harry and the Beemans—I have a feeling it goes way back. Further than Harry said . . ."

Colbie nodded, and joined him on the bed. "Me, too—in fact, when we were talking to Amanda the other day, I got the strong feeling we've met before . . ."

"Really? How's that possible? You've never been to Gillette, and I'm pretty sure she would have recognized you if that were the case."

"I don't know how it's possible—but, that's really not important right now." Colbie paused, thinking about the meeting the following day. "What if Amanda shows up at the Roundup? She would surely recognize Harry, you, and me—Hastings, too, probably, especially since he's so well-known in this state."

"I suppose it's possible—but, I think it's a long shot . . ."

Colbie knew he was right—but, a little bit of paranoia sprinkled in with common sense wasn't a bad thing. In her business, she was a young profiler when she learned anything could happen—and, it often did. "Still—if I can weave the conversation tomorrow to find out what her plans are for the rest of the day, then we'll know . . . if she's planning on going out in the late afternoon, we can get in touch with Harry, and he and Hastings can switch to a different meeting location. If she says she's staying on the ranch, then everything's a go."

Brian agreed.

"Now," Colbie continued, "we need to figure out our story for visiting the Beeman ranch tomorrow. As far as Amanda thinks, we're two nuts who decided to move to a place they picked out with a finger on the map!"

"Let's leave it that way—the more we change our story, the more unbelievable we become . . ."

Colbie moved over to snuggle under his arm. "You're right—besides, that will be a lot more fun!"

\*\*\*\*

Amanda greeted them as does any host worth his or her salt—arms outstretched, she eagerly welcomed them to their little ranch.

"How many acres?" Brian shaded his eyes with his palm. "Nothing, but . . . nothing for as far as I can see." He turned to Amanda. "I can't imagine growing up on a place like this!"

"A few acres over seventeen thousand—and, it's not what it's cracked up to be. As a teenager, I couldn't wait to get the hell out!"

"What about now? Do you feel the same way?" Colbie imitated Brian, hand over her eyes, surveying nothing but open space.

"Now? Oh, I don't know—sometimes I think I'd like to live a more city kind of life. But, once I really think about it, I wonder how I can consider leaving this . . ." As they chatted, they drifted toward several barns, one serving as the ranch vet hospital. As they neared its massive doors, Colbie felt something—or, someone—move through her, momentarily taking her breath away.

Brian noticed her slight gasp, but knew not to say anything in front of Amanda. Instead? A different tact. "Well," he commented, "It certainly is stunning—and, cold!"

Amanda bellowed a less-than-ladylike laugh, then guided them toward the house. "Please forgive me! I forgot you're tenderfeet when it comes to weather!"

Minutes later, Colbie and Brian sat in antique leather chairs, while Amanda selected a spot on the matching love seat facing her guests. "Randy offered to play butler today— he thought you might enjoy hot chocolate and homemade cookies while we chat . . ."

"Cookies?" Brian's eyes lit up at the mention of his favorite dessert—or, anytime snack. Then, as if one cue, Randy strode through kitchen saloon doors, balancing a tray with both hands. "Remind me to stay away from restaurant jobs," he joked as he put it down on the coffee table, then extended his hand. "I'm Randy, Amanda's better half!"

Colbie accepted the handshake, grinning. "You did a lot

better than I would do!"

After introducing Brian, the two couples relaxed as if long-standing friends. "Amanda tells me," Randy began, "you pointed on the map for a new place to live . . ."

"We did . . ."

"I can't imagine having the guts to do that," Amanda countered. "It seems so wonderfully reckless!"

"I suppose it was—but, we don't have any regrets, so far!" Colbie took a sip of chocolate. "Like Brian mentioned earlier, I can't imagine living on such an expanse of land— has it always been in your family?"

Amanda nodded. "Oh, yes—this property was handed down through generations since my great-grandfather . . ."

"Did he have to stake a claim?" History buff that he was, Brian wanted to learn as much as he could about the area. There was something that spoke to him about open spaces, and a rural way of life—almost as if he lived it before.

"No—but he wanted land, and he did his best to snap up as much as he could."

"This ranch has been in your family since then?"

"Yep . . ." Amanda paused, as if picturing an early century town in the middle of nowhere. "In the early nineteen hundreds, Gillette was a one-horse town, its main street lined with clapboard buildings, the road spewing up dust or mud as horses with wagons trotted by. And, Sundance? Two roads crossing that seemed to lead to nowhere . . ."

"It's so interesting," Colbie commented, "to hear about someone's genealogical story . . ."

Amanda grinned at her guest. "He's the guy who gave

me this red hair!"

"Your great-grandfather?" Colbie laughed, then pointed to her own head of gentle waves and curls. "Mine, too!"

For the next two hours, there was something nice about relaxing with the Beemans, sharing memories. Colbie's intuitive mind was on high alert the whole time, and she couldn't shake the feeling of familiarity—Brian felt it, too.

Finally, Colbie stood, always her signal when it was time to go. "Amanda, you have no idea how much we enjoyed this—we'll have to do it again . . ."

The Beeman heir gave her a quick hug. "You're always welcome here . . ."

"I hope you mean it—I plan on taking you up on it! I want to hear more about your great-grandfather . . . and, how he got into ranching."

"You may have just dug yourself into a hole—I have enough stories to last a lifetime!"

Then, quick goodbyes. "I'll give you a call in the morning," Amanda promised. "But, now? I have to start my bake-sale project!"

"Ahhh—an evening in, baking to your heart's content!"

"Sounds fun, doesn't it?" Amanda opened the front door. "Let's get together soon . . ."

And, that was it.

Colbie and Brian were soon on their way to Gillette to meet Harry and his attorney, the time and place the same as it was before spending time with the Beemans.

"Since Amanda is the heir to the Beeman fortune and

land," Colbie suggested, "it's curious she goes by Amanda Beeman . . ."

"Maybe she doesn't like Randy's last name . . ."

"Do you know what it is?"

"Nope—the subject never came up." Brian turned onto the main road leading to town. "So? What are you thinking about them?"

Colbie looked out the window for a few moments, gathering her observations. "Well—to be honest, I didn't have any feelings about Randy, and only a whisper of something when I was talking to Amanda about her great-grandfather. Other than that? Nothing . . ." She paused. "Oh—there was one thing. When we first got there and were walking toward the barns? I felt something move through me . . ."

Brian glanced at her. "Move through you? Like a spirit, or something?"

"Yes—someone young. I'm inclined to think it was the young girl with red hair."

"But, you couldn't see her—just felt her presence?"

"Pretty much—as we walked around that barn, I got the most intense feeling of sorrow." Colbie hesitated, recalling the specifics of her encounter. "Then, suddenly . . . she showed herself to me, holding out her hand so she could guide me."

"And?"

"She led me to a body . . ."

"A body? Whose?" Brian slowed as he turned onto downtown Gillette's main street.

"That's just it—I don't have any idea. All I know is as

we stood, looking at a body on a gurney, she motioned to herself, then to the body."

"Holy shit! Do you think she was trying to tell you it was her body on the gurney?"

"Maybe—but, they really didn't have gurneys back in the day. Besides, the body looked too big to be a young girl."

Brian whistled softly to himself. "What do you think it means?"

Colbie turned to look at him directly. "I don't know. I just don't know . . ."

\*\*\*\*

Harry and Jeremiah Hastings chose a table close to the back of the restaurant, already discussing Harry's case as Colbie and Brian arrived. After quick introductions, everyone ordered, listening intently to Harry's descriptions of his myriad run-ins with the Beeman boys. By dessert, he was finally starting to wind it down when Hastings interrupted. "Harry," he said, "just from what you told me in the last thirty minutes, I'm not sure . . ."

"Not sure about what?"

"Let's face it—when a jury hears how many times you

wanted to smash a Beeman boy's face—well, it doesn't look good . . ."

"Do you have to tell them about every time?"

Hastings glanced at Colbie and Brian. "What do you think?"

"I think the more Harry is aboveboard and honest, the jury will take that into consideration. At least it shows he's not hiding anything . . ."

Harry and Hastings sat quietly, chewing on what Colbie told them, both knowing she was right. Harry's attorney already knew the answer to his question, but he was hoping Colbie's point of view would bolster convincing his client.

Then, Colbie drained her water glass, leveling her most serious look at Harry. "I'm sorry, Harry—as I listen to you, I get the distinct impression you're not telling the whole truth. Like the time you pulled a gun on one of the Beemans last spring . . ." As she listened to the words coming out of her mouth, she couldn't believe how insulting they were. How could she intimate her uncle was a liar? *But, the gun? Where did that come from*, she wondered, as she waited for Harry's response.

Harry met her eyes with a stare of his own. "How do you know what I said, or did?"

Colbie didn't break his gaze. "You're right, Harry—I don't know . . ." Theirs was a conversation requiring privacy, and she didn't want to jeopardize any headway he made with Hastings—although, she supposed it were too late for that.

But, Hastings wasn't going to let it go. "What gun, Harry?" He sat back in his chair, waiting for an acceptable answer.

Colbie suspected Harry's lawyer wanted to head out and never come back, but she knew that wouldn't happen. Still, Harry needed to know he had to be truthful with his lawyer at all times, without exception. Lie to your attorney? Well— it's a good way to get convicted.

"I'll ask again—what gun?"

Hastings waited.

With a scorching look to his niece, Harry's shoulders slumped. "Okay! Okay! It wasn't anything, really . . ."

"I'll tell you if it's anything . . ."

Harry polished off the rest of his soda, then leaned back in his chair. "Last spring," he explained, "I heard the dogs barking after Evie and I went to bed . . . well, I didn't think too much of it, until I heard what sounded like a yelp." He paused, the image of that night alive in his brain. "So, I decided to check on it—I grabbed my shotgun, and headed for the barn . . ."

"What happened?"

"Before I reached the barn doors, I nearly tripped over Sophie—she lay there bleeding, her breathing shallow."

"But, she didn't die," Colbie interjected. "She hangs out with me every morning while I drink my coffee . . ."

Harry nodded. "It was by the grace of God she didn't . . ."

"Then what happened," Hastings prodded.

Harry sighed, draping his right arm over the back of his chair. "I knew the son of a bitch who did it—the young Beeman kid, that's who . . ."

"How do you know?"

"Because I saw him hightailing it out of there. He wasn't anymore than five feet from me when he took off running—I raised my shotgun, cocked it, and aimed. I let off two rounds, reloaded, and waited for him to come back to confront me, but he never did." Harry paused. "Good thing, too—he would have been six feet under if he had . . ."

"Did the Beemans call the sheriff about it? You're taking pot shots at him, I mean . . ."

"Hell, no! Why would they? So I could accuse them for nearly killing my dog?" Anger flashed in Harry's eyes. "That would have been a pretty stupid thing to do . . ."

Colbie and Brian sat, listening to building emotions. Harry again shot a scathing look, as if blaming her for the timbre of the conversation.

"I can see how traumatic that was for you, Harry—but, can you see how important an incident like that might be in a court of law?" Colbie hesitated, glancing at Hastings who sat silently, his chair backed up against the wall. "The fact you fired off two rounds," she continued, "and didn't hit him? That tells me you didn't want—or, try—to take him down." Colbie waited a moment. "I don't think you have gunning another man down in you, Harry . . ."

Harry sneered, a dark look descending on his face. "How do you know what I'd do? You haven't been around me for decades—the fact is you don't know shit about me!"

Colbie stood, then Brian. "You're right, Harry—I don't know a damned thing . . ."

# Chapter Five

"I told you, Hattie Pearl—I met them standing in line at the Roundup!" Amanda didn't try to mask her exasperation.

Over passing months, Hattie Pearl's deterioration was noticeable to just about everyone—everyone, that is, but Hattie Pearl. Still, her loving granddaughter did what she could to make sure she was comfortable, but, when Amanda was left to the privacy of her own thoughts?

The Hattie Pearl situation was less than desirable.

Stories of her grandmother's youth at the Thanksgiving table sparked visions of a young woman left to her own devices from an early age. "My father—your great-grandfather," she would say to Amanda, "wanted nothing to do with me, and he left my mother to seek his fortune doing God knows what." Eyes rolled, of course, and nobody ever wanted to pick up the thread of that conversation. "His only son, my brother, couldn't stand the abuse, and he finally struck out to find his fortune in this God-forsaken state . . ."

Yes—it was lovely conversation for a holiday table.

Amanda glanced at her husband as she recalled their last Thanksgiving dinner as a complete family, barely a year ago. Three funerals and a declining grandmother later, things certainly changed if she looked at it from a death standpoint. After all, losing two sons and a grandfather was a horrible thing to endure—but, she couldn't help praising herself about how well she was getting along without them. She was certain some labeled her as calloused, but, inwardly, she countered the claim with her innate understanding she really didn't want to be a mother, anyway. According to her, it wasn't in her DNA—a trait, she heard, inherited from her great-grandfather.

And, what of Randy? Often spoken of in hushed tones at church, Amanda's husband was nothing more than a servant. That knowledge, of course, was perfect fodder for questions such as, "Why does he stay with her?" Gossip swirled around Sundance and Gillette, but there was never truth put to their suspicions.

The answer was simple—money. Inheritance. Freedom.

Even so, it was clear Amanda Beeman needed a break from the apparent rigors of every day ranch life. "How about," she cajoled her husband as he busied himself dusting knickknacks on the fireplace mantle, "how about if we head up to Deadwood for a couple of days?"

"And, leave your grandmother?"

"I'll ask Mrs. Constantine to stay with her—she'll be fine!"

Randy wasn't comfortable with that idea, but when

Amanda put her mind to something, she wasn't going to give up. "When do you want to go?"

"Tomorrow! I already put the bug in Mrs. Constantine's ear . . ."

A resigned sigh. "Of course, you did . . ."

Amanda returned her attention to her grandmother. "Did you hear that, Hattie Pearl? Randy and I are going to be gone for a few days, but Mrs. Constantine will be here to look after you . . ."

Hattie Pearl smiled. "I heard—you two have fun!"

Amanda kissed her grandmother on the top of her head. "We will, Grandma—we will!" With that, she nearly twirled out the door, excited at the prospect of a three or four-day reprieve.

Hattie Pearl watched as Randy dutifully followed her granddaughter, disgust registering in her eyes. *You think I don't know what's going on,* she thought as Randy gently closed the door. *You wretched child! You wretched, wretched, child!*

\*\*\*\*

"I think you're overreacting, Harry—I'm sure Colbie didn't mean anything by it. After all, she's an investigator . . ." Evelyn paused, thinking about how she was going to mention to her husband his niece wasn't only an investigator—she was a psychic investigator. Since Colbie confided her true career, however, Evelyn thought it best to keep Harry in the dark about it for a while. It was the sort of thing he didn't believe in, and she was sure learning of Colbie's abilities would push him away.

"Calling me a liar? That's something I can't forgive!"

"I don't think she meant to call you a liar . . ." So, as much as she wanted to avoid it, it was time Harry knew the truth.

Evie sat beside him, taking her hand in his—she could feel the tension in his fingertips, and she couldn't imagine the stress he must feel. "Have you ever talked to Colbie about her work?"

"Her work? No—should I have?"

"Well, I think if you knew the extent of it, you wouldn't be so quick to accuse her of things such as lying . . ."

Harry pulled his hand away, leaning back so he could see her face clearly. "What the hell are you talking about?"

Evelyn took a deep breath and, fifteen minutes later, Harry knew everything about Colbie—and, Brian. She could tell by the look on his face he was doubting her story—but, assuming Colbie's background could be verified, there wasn't anything he could do but believe her. "She can be a huge help to you, Harry—if you'll let her . . ."

Her husband sat for a moment, considering Colbie's intuitive abilities. He, of course, thought it was a bunch of crap—but, if she could help him, then it was worth having her around. "I'll apologize to her in the morning," he promised. "I jumped the gun, and I'm hoping she'll bring something to my case . . ."

"She will—I know she will!"

\*\*\*\*

Next morning, Harry kept his word, taking Colbie aside, apologizing for his snarky behavior at the Roundup. The apology came at just the right time, too—by the time breakfast was in the books, Colbie felt it was time to mention the little red-haired girl.

"I felt her several times since we've been here" she explained, "and I have the feeling she's important to this investigation—but, I don't know why . . ."

Harry leaned forward, placing his forearms on his knees. "How old was she?"

Colbie thought for a moment. "About nine—maybe a shade younger . . ."

"And, she had red hair?"

"Yes—a burnished red. And, curly. In fact, now that I think about it, her hair is the same color as Amanda Beeman's."

"Amanda Beeman? How do you know what color her hair is?"

Colbie grinned at her uncle. "We just went over that, Harry—I just know . . ." Then, Colbie burst out laughing! "I'm pullin' your leg—Brian and I met her at the Roundup several days ago when we stopped in for lunch . . ."

"Before our meeting with Hastings?"

"Yes—I forgot to mention it . . ."

The way Harry was reacting to learning Colbie and Brian spent lunch with Amanda Beeman, she figured it wasn't the best time to bring up they'd been to the Beeman ranch, too. "Let's get back to the red-haired girl—do you have any idea who she is?"

Harry looked at Evelyn. "I remember hearing a story about a tragedy on the Beeman ranch decades ago—Amanda Beeman's mother . . ." He paused, attempting to mentally verify his information. " . . . which would be Hattie Pearl's daughter . . . was playing in the barn with her sister, when a beam crashed to the ground, instantly killing the young girl. LaRee was her name, I think . . ."

Colbie sat up, instantly captivated. "What about Amanda's mother? What happened to her? Do you know how old she was when the accident occurred?"

"Not really—all I know is Amanda's mother was quite a few years older than her sister. In fact, she was almost a mother figure to her . . ."

"What does Amanda's mother look like?"

"The only thing I remember is the red hair—just like her grandmother's . . ."

"And, Amanda . . . and, LaRee."

"Don't forget the Beeman boys—they were the spittin'

image of their mother . . ."

"What about Amanda's grandfather? It seems—from what you're saying—the women in the family were those with the power . . ."

Harry didn't answer the question directly. "That's right. Although, when Hattie Pearl married, she and her husband were considered the heads of their family. True patriarch and matriarch, if you know what I mean . . ."

"I'm not sure I do . . ."

Harry looked at Colbie with a glint of disdain in his eyes. "Everyone in these parts know they ruled with an iron hand. That's one reason I hated the Beeman boys—they were spineless, and weak. They always carried weapons with them while they were on the ranch—in their minds, it was the only way they could get respect. Everyone knew they were always packing . . ."

"Don't most ranchers carry weapons? It seems a logical thing to do . . ."

"Yes, but that's for varmints of the four-legged variety."

Colbie took a few seconds before asking her next question. "What happened to Amanda's mother? Is she around?"

Harry shook his head. "Nope—I don't really know what happened to her, but, as far as I know, she's not in the picture."

Colbie scribbled down a few notes on a paper napkin. "When was the last time Amanda's mother came around?"

Harry thought for a moment. "Thirty-five years—a little more, a little less . . ."

"That's a long time to stay away from family—what do

you know about her?"

"Well—she was an odd sort. But, then again, I only met her a few times, so I can't really say. What I do remember is she was timid and frail—as though she were haunted by something evil. Something sinister . . ."

"And, you're sure LaRee was the red-haired girl's name?" For Colbie, knowing her name was an important bit of information—if she could communicate with her, it would be much easier if she used her name.

"No, I'm not sure, but I think that's it—don't take that to the bank, though."

Colbie smiled at her uncle. "I won't, Uncle Harry," Colbie promised. "I won't . . ."

\*\*\*\*

Harry and Jeremiah Hastings met several times before the attorney headed back to Laramie, although little was decided except an exorbitant price for his services. Harry swore he told him everything, but, after lying to him once, Hastings wasn't so sure. Still, after a three-hour, clandestine meeting with Colbie and Brian, he was convinced she could be an integral part of the case as well as instrumental in Harry's telling the truth—all of it. That meant, however, she and Brian would have to stay in Sundance considerably longer than first anticipated.

When he broached the subject, Brian was all for it, but Colbie needed to assess how long she could be gone from her business. Tammy, of course, was taking care of things while she and Brian were away, but Colbie was ready to get back to work. However, after a few days to consider Hastings's request, she agreed it was in Harry's best interest to stay.

"I don't know if I made the right decision," she commented as Brian pulled out of the drive, heading toward the Beeman's ranch. "But, bailing on Harry? I couldn't do it."

"I don't blame you—you'd never forgive yourself."

Colbie grinned at him. "You know me too well . . ."

"True . . ." Brian paused as he slowed behind a feed truck taking up most of the road, changing the subject as he tried to peer around it. "Does Amanda know you're coming?"

"No—I don't think she'll mind, though, if we stop in unannounced . . ."

"I hope not . . ."

Twenty minutes later, Brian eased their car through the Beeman's ranch gate, wishing he rented an SUV rather than a sedan. *A rookie move*, he thought, the car rattling the cattle guard between gateposts as he headed for the circular drive in front of the house.

"Weird," Colbie commented. "There's not much energy here today—everything seems so quiet . . ."

"Maybe you should have called . . ."

She shot him a look. "I'll knock . . ."

Brian watched as Colbie climbed the steps, then rapped loudly with the knocker on the front door. She waited, then tried again. Nothing. But, as she was about to leave, the door opened, revealing a face she didn't recognize. "Who are you," the woman asked, her eyes scanning Colbie from top to bottom.

"Colbie Colleen—is Amanda here?"

"No."

"Oh, no! I'm sorry to intrude . . ."

"She won't be back for a few days . . ."

Colbie managed her best crestfallen smile. "Oh—okay." She glanced at Brian, then back at the woman peering at her from around the door. "Do you mind if I use your restroom?"

The woman hesitated, then nodded, holding the door for Colbie. "It's the second door on the right . . ."

"Thank you!" Then she extended her hand. "You know my name, but I don't know yours . . ."

The woman hesitated, uncertain whether she should accept the handshake. "I'm Mrs. Constantine—I'm staying here with Hattie Pearl until Amanda and Randy get back from Deadwood."

"Deadwood? How fun! I've heard of it, but I've never been there . . ." She glanced down the hall. "Second door?"

Mrs. Constantine nodded.

Just as Colbie started down the hall, a voice called to them. "Caroline? Is that you? I thought I heard voices . . ."

"It's someone for Amanda," she called as she pointed Colbie down the hall.

"Who is it?"

"She says her name is Colbie Colleen . . ."

"Oh! Amanda told me about her—I think they met at the Roundup. Bring her to me so I can meet her . . ."

Colbie rejoined Mrs. Constantine in time to hear the voice's request. "Meet who?"

"Hattie Pearl—Amanda's grandmother."

"I'd love to meet her! Lead the way!"

Mrs. Constantine guided her toward a sitting area in the great room to a small, wizend woman looking as if she were swallowed by a chair three times her size. "Hattie Pearl, this is Colbie Colleen . . ."

Colbie held out her hand, offering a gentle handshake. "It's a pleasure, Hattie Pearl!"

The elderly woman smiled, motioning to the chair beside her. "Thank you—now, sit. Tell me—how do you know Amanda?" She paused, wrinkling her eyebrows as she tried to remember something. "Weren't you here a few days ago?"

"Indeed, I was! Brian and I spent a couple of hours here with Amanda and Randy . . ."

"I thought so. I recognize your voice . . ."

Colbie grinned. "Amanda was telling me about some of your ancestors, and how they claimed your land. I found it absolutely fascinating!"

Hattie Pearl laughed, leaning forward to pat Colbie's hand. "Oh, it's interesting, alright! What did she tell you?"

"Not enough! That's why I thought I'd stop by today—I

told her I wanted to hear everything about her great-grandfather . . . I'm sorry I don't remember his name."

Hattie Pearl laughed out loud, her delight resembling a soft cackle. "Oh, there are plenty of stories about him! His name? From the time I remember, his name was 'Buzz'—why, I don't know!"

"That's it! Buzz!" Colbie leaned back in her chair, making herself comfortable. "If I remember correctly, Amanda said he homesteaded in Sundance around the turn of the century."

"Yes—but, a little later than that—it was a good ten years into the next century."

"Where was he from?"

Hattie Pearl tucked a wool blanket around her legs, then focused on Colbie. "Are you warm enough, Dear?"

"I'm just fine, thank you . . ."

Amanda's grandmother took her time getting situated, then picked up where she left off. "Buzz was born near Wheaton, Minnesota, in September of 1893, and he moved with his parents when he was around thirteen. Up until then, he was a good boy—or, at least, his parents thought so. They were quite disappointed in their eldest son when, at age sixteen, he started hanging out in the pool halls, drinking booze."

Colbie's eyebrows arched. "Really? I imagine that behavior was frowned upon, especially to church-going folks."

"Oh, it was! Buzz's family were strict Baptists, and they didn't allow card playing . . . although, I remember someone saying all of them were fond of sweets, and ate too much sugar."

Colbie smiled at the old woman. "I'm guilty of the same thing," she confessed. "It's my Achilles heel!"

"Don't tell anyone," Hattie Pearl whispered, "but, *I'm* guilty of the same thing!" She chuckled, winking at Colbie. "So, at that time, she continued, "school only went to grade eight, and everyone seemed to go to a local college after that. But, not Buzz—he refused to attend, and opted to train as a barber."

"How did that go?"

"Well, Buzz got into many scrapes which his father—as Justice of the Peace—managed to resolve. By the time he was twenty-one, Buzz was a grain buyer, probably on his father's recommendation."

"At least it was a job!"

"True, but that was about the time he decided to marry a neighbor girl—Rose, I think—and she was twenty years old. For some reason—probably because her family didn't approve—they traveled to get married at a Baptist parsonage in February of nineteen fifteen."

"Were they allowed to marry that young?"

"Oh, good heavens, no! Buzz's sister—she was nineteen— and, his first cousin . . ." Hattie Pearl's voice trailed as she tried to remember the details. "He was twenty, I believe . . ."

"They were witnesses?"

"No—neither was old enough because they had to be of legal age."

"Twenty-one?"

Hattie Pearl nodded.

"Since the witnesses weren't old enough, did Buzz wind up marrying Rose, anyway?"

"Well, now—that's the thing. He did make an honest woman out of her . . . but, it didn't really matter. Buzz Beeman was going to do whatever he damned well pleased." Hattie Pearl shot Colbie a knowing look. "Including drinking and cheating . . ."

Again, Colbie's eyebrows gave away her surprise.

"Oh, yes—by the nineteen sixteen census, Buzz was a grain buyer in two elevators. Still, he was always getting into trouble, and that didn't change when they had a baby boy in May of nineteen sixteen.  Then, they adopted another baby boy, but, as I understand it, Rose always suspected the child belonged to Buzz."

"Then what happened?"

Hattie Pearl sighed as if she had the weight of the world on her shoulders. "Well, at some point, Buzz took up with a nurse—Elizabeth Hawkins. In nineteen thirty-eight they had a son and, in nineteen forty, a daughter, Ida May—both with the Beeman surname on their birth certificates."

Colbie shook her head as if clearing cobwebs. "Wait—I'm confused. Did Buzz divorce Rose somewhere along the line?"

"No—in fact, there was some talk that Buzz married Elizabeth, but that can't be true since he was still legally hitched to Rose. There was also some scuttlebutt that Buzz—much later—told someone in the family he didn't marry Elizabeth, and people assumed they were married. Apparently, when they moved from town to town, folks automatically called her Mrs. Beeman. Even at that, Buzz continued to change his name whenever it suited him."

Colbie glanced at her watch. "Good heavens! Brian will be furious with me!" She looked at Hattie Pearl with a fondness unfamiliar to her. "I really have to go—so, what happened to Buzz?"

Again, Hattie Pearl sighed. "So much tragedy," she said. "He moved from place to place until he finally wound up in jail for stealing a necklace from a drugstore—eighteen months, I think. No one really knows, and Buzz wound up passing away in jail in nineteen forty-nine—five days before he was to be released."

"What did he die of?"

"The final determination was coronary thrombosis, although the coroner thought he had a heart attack before that . . ."

Colbie sat for a moment, trying to digest Hattie Pearl's story. If half of what she told her were true, there were probably some interesting behaviors passed down through generations. *Certainly*, she thought as she rose to leave, *the Beeman boys were a little off the rail . . .*

"Hattie Pearl, I can't tell you how much I enjoyed hearing about your family, and spending time with you! I hope we have the opportunity to do so again . . ."

Hattie Pearl smiled, offering her hand to Colbie. "You're welcome here any time . . ."

A few minutes later, Colbie sat in their car, apologizing profusely to the man who waited for her. "I'm so sorry! But, I know you'll understand—I met Hattie Pearl, and she told the complete story of Amanda's great-grandfather . . ."

"And?"

"The family sounds a little screwy if you ask me!"

# CHAPTER SIX

His defense? Make it look as though the Beeman boys were petulant instigators who didn't give a rat's ass about anyone or anything except drilling for riches on their family's ranch. *That,* Jeremiah Hastings thought, *can be their undoing . . .* By making the two great-grandsons appear to a jury as unhinged and self-absorbed, Harry Fenamore had a fighting chance. And, from what Hastings learned from his research, the Beeman's weren't strangers to a bar fight or two. Or, more. *The inability to harness one's emotions always goes a good distance toward reasonable doubt,* he considered as he took a break, cigar in hand. *Even so, that bit of information only speaks to character—it doesn't speak to hard evidence supporting the claim Harry murdered both of them . . .*

Harry's was one of those cases that could go either

way—undoubtedly, the jury could be convinced Harry was a killer without remorse. Or, they could believe the Beeman's were so out of control, anything was possible. But, after talking with Colbie for more than an hour about that topic, he was becoming more convinced of his client's innocence. The main problem with the prosecution's case was it didn't answer the fundamental question of why Harry would have shot the Beeman boys, let alone in different places. Yes, that would speak to premeditation, but that was about all.

Three weeks shy of having Harry for a client and being paid for her services by Jeremiah Hastings, Colbie's and Brian's research unsheathed several items she was certain the Beeman family would prefer to keep buried. A few hours in the county courthouse revealed the boys were in trouble from the time they turned to teens. Brought up with the idea they were better than everyone else, each great-grandson had no compunction about humiliating, harassing, or haranguing those managing to get themselves on the boys' dark side. Not only that, as the third generation of Beemans on the ranch, ancestry alone entitled them to a high horse, didn't it?

Of course, it did.

From the time the boys turned sixteen, they commanded a presence on the streets of Sundance which, over all, didn't account for much—too small for their kind of persuasion. As a result, they took their unpleasantness to Gillette where they fared marginally better, but, again, it wasn't enough to quench the thirst they had for superiority.

An unquenchable thirst.

\*\*\*\*

Harry wasn't having any of it, and made no bones about telling his family and Hastings so. From the time he remembered the Beeman boys as fledgling teenagers, he told Evelyn they were of bad blood. Bad seeds. "I don't know what's in their past," he said, "but one thing I know for sure—it ain't good."

Silently, she agreed, privately hoping her husband was right. It could help his case—it was an interesting comment and, when she repeated it to Colbie, her house guest agreed there was a feeling about the Beemans she couldn't quite describe, or put to rest. The story about Buzz Beeman's life was proof of that. It was the familiarity, though, that kept tugging at Colbie—the Beemans weren't anything to her, so why did she have the feeling she heard it before?

"It doesn't make sense to me," Evelyn commented as she joined Colbie in the great room after dinner. "And, I'm afraid I can't be much help when it comes to the Beemans—I rarely saw them. Harry was always the one to deal with their dissatisfaction . . ."

"Dissatisfaction? About what?"

"Life in general—Harry will tell you they were spineless, and would do everything they could to elevate themselves in everyone's minds. But, townsfolk in Sundance and Gillette weren't buying their brand of intimidation, so when they were flicked away like an annoying mosquito? Well, the boys didn't take it very well . . ."

Colbie sat quietly, thinking about her time at the Beeman ranch—about Amanda. About Hattie Pearl. "What can you tell me about Amanda," she finally asked.

It was Evelyn's turn to be quiet for a moment before answering. "Amanda Beeman isn't who she wants people to see . . ."

"Why do you say that?"

A shadow flickered across Evelyn's face, accentuating new lines digging themselves deeper with passing days. "Let's put it this way—Amanda Beeman will be as nice as pie in conversation. It's when she's out of earshot that puts her in a different category . . ."

"I'm not sure I understand . . ."

Evelyn squared her eyes on her niece. "She's a liar—you can't believe a word that comes out of her mouth . . ."

"How do you know?"

That, Evelyn knew, was the tough part—she didn't know. All she had to base her comment on was a dark feeling, and that wasn't enough to help Harry win his case. "I wish I could give specifics, but I can't. But, ever since I met Amanda Beeman, I had the feeling things aren't quite right with her—she can't be trusted."

Colbie shook her head. "Your feelings aren't going to hold much water in a court of law . . ."

"I know—but, don't you feel it, Colbie? Can't you feel there's something dark at work with Amanda Beeman?" Evelyn's eyes filled with tears as she thought of the pain the Beemans caused her family. "Did you meet her grandmother?"

"I did—she was fascinating!"

"Well, I'd keep my distance if I were you—do what's needed to help Harry, but anything other than that? Keep your distance . . ."

Colbie watched her aunt as a darkness crept over her. "What aren't you telling me?"

Evelyn bristled slightly. "I told you everything I know— but . . ." She paused, then dropped her voice to a whisper. "Don't you ever just get a feeling about someone, and it tells you to stay away?"

Colbie nodded—of course, she did.

"That's how I feel about Amanda Beeman—there's a darkness in her as sure as I'm sittin' here . . ."

"Do you get such feelings often—about other people?"

"All the time—but, some feelings are stronger than others . . ."

Colbie felt a blush of excitement thinking about what her aunt confided—was Evelyn her link to an intuitive ancestral past? She knew her mother didn't have a lick of psychic ability, and Colbie always wondered if there were anyone else in her family who did. But, Evelyn? "I know exactly what you're talking about—the same thing happens to me . . ." The two women fell silent, neither voicing the obvious implication. "Do you," Colbie finally asked, "think you're a sensitive?"

Evelyn nodded. "I know I am . . ."

\*\*\*\*

"It's weird—I never thought I'd meet someone in my family who has abilities similar to mine . . ." Colbie stood at the bathroom door, tying her bathrobe belt around her waist.

"Why's it weird? I'd think you'd like having someone in your corner . . ."

"I do—but, if Evelyn is a sensitive, wouldn't my mother have noticed it when they were growing up? If she did, she never said a word!"

Brian took his time unwrapping his favorite candy bar before focusing on Colbie. "Maybe—but, you have to admit, it's not a typical topic of conversation."

Colbie nodded, disappeared into the bathroom, then reappeared five minutes later. "Well—it really doesn't make any difference. If Evelyn ever wants to talk about it, she knows she can come to me . . ."

She crawled into bed, then clicked off the small light on her nightstand. Making herself comfortable, she lay back and closed her eyes, inviting her intuitive mind to provide her with good and valid information. Instantly, images flowed, most zipping in and out—a few, however, took their time, allowing Colbie the opportunity to focus on each one. A vintage hotel clipped her peripheral vision, as if its importance were minimal. Then, a casket. Nothing fancy— more like a pine box in a grade B cowboy movie.

Colbie knew better than to analyze each vision as it appeared before her, soon shattering and splintering as another took its place.

Then, everything changed.

Suddenly, she found herself walking a solitary country

road—focusing on her feet, she paid little attention to anything around her, barely noticing as a man in overalls approached, a young girl dressed in a tattered, white dress in tow. Did she know them? Then, as quickly as they drew near, Colbie backed away, unsure. The two coming toward her stopped, and she recognized the young girl as LaRee Beeman—red, curly hair was streaked with dirt, her face revealing a life not fit for a young child. *How can that be,* Colbie wondered. *LaRee Beeman was Amanda's aunt—the time period doesn't fit...*

Her legs jerked as the vision dissipated, morphing into a series of small objects from a different time. Two, tarnished, silver napkin rings. A washbowl and pitcher. An empty picture frame. Eyelids fluttering, Colbie watched as each symbol appeared and vanished until there were no more. Slowly, she coaxed her body and mind from meditation, then opened her eyes.

"That was interesting..." Brian lay on his side beside her, watching as Colbie transported from one vision to another.

"I bet it was!" Colbie took a moment to focus on him. "Everything was from a hundred years ago—including LaRee Beeman. She was with a man who was walking with her on a country lane..."

"LaRee? But, that doesn't make sense—she wasn't around a hundred years ago..."

Colbie nodded. "I know! So, that makes me wonder if I were really seeing LaRee, or someone else who came before her..."

"You mean a relative of hers?"

"Exactly—I think the girl I saw in my vision may be Buzz's daughter. And, I think the guy was Buzz..."

"I don't get it—why would your visions have anything to do with the Beeman family? You're here to help Evelyn and Harry—it seems your visions are showing you a different direction."

Colbie sighed, then rolled onto her side to look at him. "I don't get it, either. But, now I know I still have my intuitive abilities—you know I was doubting that when we returned from Switzerland . . ."

Brian pulled her close. "Good! But, I never doubted you for a minute!"

\*\*\*\*

By the time winter crocuses poked their heads through melting snow, Harry's case was nearing its trial date. Colbie and Brian never thought they'd still be there, but, as Harry's nerves deteriorated, both knew their hanging around was a good idea. Evelyn retreated further into herself, often opting for an early bedtime just so she wouldn't have to deal with things. It wasn't that she was weak—just tired. Keeping Harry on an even keel wasn't the easiest thing, and she found herself taking up slack on the ranch. Of course, Colbie asked why she didn't hire a ranch hand, quickly learning they weren't that easy to find. "A good hand," Evelyn explained, "is like finding a four-leafed clover—you only get lucky once in a while."

She was right. At Colbie's insistence, Evelyn advertised for an experienced ranch hand, but it yielded nothing. It wasn't the money—Evelyn offered a good salary, leaving Colbie wondering if there were another reason hands from Sundance or Gillette didn't express an interest in the opportunity.

Harry, however, didn't think he needed help, grousing every day as he walked out the door he could take care of things on his own. Colbie and Brian noticed fleeting moments of his changing personality, but Evelyn refused to acknowledge the stress was getting to her husband. She knew him as a strong, self-sufficient man who needed nothing from anyone, and having family near was enough for him. The thought he may be found guilty of murder was inconceivable—and, it was a thought he couldn't tolerate.

Nor, would he.

\*\*\*\*

Mid-March, Colbie and Brian listened to sirens blaring as an ambulance and fire truck streaked up the road in front of Harry's ranch, shattering the country quiet. Evelyn stepped onto the porch, drying her hands on a terrycloth towel. "That's something we never see," she commented as the sounds began to fade. "The last time was when they found the Beeman boys . . ."

Colbie glanced at her aunt, then down the road, following the screeching sound. "Are there ranches in that direction other than the Beeman's?"

"Not really—we're the last two working ranches on this side of the county . . ."

"I know what you're thinking," Brian interjected, "but let's not get ahead of ourselves. Out this far, I imagine cars go at a pretty good clip—there could be a wreck. Just because they're going toward the Beeman's doesn't mean they're headed there . . ."

Colbie knew Brian was right, but logical thinking wasn't jibing with her feelings. Something was wrong at the Beeman's, and she damned well knew it. "Maybe—still, let's see if we can track them . . ." Before she could finish her sentence, she was heading for the car.

Brian checked his pocket for the keys, glanced at Evelyn with an apologetic look, then followed Colbie's lead. Within minutes, they were on their way west toward the Beeman's. "This could be a wild goose chase, you know . . ." Brian scanned the endless prairie in front of them. "It's probably nothing—think of all the times ambulances are dispatched, and it turns out the call was bogus."

"Give me a break! There's something going on at the Beeman's, and we need to find out what it is!"

Just as Colbie was about to explain her thinking, a sheriff's SUV screamed past them, providing a perfect map. It slowed as it neared the Beeman ranch, then turned toward the massive gate.

"I thought so . . ."

Brian parked on the side of the road about one hundred feet from the drive, constantly checking the rear view mirror. They watched as paramedic personnel approached the house, joined by the coroner moments later.

"Somebody died . . ."

Brian glanced at her, then back at the ranch house. "Only four people live there, plus ranch hands—maybe one of them got hurt, and didn't make it . . ."

"Maybe—but, do you remember the vision I had when the red-haired girl showed me a body on a gurney, then pointed to herself?"

"Yep—do you think this situation is what she was referring to?"

"I'm sure of it . . ."

Brian glanced at her. "So . . . the ranch hand theory is out?"

She grinned at him, then refocused on the house. "Pretty much . . ."

"If this is something more than a natural occurrence, you know this will be a crime scene. I'm not so sure it's a good idea to hang around—we don't want the sheriff catching wind of our being here, especially with Harry's trial coming up . . ."

"You're right. Let's get out of here—we'll find out soon enough what's going on." She flipped down the visor, and flicked open the mirror. "I don't look too bad—Gillette for dinner?"

Brian laughed, and pulled onto the road. "Sounds good to me!"

# CHAPTER SEVEN

They decided on a restaurant other than the Roundup. Colbie didn't like the idea of being recognized, and having been to the popular restaurant twice didn't bode well for anonymity, especially if she and Brian showed up a third time. Amanda clearly knew the staff there, and it wasn't a stretch to think word of Colbie's and Brian's patronage would find its way to her. That wasn't all—it was a good bet the Beemans hired a private investigator—or, more—to keep an eye on Harry. Chances were good they knew Harry had people staying with him—if so, what did they know about Brian and her?

Colbie tried to get in touch a few times after she had her conversation with Hattie Pearl, but Amanda didn't respond. Perhaps it wasn't unusual, but Colbie couldn't help thinking Amanda's silence signaled anger or dissatisfaction about something. On the other hand, maybe she decided she really didn't care for Colbie and Brian, so why keep up false pretenses?

She didn't consider Amanda consulted the Internet to find out what she wanted to know . . .

\*\*\*\*

"Can I get you anything else?"

Colbie smiled at the server, placing her napkin on the table. "No, thank you—that was one of the best meals I've had in a long time!"

The waitress grinned, checking the table. "That's local beef—some of the best around!"

"Really? Where?"

"A ranch outside of Sundance—Beeman's Circle B, I think . . ."

"No kidding! We were out that way today . . ." A dramatic pause. "Something was going on . . ."

The server glanced at her station to make sure no one needed her. "I heard about that . . ."

"What happened?" Colbie put on her most innocent

expression. "I hope everything's okay . . ."

The waitress shook her head. "Not for the grandmother, it isn't . . ."

"What do you mean?"

The young woman leaned close to Colbie, her voice a low whisper. "I heard it was murder . . ."

Brian watched as Colbie tried not to choke on the last crumbs of her dessert. "Murder? Whose?"

"That's what I said—the grandmother!"

Colbie sipped her water, trying to regain her composure. "How do you know what happened?"

"My best friend texted me . . ."

Colbie had the feeling there was more to the girl's story, but it was critical she didn't sound too interested. "Wow! What a friend! It must be nice to get the latest news before everyone knows about it!"

The server laughed, brushing an errant crumb off the table. "Oh, that's only because I used to date Bobby Beeman eons ago . . ."

"Oh—I don't know who that is . . ."

"Sure you do! He was murdered a few months back—it was plastered all over the news . . ."

Brian slipped his arm around Colbie's shoulders. "I think I remember that . . . did they ever find out what happened?"

She shook her head. "No—but they arrested a guy a while back. That's about all I know . . ."

Colbie took over. "How are you? How did you deal with your boyfriend's death?" Feigning emotional concern always worked.

"It was rough, at first—but, then I remember what an ass he was—so, I guess I don't feel too sorry for him . . ."

"You mean he abused you?"

Sorrow crept into her voice. "Yes, I'm embarrassed to say. Eventually, though, I told him I was leaving . . ."

"What did he say?"

"Nothing—he didn't care . . ."

\*\*\*\*

"I can't believe Hattie Pearl is dead!" Colbie stood at the car, her hand poised to open the passenger door. "She seemed just fine when I saw her . . ."

Brian agreed. "I know—I can't believe it, either. But, consider the source . . . we don't know the waitress at all, so how believable is the story about her friend texting her about Hattie Pearl's murder? Not only that, who's her friend?"

"And, how did her friend find out? Was she there?" Colbie paused, laying out possible scenarios in her brain. "The first thing we have to do is find out if Amanda's grandmother really is dead. If that's the case, then we need to know how she died . . ." Colbie climbed in the car, sliding the leftover containers between them. "Here's another question—when the little red-haired girl pointed at the covered body on a gurney, was she pointing at Hattie Pearl?"

"That would be my guess . . ."

"Mine, too. If you ask me, losing four people in one family in a year's time is a little more than a coincidence."

"Losing them to murder—if what the waitress says is true—is a hell of a lot more than a coincidence!"

"You're tellin' me—they're dropping like flies at the Beeman ranch . . ."

"So—the question is why. Who has what to gain?"

"If Hattie Pearl is dead, the only family member left living at the ranch is Amanda—and, her husband."

The implications were staggering, leaving Colbie and Brian to wonder privately if Amanda were at the source of Uncle Harry's troubles. There was something about the remaining Beeman Brian didn't like, and he agreed with Evelyn—Amanda was a liar. Did he have proof? No. But, the few times he was around her, his skin crawled, and he couldn't wait to leave. His reaction was, perhaps, something he should have told Colbie, but he didn't think it accounted for much at the time. Now? He wasn't so sure.

Colbie's suspicions tracked Brian's, but she wondered if Amanda were responsible for more than Hattie Pearl's passing—although she refused to pile a murder accusation on someone without knowing the facts, her intuitive senses were at full attention. "How long ago did I meet Hattie Pearl?" She glanced at Brian, then focused again on the road.

"Remember a couple of days ago when I was in my intuitive mind, and you were watching me? We were getting ready for bed."

"I remember . . ."

"We talked about LaRee Beeman's appearing in my vision as the young girl, but I didn't tell you the rest of it . . . I also saw a vintage hotel, and a pine-box casket."

"You mean a cowboy casket?"

"Exactly!"

He glanced at her. "That makes two things representing a body—the first one was the gurney with a body on it, and the second is the pine-box casket. They have to represent someone's death . . ."

"I think they do—Hattie Pearl's. I think the vintage hotel signifies the era of my visions. I'm thinking mid to late eighteen hundreds . . ."

"That also tracks with your vision of the guy and the little girl—you said they could be Buzz and LaRee. But, the LaRee thing doesn't make sense because of time frame."

"I know—I'm beginning to think the girl with Buzz wasn't LaRee, but Hattie Pearl when she was young . . ."

"That makes more sense . . ."

"Especially because there's a strong family resemblance—that red hair is a defining trait of the Beeman family." Colbie thought for a moment before continuing. "I remember I had the opportunity to meet the daughter of my best friend in high school. The daughter was about twenty-six and, when I met her, it struck me she didn't look anything like her mom or dad. Then, in the middle of dinner, it came to me—she was the spittin' image of my friend's mother. And, I mean the spittin' image!"

Brian laughed, reaching over to squeeze her hand. "Kind of the same thing in your family—you and Evelyn have the red hair . . ."

"So did my grandfather—although, I never had the chance to know him. He passed when I was very young— Mom told me he had the red hair, too . . ."

"What about his father? Your great-grandfather . . . how far back does the red hair go?"

Colbie laughed, recalling how much she didn't know about her family. "You're asking the wrong person—I don't have any idea. If you're curious, ask Evelyn—she has a pretty good handle on our family lineage!"

****

By the time they reached Evelyn's and Harry's, the situation at the Beeman ranch hit the airwaves. A small radio station broadcasting from Gillette picked it up first, and it wasn't long until television stations informed their viewers the Beeman family was, once again, in the news.

Evelyn had the small T.V. in the kitchen tuned to a local channel, and she sat at the ranch table, clutching a mug of coffee. "Did you hear? Hattie Pearl Beeman is dead!"

Colbie  wriggled out of her jacket, hanging it over the back of a chair. "We did hear, but not from the media . . ."

Evelyn turned to look at her. "Meaning?"

"Our waitress at the restaurant told us—it seems a friend of hers texted her about Hattie Pearl shortly after it happened . . ."

"How did the friend know about it?"

Colbie glanced at Brian, then shrugged her shoulders. "That's what we want to know . . ."

Evelyn refocused on the television. "They're not saying how she died . . ."

"They probably won't until they have an autopsy report— the last thing they want is to get in a mess by reporting false information."

"I'll bet it has something to do with Amanda . . ." Evelyn's face set as she thought of the only Beeman heir.

"Perhaps—but, Hattie Pearl was elderly. She easily could have passed due to natural causes . . ."

Colbie's aunt whirled around, her eyes dark with anger. "Is that what you think, Colbie? Is that what you really think?" She didn't wait for an answer. "Hattie Pearl didn't die from old age. Or, dementia. Or, a medical problem . . ." Evelyn paused for a deep breath. "She died at the hands of Amanda Beeman—you mark my words!" Tears welled in her eyes as the torment of the last months finally fractured the dam. "Excuse me . . ."

Colbie and Brian were silent as Evelyn got up, grabbed her mug, and left the kitchen. Brian waited until she was out of earshot before focusing on Colbie. "What the hell just happened?"

"I can't say I blame her—she's been dealing with Harry's problem for months, and Hattie Pearl's death is a catalyst for many questions regarding the murders of the Beeman Boys."

"Do you think she's right?"

"About Amanda's being involved with Hattie Pearl's death? It's possible—so many deaths within a year's time is highly unusual, and someone is going to take notice."

Brian was quiet for a few moments as he watched live coverage from the Beeman ranch. "How long until the trial starts?"

"Two weeks . . ."

"Then, we need to get our butts in gear . . ."

\*\*\*\*

Jeremiah Hastings watched the broadcast, savoring a drink. After a tough day in court, he figured he deserved a little bit of good news—such as the possibility of Harry's innocence from a jury's perspective getting a whole lot better. He was quick to mentally calculate the Beeman body count within the last year, convinced only a total moron would believe the deaths were coincidental. *There's no way,* he thought as the news anchor wrapped a live segment from the ranch. *There's no way on God's green earth . . .*

Trial preparation to that point wasn't proceeding particularly well. With few witnesses willing to step up on Harry's side, Hastings feared the case was tilting toward the prosecution simply based on numbers—there were probably only two or three character witnesses he could count on during Harry's defense.

Not the best situation.

Unfortunately, his client was a man of few friends—not because he was unlikeable, but because he chose a more reclusive lifestyle. It suited him and, not too long after he married Evelyn, it suited her, too. Of course, he couldn't ignore society in its entirety, and it was that obligation placing him directly in front of the Beeman boys on several occasions. Somehow, the boys managed to infiltrate a few local organizations to which Harry belonged, and it was there he got his first real look at how despicable the boys could be—especially Bobby. "A nasty piece of work," Harry told his attorney when he first met him. "He'd murder his own grandma if it meant he had total access to the ranch."

At the time, Hastings wasn't entirely sure Harry's observation was based on pure hatred of the boys, or whether it had an element of truth. After a couple of months of working on his case passed, however, he had little doubt he could get an acquittal. Why? Because the Beeman boys' reputation succeeded them, and Hastings suspected the prosecution was having a hell of time rounding up anyone who would vouch for someone they didn't like. *If Harry has only two or three great character witnesses, the prosecution probably has fewer . . .* The truth was each side had little to go on which, perhaps, put Harry in a good position. Coupled with the news of Hattie Pearl's unfortunate passing? *They may as well concede now,* Jeremiah thought as he drained his glass.

Although there was no one there to see, with the sunlight just right Jeremiah Hastings looked like a man who experienced the best and worst of life. As he neared a foreseeable retirement, seldom did he look forward to going to court—somewhere, he lost his taste for the judiciary kill. If he lost? Well, that was okay, too—except he rarely didn't bring home a win for his client.

That would be unacceptable.

# CHAPTER EIGHT

Colbie figured there would be little or no evidence corroborating the thought Amanda Beeman was responsible for her grandmother's death. According to Evelyn, however, it was possible—and, probable. And, although the majority of people in the Gillette and Sundance areas forgot about Hattie Pearl's passing five minutes after it happened, Colbie knew instinctively Evelyn was right— the more she tuned into the Beeman heir, the more she was certain Amanda's grandmother passed at the hand of her granddaughter. *That may be*, Colbie admonished herself, *but Hastings didn't hire me to investigate Hattie Pearl . . .* still, she had to consider if Amanda were capable of murdering her own grandmother, the possibility existed she could have killed her own sons. Knowing that, she had to turn the investigation toward the Beeman heir.

It was in Harry's best interest.

As soon as the news of Hattie Pearl's death reached Jeremiah Hastings, he was on the phone to Colbie, hoping to discuss her take on the events at the Beeman ranch—what began as a thirty-minute conversation turned into nearly two hours of devising a trajectory for Harry's defense. If they could deflect attention from him and turn it toward Amanda, Hastings' knew Harry stood a good chance of beating the charge.

That, unfortunately, wasn't going to be easy.

It was clear to Colbie the last Beeman standing wasn't interested in continuing their neophyte friendship. She wasn't sure why, but it probably had to do with Hattie Pearl's telling her granddaughter she had a lovely conversation with Colbie. Or, Amanda learned of Colbie's professional career. There was a third possibility, too—Amanda may have learned Colbie was related to Evelyn and Harry. But, no matter the different possibilities, none of them were good, and Colbie imagined each could throw Amanda into a bitchy snit.

So, since getting close to Amanda as a friend was out, her next best choice was heading into Gillette to speak with the waitress who dated Bobby Beeman. When she and Brian met her a few evenings prior, Colbie had a feeling the waitress wasn't telling all she knew—and, the first thing Colbie wanted to know was how the server's friend knew about Hattie Pearl's passing. *Was she there?*

Colbie entertained that question as well as others as she turned onto the main road heading toward Gillette. *This is where the case changes*, she thought as she noticed dark rain clouds settling in. A portend?

She hoped not.

\*\*\*\*

Amanda Beeman offered the family attorney a drink or a cup of coffee—whatever he preferred. "Scotch—neat," he replied without stopping to think it may be a little early. But, since he would undoubtedly be subjected to Amanda's rants for the next hour, he figured it best to be . . . fortified.

"I have a lot I need to discuss today . . ." Amanda eyeballed the amount she poured into his glass. "With my grandmother's passing, I guess that means I'm in charge."

Her attorney grunted as he sat in the overstuffed chair in front of the fireplace. "Don't count your chickens, Amanda— things change . . ."

She shot him a dark look. "What do you mean, 'things change?'"

"Nothing, really—but, with an estate the size of Hattie Pearl's, it's not unusual to have a family member scurry out from under the woodwork just in time to contest the will."

"Well—that can't happen because I'm the only one left. No other Beeman's on the horizon, as far as I know. Besides, if there were, no judge in his right mind would go against me in a court of law. It wouldn't make sense . . ."

"Perhaps—but, for now, it's a moot point. According to Hattie Pearl's will, she wanted a full autopsy . . ."

Amanda tried to quell her sudden anger as she placed her cocktail glass on the end table. "An autopsy? What the hell for? The woman was ninety-seven for Christ's sake!"

"I know, I know—still, we have to abide by the terms of

her will. I notified the coroner this morning . . ."

Amanda sat back, picking up her glass, shaking it slightly to separate the ice cubes. "Can't you tell him to forget it?"

"Nope—he assured me he would begin the procedure this afternoon . . ."

"Then I contest the autopsy . . ." Her eyes turned steely as she thought of Hattie Pearl. "What do I have to do?"

"Seriously, Amanda? You want to go that route? It can wind up being a bigger mess than you know . . ."

"Oh, please—you know as well as I, Hattie Pearl died from natural causes!"

The attorney watched her carefully, certain there was more to her protestations than she was letting on. "What do you have against an autopsy," he asked, his tone laced with accusation.

"I don't have anything against them when they're necessary—and, an autopsy isn't necessary when it comes to Hattie Pearl." She thought for a moment. "Who pays?"

"For the autopsy? Well, when it's requested by the deceased, I imagine the deceased's family foots the bill . . ."

Amanda snorted with disgust. "I'm not paying for it, I can tell you that!"

"Well, you'll have to take that up with the coroner's office. I'm sure they have the information you need about who's responsible for what. All I know is I have to abide by the wishes of my client, and Hattie Pearl requested an autopsy. That's it . . ."

"That's it, my ass . . ." Amanda swigged down the last of

her drink, determined no one was going to tell her what to do when it came to her own family. "What about the ranch? I assume my grandmother made provisions for that . . ."

"She did . . ."

"Well?"

"I'll be having an official reading of the will, but it won't be until after the autopsy . . ."

"After the autopsy? Why?"

Her attorney leveled his eyes with hers. "Because things are subject to change . . ."

Amanda met his gaze. "That's bullshit, and you know it."

"Perhaps—but, that's the way Hattie Pearl wanted it . . ."

Amanda was increasingly aware she wasn't going to win her argument that day—time for a change of subject. "What's going on with the trial?"

"It starts in a couple of weeks . . ." The question was one he didn't expect. Up until then, Amanda Beeman exhibited no interest in the trial against Harry Fenamore, even though she was the one instigating the murder charge.

"We'll win?"

"Probably—although, I have to be honest . . . it's a circumstantial case."

"Why? Everybody knows Bobby and his brother were hassled by Harry Fenamore from the time they were old enough to drive."

"Enough to make Harry want to kill them? That seems

a little far-fetched . . ."

Amanda stood, cutting their conversation short. "Perhaps you're not the one to be trying our case, if that's the way you feel . . ."

The attorney also stood, poised to meet her verbal challenge. "You may be right, Amanda—I can get a continuance, and you're free to hire whomever you please. That will, at least, provide a little time for someone new to work hand-in-hand with Marshall Sage, and get up to speed."

She walked him to the door. "I'm sorry, Rory—but I think I need someone in my corner with a little more killer instinct. I'll start contacting someone to replace you first thing in the morning . . ."

With that, he was gone. No thank you for his forty years of impeccable legal service to the Beeman family. No thank you for getting the trial against Harry Fenamore up and running.

Not a thank you to be had.

\*\*\*\*

Having been a waitress at a small diner during high school, Colbie had the foresight to call the restaurant for a quick conversation with the young server who dated Bobby

Beeman rather than showing up without notice. It was too bad she couldn't remember the server's correct name, asking for Sarah when the front desk hostess answered the phone. "Do you mean Sari," she asked.

"That's it! Is she available? I know you're getting ready for the dinner shift, so I won't keep her . . ." With that promise, the hostess politely asked Colbie to hold and, within moments, Sari was on the line.

"Sari? This is Colbie Colleen—you waited on me a couple of nights ago . . ." It was obvious the waitress was searching her memory banks to place the woman's voice. "With all the people you wait on, I'm sure it's difficult to remember me—we talked about your dating the great-grandson of the elderly woman who died a few days ago . . ."

"Oh! I remember! What can I do for you?"

"Well, you really piqued my interest . . . is it possible to meet soon? I'd love to hear more, and it's a great story for the book I'm working on . . ."

"A book?" A momentary silence. "I'm not sure what I can tell you . . ."

Colbie laughed as if she were talking to her best friend. "I figured you might say that—but, I'm creating a character that reminded me of the boy you dated, and I'd love to hear your perspective of the relationship . . ."

Sari thought for a minute before consenting. "Alright—I guess that would be okay . . ."

"Excellent! I promise I'll mention your name in the acknowledgments!"

It was a go—three o'clock the following day.

\*\*\*\*

Finding an experienced lawyer turned out to be more difficult than Amanda thought. If she were lucky enough to speak to one instead of an assistant, she might have been able to make a quick decision. Instead, she found herself waiting for return calls—a situation she found appalling.

"You'd think with the mention of my name, they'd pick up the damned phone!" She cast a scathing glance at her husband, as if he were responsible for the lack of personal communication.

"Maybe they knew it was you . . ." The second the words left his mouth, Randy knew he made a mistake. He also knew, however, how demanding and unappealing his wife could be. Truth be told? He didn't blame any attorney for not wanting to talk to her.

"What the hell do you mean by that?"

Time to tap dance. "Nothing—I didn't mean it the way it sounded . . ."

"Then what did you mean?"

"I meant they probably knew about your case against Harry, and they didn't have the time to talk to you when you called. It wouldn't be a short conversation—that's all . . ."

Amanda peered at him over the rim of her glasses—she knew it was a line of crap, but she didn't feel like arguing.

Another truth? Randy could've cared less about the trial—it didn't involve him, and he could understand why someone would want to off Amanda's boys. They were spoiled, barbaric brats—even as adults—and it was an unspoken surprise when they didn't wind up dead sooner than they did. Yep—the way Randy saw it, life was easier without the Beeman bastards around.

Then there was everyone and anyone in Sundance—they knew Amanda and Randy were an odd pair. In public, he doted on his wife, affording her every inch of respect and adoration he could muster. In private? Their relationship wasn't based on public opinion, and arguments were a daily sport. Amanda loved to belittle him, and Randy hated taking it—so, when he had the opportunity to witness Amanda's being taken down a peg by something as petty as a personal conversation with an attorney she didn't know—well, it put a smile on his lips.

Few in Sundance and Gillette remember the 'old Amanda'—the girl who exuded confidence no matter the situation, although 'confidence' may be the wrong word—arrogance was more like it. When she headed off to college, she returned with an attitude rivaling the haughtiest of rich bitches, and she didn't hesitate to let everyone know she was the new manager for Beeman ranch.

That was when she met Randy Howard.

A year older than Amanda, Randy graduated from the University of Wyoming with a degree in business—it seemed the easiest thing to do. Grades weren't of utmost importance to him, and the sole purpose for going to college was to get away from his parents in his backwater hometown in southwest Wyoming. Ranching was a way of life for him—although he deemed the work much too difficult—and it was his experience in all things rustic that attracted him to Amanda when she blew into town shortly after her graduation. She represented what ranching could be—not what he knew it to be.

It was at a local ranchers' meeting when they met and, from then on, they were inseparable—just Amanda and him.

And, her two-year old boys.

****

Colbie was pleased Sari was on time for their meeting—her intuitive senses told her the young waitress was honest and forthright, speaking to her overall character. Without having the opportunity to meet Bobby Beeman, Colbie wondered what she saw in him, especially because he was known as a rich, punk rancher from Sundance. *Maybe it's a bad boy syndrome*, she thought as Sari waved to her.

"Am I late? There was a wreck ahead of me, and I swear I was waiting for hours!"

Colbie laughed, motioning for her to sit down. Spring was in full swing, so they decided to meet at a small park not too far from Sari's restaurant. "You're fine! Although, I have to laugh—I'm used to massive traffic jams, and I can't imagine a major tie-up in a small town like Gillette!"

"Trust me, we have them—the worst is outside of town when ranchers are moving cattle, and they're crossing the road!" Sari tossed her jacket on the arm of the bench, then sat next to Colbie. "So—what do you want to know?"

Colbie angled her body so she could face her. "To be honest, I'm not sure I know! Why don't you start at the beginning of your relationship with Bobby—what attracted you to him?"

Sari grinned. "What attracted me to him? He was drop dead gorgeous, that's what! And, I'm a sucker for red, curly hair!" She paused, thinking about how good their relationship was in the beginning. "I don't know—there was just something about him I really liked . . ."

"I get it—how long were you together?"

"Nearly four years—it wasn't until after his grandfather died that everything started to change . . ."

"In what way?"

Sari glanced at two kids kicking a soccer ball close to their bench. "I don't know much about his brother, but Bobby started to get real quiet—like something was bothering him."

"Do you have any idea what it was?"

"No—like I said, he was real quiet, and there were days he barely spoke to me. It was like he was mad about something, but it wasn't me—he just ignored me like I didn't exist . . ."

Both sat for a few moments thinking about Bobby Beeman, and what could have caused such a change in personality. Colbie tried tuning into Sari as she sat beside her, but it wasn't easy. The server had her guard up, exhibiting a western reserve often found in those who lived a rural existence—or, so she heard.

"Did Bobby ever confide in you what was causing his anxiety—at least, I'm assuming that's what it was . . ."

"No—but I always thought it had to do with his mother. She was a real piece of work, if you know what I mean . . ."

"Explain . . ."

"Well, for starters, she was always yelling at him, telling him he was 'a no good piece of shit.' And, whenever she went on a screaming spree, he tucked his tail and ran like a whipped puppy."

"Do you think he was scared of her?"

"I think it was more than that—I think he was petrified of her. I also think that's why he acted like such a tough guy when he was out of her sight . . ."

Colbie nodded. "That's very insightful . . ."

"It wasn't just me who noticed the change in him—my best friend saw it, too. That's how she knew about the grandmother's murder so fast—she stopped by the ranch."

"Why did she do that?"

"Because I asked her to—Bobby had some things of mine, and I figured it was about time I got them back. Except, I didn't want to be the one to go there . . ."

"So, she went for you . . ."

"Yep—she got there just as the paramedics arrived."

Colbie recalled the same scene as she and Brian parked on the side of the road, watching through the binos. As she scrolled through her memory of that day, she didn't remember seeing anyone else other than rescue personnel and the coroner.

"And, that's how you found out about Hattie Pearl's death?"

Sari gently picked up a lady bug climbing on her shoe, placing it in the grass beside her. "Yep—I still don't know the details, though. I haven't had time to talk to my friend . . ."

"What do you think happened?"

Sari squared her body to Colbie. "What I really think?"

Colbie nodded.

"I think Amanda Beeman is as guilty as they come!"

"For Hattie Pearl's death—or, the Beeman boys?"

Sari hesitated. "I haven't told anyone this . . ."

Colbie waited a moment before acknowledging her indecision. "Sari—it's okay."

The young waitress suddenly appeared timid, as though remembering something unpleasant. "Okay—but, if it ever comes down to it, I won't admit anything . . ."

Colbie smiled. "Agreed. So . . ."

"So—I think Amanda Beeman killed Bobby and his brother, and I think she took Hattie Pearl out of the picture, too." Sari gave her the 'there—I said it' look as if silently apologizing for speaking her mind.

Colbie gave her hand a quick pat. "Well, I can tell you if you're thinking it, then other people are, too . . ."

"Really? You think so?"

"I know so . . ."

For the next hour, Colbie allowed Sari to spill her guts about everything—how she really felt about Bobby Beeman, the abuse, and his refusal to acknowledge her as someone who mattered. Finally, Colbie stood. "Sari—you've been a big help. Do you mind giving me your cell? If I have any questions, it will be easier to shoot you a text . . ."

Moments later they parted, Sari wondering if she did the right thing, Colbie thinking about what she could do with her newfound information. What she told Sari was true—more than one person was undoubtedly considering Amanda Beeman in all three murders. It was only a matter of time until a river of emotion overflowed its banks, revealing motivation for the killings.

Who would be trying to choke back those emotions was the question . . .

# CHAPTER NINE

66 I don't know if I can do this . . ."

Colbie grasped Evelyn's hand, giving it a loving squeeze.

"Of course, you can—Brian and I are in your corner. And, remember—I'll be counting on you to tell me what your intuitive feelings are during the trial . . ." It was a gentle reminder that Evelyn needed to be Brian's and Colbie's eyes and ears while they dug in trying to find enough evidence pointing to Amanda Beeman's culpability for the murder of her two sons.

Evelyn drew a deep breath to gather courage, then headed toward the courthouse's heavy front door. "You're right—besides, I know Harry didn't kill those miserable Beeman boys. The truth puts justice on his side . . ."

Colbie watched her aunt steel herself, ready to tackle

whatever lay in front of her. But, the truth?

Harry Fenamore was in a situation.

Of course, Colbie updated Jeremiah Hastings about her conversation with the young waitress and, he, too, agreed Amanda Beeman should be investigated—the problem was there was so little time. He anticipated the trial lasting no more than two or three weeks, so Colbie's targeted investigation of Amanda had to be precise—there was no room for error.

That meant she and Brian needed to split their time— Colbie would scour courthouse and library records again, while Brian surveilled Amanda and Randy Beeman. Colbie also had the feeling if she could have a conversation with Amanda's husband—alone—she might get a clearer picture of what really happened the night the Beeman boys were gunned down. *That*, she thought as she settled Evelyn in the courtroom, *would be a miracle of miracles . . .*

Evelyn whispered goodbye as Colbie turned to go. "I'll pay attention to everything!" She tapped her yellow legal pad with her pen. "I'll see you this afternoon—good luck!"

\*\*\*\*

Colbie set her sights on a day of sifting through legal docs and newspaper clippings to find something Hastings could use to acquit Harry. And, although the main library was helpful, it didn't take Colbie long to realize she needed a library with comprehensive state records—that meant a half-day's drive to Cheyenne. *Not today,* she thought as she checked her watch. *Besides, I'm not going without Brian . . .*

Just as she was about to call him, he checked in to see how the research was progressing. "Not great," she confided, privately thinking there may not be much she could do to help Harry. "I think we need to head to Cheyenne to check out state records . . . I have a strong feeling Amanda's name is going to crop up—but, not if we stay in Gillette."

"Is this an intuitive thing?"

Colbie smiled. "Yes, it's an intuitive thing. What do you think?"

"You want me off surveillance?"

"Well, I don't *want* you off of it, but I don't feel like making that drive by myself . . ."

"Understandable—for what it's worth, I staked out the Circle B for the morning, and I saw Amanda for a grand total of about two minutes."

"What was she up to?"

"Nothing—she talked to a couple of ranch hands, and fifteen minutes later I saw them peel out. My best guess is she fired them . . ."

"Fired them? Why? One would surely think she needs all the help she can get running that place . . ."

"That's what I thought—maybe, though, she's already

making plans to sell. If that's it, she knows she can work the ranch with a skeleton crew until the cattle are sold to market. Especially coming into summer . . ."

"Or, another rancher . . ."

"Doubtful—but, you never know. It could happen . . ."

Colbie was quiet for a moment, considering the possibilities. Could Amanda really run a seventeen thousand acre ranch on a skeleton crew? Maybe, but it seemed to her life on the ranch would be busier during fair-seasoned months—not because of the cattle, but all the other things needing attention for a well-run, full-scale operation. "If she's already making plans to sell, she's placing herself in the judicial crosshairs . . ."

"Agreed . . ."

"And, let's not forget Grandpa Beeman—he passed only a year ago. If we're considering Amanda's murdering her own two sons . . ."

"And, Hattie Pearl," Brian interrupted.

" . . . we have to consider she murdered her grandfather, too."

"It's going to be incredibly difficult to prove any of it, unless you convince Hastings to request an exhumation."

"Which reminds me—Hattie Pearl's autopsy findings are supposed to be available tomorrow. Finally!"

Brian chuckled. "Is it just me, or does everything move slower in the west?"

"It's not just you—but, I have to admit, it's growing on me."

"Seriously?"

"So? What's wrong with that?"

Brian bellowed a gut laugh. "I never thought I'd hear you say you're okay with a slower pace . . . you! The woman who travels the globe, solving exciting cases!"

"Oh, please—anyway, are you up for taking an impromptu trip to Cheyenne?"

"Yep—when do we leave?"

"Tomorrow, first thing . . ."

\*\*\*\*

Marshall Sage stood, buttoned his suit coat, and leveled his eyes on the jury foreman. "My name is Marshall Sage." His voice was clear. Concise. Clipped.

Then, the proclamation. "Harry Fenamore is a killer!"

Evelyn gasped at his words, though she knew to expect a venomous assault against her husband. "The prosecutor will be a pit viper of a man," Colbie warned. Still, his pit bull approach sparked uncertainty. Yes, she had faith in Jeremiah Hastings, but the man crossing to the juror's box was convincing. One glance at them told her that . . .

She watched as he paused, letting his words sink in with each juror seated in front of him. "In fact," he continued, "there was a time his guilt wouldn't be up for discussion! There was a time not too long ago when men like him met their fate at the hands of those who judged outside the confines of the law—gibbeted in the middle of the night, the hangman gone by morning!" Of course, few, if any, knew what 'gibbeted' meant, but they could guess.

He paused when someone in the back of the courtroom whispered agreement as if attending a revival meeting packed with hopefuls seeking healing from a self-proclaimed conduit of God. "But," he continued, "that's not how we do things now—a man must be proven guilty by a jury of his peers before paying penance!" A pause. "That responsibility, Ladies and Gentlemen, falls to you . . ."

Evelyn noticed Juror Six glance downward, refusing to meet the prosecutor's eyes.

"Now," Sage continued, "from the simple fact Gillette isn't an urban hub, it's entirely possible you know Harry Fenamore—or, know of him. The defense will paint him as a pillar of the community, and you might know or think him to be just that—a best friend in waiting if you give him the chance. But, what kind of best friend will shoot you, blasting your guts all over a bridge at Harrelson's Gap?" He paused as he slowly walked the length of the jury box. "What kind of friend—or, acquaintance—will rip your body apart with a shotgun?" A glance at the juror directly in front of him. "And, what kind of friend will leave you there to be ravaged by critters of each . . . and, every . . . kind?"

Marshall Sage backed away from the juror's box, crossing his arms. "I'll tell you . . .

The Harry Fenamore kind."

\*\*\*\*

Amanda stood in front of her husband, clutching a thumb drive in her clenched first. "I knew it," she cried. "I knew it!"

Randy refused to flinch as a small speck of spit splatted on his face. "Knew what?"

"Colbie Colleen! I knew damned well she was a fraud!"

"A fraud?"

"Yes! A fraud! She's a psychic behavioral profiler—and, a successful one!"

That was news he wasn't expecting to hear! Randy grew quiet as he considered how Colbie Colleen could ruin what Amanda and he worked so hard to achieve. They were almost at the end of their run and, soon, the ranch would be little more than a distant memory—they could retire, enjoying the life they were meant to have. "How do you know?"

"I hired our investigator to take a hard look at her . . ."

"Let me guess—his findings are on that thumb drive."

"Everything that bitch told me was a lie! She and that boyfriend of hers never picked Wyoming as a place to live, and I'll bet she's here because of Harry . . ."

"Harry? You mean she's working for him?"

"Yep—that's exactly what I mean . . ." Amanda glared at her husband, eyes flashing with anger. "The question is what are you going to do about it?'

Randy's face set. "I'll take care of it . . ."

\*\*\*\*

As Colbie expected, Evelyn took comprehensive notes during opening day of Harry's trial, all the while watching him in the defendant's hot seat. Hastings sat beside him, scratching hurried notes as he listened to the prosecution's opening statement, occasionally leaning close to Harry, whispering something only the two of them could hear.

For all of his bravado, it was clear to anyone looking Harry Fenamore was scared. His face no longer looked like a well-seasoned rancher, skin leathered by an unrelenting sun—over the months since his arrest, his weight tumbled, giving him a slightly gaunt appearance as he concentrated on the prosecuting attorney's every word.

"Marshall Sage is the main prosecutor," Evelyn explained as Colbie flipped through her aunt's notes after dinner. "But, of course, you knew that . . ."

Colbie glanced up at her aunt, smiling. "Yes, I did know—but, your notes are on par with a seasoned attorney! I particularly like jotting your questions in the margins—well done!"

Evelyn beamed at the compliment. "Thanks—I tried to think like you . . ."

"How's Harry?"

"He's fine—he should be home any time now. You can ask him yourself . . ."

Again, Colbie flipped through Evelyn's pages of notes. "What's your impression of Marshall Sage," she asked, not looking up.

"Well, he's young—and, he seems hungry to make a name for himself among his colleagues . . ."

"Like Jeremiah Hastings?"

"Yes, now that you mention it . . ."

"What about your intuitive observations?"

Evelyn paused. "I think the thing that stood out the most is Marshall Sage's unyielding commitment to convict Harry—and, he'll do whatever it takes to do so . . ."

Colbie sat back in her chair, glancing at Brian. "To the point of being unscrupulous?"

"Maybe. No—I don't know!"

The fact Evelyn mentioned her strong reaction to the prosecuting attorney clued Colbie into the depth of Evelyn's ability—an ability she seldom used for a particular reason. Up until Harry's trial, any intuitive visions were of little or no consequence. Having the ability to help Harry and Colbie much like her niece conducts a profiling case, however, was something she never considered or thought possible.

"Did you get a chance to talk to Hastings after court adjourned?"

Evelyn nodded. "Yes, but not for very long. He said he expects to address the jury tomorrow with his opening statement . . ."

"Did he seem comfortable?"

"Yeah—but, then again, he always comes across as completely unflappable, so it's hard to tell."

"I agree—he's hard to read." She winked at her aunt. "But, you—and, I—have a secret weapon!" Finally, she noticed Evelyn's shoulders relax.

It had been one hell of a day.

# CHAPTER TEN

Colbie turned in before Brian, exhausted. Leaving the next day meant getting up before dawn so they could be in Cheyenne by the time the courthouse opened— if they were going to make such a long trip, they should maximize their time, researching.

She clicked off the lamp on her nightstand, her eyes adjusting to the slight glow of a night-light by the bathroom door. As her body relaxed, images formed in her mind, twisting and turning until they came into clear focus— Harry. LaRee. Then, something more disturbing—a vision of Buzz, his body splitting in two, straight down the middle.

Colbie watched until his figure disappeared.

Drifting deeper into meditation, each muscle relaxed as she envisioned a healing cocoon encapsulating her body. From her feet to the top of her head, a soothing warmth enveloped her, its white light reaching the depths of her soul, cleansing her from the day's frustrations. Then, suddenly, her intuitive mind jerked harshly back into her body, leaving her with remnants of a forming vision she didn't understand. Buzz stood before her with two young women—one on each arm, right hands lovingly placed on their swollen bellies. As far as Colbie could tell, both looked as if they were ready to deliver—but, the young woman on Buzz's left sneered as her eyes met Colbie's.

*What the hell does that mean?* She waited as her mind cleared, bringing her gently back to reality. *Why are there two?*

It was a question she soon would answer.

****

"How much longer?"

Brian looked over at her, then refocused on the road. "Getting antsy, are we?"

Colbie grinned, returning the gesture. "Not antsy, really—I just have a strong feeling we're going to uncover something that will shift Harry's case in a totally different direction. I'm just eager to get started . . ."

"Shift it how?"

"I don't know—but, I'm pretty sure I'll know it when I see it . . ."

Brian glanced at the clock on the dashboard. "To answer your question, we're about an hour out . . ."

"That's not bad—we'll be at the courthouse right after it opens."

She turned her attention to the passing prairie, recalling her vision the previous night. *Two pregnant women? Maybe,* she thought, *Buzz liked sewing his seeds a little too much—* but, as she thought about it, Colbie realized straying from the marital bed was a common occurrence no matter the century. *What happens in Vegas, stays in Vegas . . .* She smiled to herself as she mentally quoted the popular television commercial.

She was right, too. Women often turned a blind eye to their husbands' infidelities, especially when it benefited them personally or financially. *Not so different than today,* she thought as the sun claimed its rightful position in the early-morning sky.

*Not so different, at all . . .*

\*\*\*\*

It turned out they were closer than Brian thought— within the hour, they sat at a small table in the courthouse, public files carefully organized in front of them.

"Where to do you want to start?"

Colbie opened the file closest to her. "We have a lot of material to cover . . ." She twisted open a bottle of water, then leaned back in the hard chair. "Doesn't it seem a little weird that when I asked the clerk—Velma was her name, I think—about the Beeman boys' public documents, it took her all of two seconds to put her hands on them?"

"Maybe she's been working here for God knows how long—did you look at her? She's no spring chicken—she'd know where everything is." Brian paused, thinking for a second. "But, what she gave us doesn't include digital files— and, since we're in Cheyenne, you know the system is going to be a little more technologically oriented."

"True . . . well, let's tackle the digital thing later. For now, let's sift through what we have—hopefully, we'll find something Harry can use."

And, that's what they did. Sift. For five hours. Straight through. Brian finally plucked off his glasses, then rubbed his eyes. "Nothing—I can't believe we didn't find anything."

"Neither can I . . ."

"What say we grab some lunch—my eyes are going goofy . . ."

"I'm starving, too—but, I'm not ready to give up!"

"Well . . ." He placed his glasses on the table, then focused on her. "That makes sense—if you think something is here, I'm game. We'll find it . . ."

"I love your optimism," Colbie grinned. "But, I have a feeling you're right. I know we're close, and it's not going to be in the digital files."

"How do you know?"

"Same old, same old—I have a feeling . . ."

\*\*\*\*

She paid particular attention to Juror Six as they filed out. Evelyn thought the woman resembled a field mouse, skittish and timid at the slightest movement, and she couldn't help but wonder why the attorneys passed her through the jury selection process. *There has to be a reason,* she thought, watching the door to the inner sanctum of the courtroom close behind them. She soon forgot the juror, however, as her mind launched into a recap of the prosecuting attorney's opening statement.

There was no mistaking his intent—bring Harry Fenamore to his knees, warranted or not. To Harry's wife, Marshall Sage seemed more interested in his won-loss record than making sure justice was served—in her mind, he was the lead player in the precarious game of life, or death. If he succeeded in convincing the jury of Harry's guilt? Well—the fact Wyoming hadn't enforced the ultimate sentence since the early nineties served as little consolation.

Sage's performance was flawless—long, but flawless—

and, by the time he wrapped up his opening statement, it was pushing noon. The judge called a recess, the courtroom emptying soon after.

Except for Evelyn.

She sat alone in the first row, directly behind the defendant's table, hoping to feel a glimmer of her husband's soul. Oh, she knew it was silly, but maybe—just maybe— she could latch onto him if only for a second. Closing her eyes, she pictured him as she always did—Levi's and cowboy boots. That's who he was—the kind of man who always stood up for the underdog or downtrodden until circumstances convinced him otherwise.

Then, something she never imagined happened as she sat silently. The young girl with red hair appeared in a soft vision—that was the only way Evelyn could describe it—beckoning to her, holding out her hand for Evelyn to grasp. Then, as quickly as the red-haired girl appeared, she was gone, replaced by a vision of an empty bed, lingering a moment before shattering.

"Ma'am?"

No response.

"Ma'am? Is this yours?" A young man dressed in coveralls—his shirt looking as if it hadn't seen a washing machine in a month of Sundays—stood to Evelyn's right, holding a white cotton scarf, waiting for her to acknowledge him.

"Oh—yes. Thank you . . ." She took the scarf, holding it gently to her cheek, her voice choking almost imperceptibly with tears.

"Where did you . . ." She looked up, then at her hands.

There was nothing.

No one.

**\*\*\*\***

Amanda Beeman's mood wasn't any better than the previous day's, and she did nothing but harp at her husband until her grousing reached his breaking point. "I said I'd take care of it," he screamed as she hurled one of Hattie Pearl's knick knacks whizzing past his head.

"When? When are you going to take care of it? Today? Tomorrow? Next week?"

Randy knew better than to answer. He snatched his jacket from the back of an antique chair, shooting a final glare at his wife, then strode from the room in a controlled rage.

"When, Randy? When, you worthless son of a bitch!"

As her voice trailed in a flurry of profanities, her loving husband was already out the door. *That's the last time*, he promised as he headed for his truck.

*The last time . . .*

****

Colbie's phone chirped just as their server placed a heaping plate of fish and chips in front of each of them. "Holy cow! That's a lot of fish!"

Brian grinned at the waitress. "Everything's bigger in the west!"

She laughed. "Better, too!"

Moments later, Brian was the first to dig in. "Are we going back to the courthouse, or somewhere else?" He dipped a piece of cod gently in tartar sauce, then looked at Colbie expectantly.

"Well, I've been thinking—since we dug through the available files at the courthouse, let's head to the main library to check out land transfers in the state. They should have records going way back . . ."

"Land transfers? What does that have to do with Harry's trial?"

"Maybe nothing—but, we didn't find anything of importance at the courthouse, so it makes sense to try something else . . ."

Brian was quiet as he considered her idea. "I see your point, but what does a land transfer have to do with Harry? We know when he and Evelyn inherited the ranch . . ."

Colbie put down her fork and sat back, meeting his eyes with a serious look. "I'm not talking about Harry . . ."

"If not Harry, then who?"

"Amanda . . ."

He stopped eating for a moment. "Why?"

"You have to admit, she's been on our radar for a while now—and, I'm convinced the Beeman ranch is smack dab in the middle of our investigation."

"Maybe—but, as far as I can tell, you only have a suspicion. That's not a lot to go on when we have so little time to come up with something Hastings can use for Harry's defense."

"Only suspicion?"

"Okay, okay—I didn't mean that the way it sounded. I meant it's going to be tough to come up with something solid—we don't have much time to investigate . . ."

"You're right about that—still, I know in my gut Amanda Beeman is the root of Harry's problems. Did she take out her own two sons and grandparents? I don't know—maybe."

Colbie checked the address of the main Laramie County Library on her phone. "It's not far from here—let's try that. Then, if we don't find anything, we can take another stab at the courthouse in the morning."

Brian nodded. "Are we planning to leave tomorrow afternoon?"

"I think so—I couldn't get in touch with Evelyn, so I'm assuming she's in the courtroom. I don't want to be away from her for long—she's more fragile than I thought."

"It's Harry I'm worried about . . ."

"Me, too—he looks like crap lately. I swear he's lost at least twenty pounds . . ."

Brian glanced at her before tackling another piece of fish. "So, that's it? Library today, courthouse tomorrow?"

"Courthouse tomorrow, if needed—if we find what we're looking for, we can take off in the morning."

"Sounds like a plan—who called?"

"I totally forgot!" Colbie swiped her index finger across the phone screen. "Evelyn."

"Did she leave a message?"

"Text. She wants me to call her back . . ."

Brian scoped out her plate. "Eat your fish—the call can wait. You need to keep your strength up . . ." He flashed a heart-warming grin.

"You sound like my mother!"

# CHAPTER ELEVEN

66 Ladies and Gentlemen—my name is Jeremiah Hastings."
A dramatic pause as he turned to look at his client,
then back at the jury. "I'm going to cut to the chase—
Harry Fenamore had nothing to do with the untimely and
unfortunate deaths of Bobby and Maximilian Beeman—
and, I'll show you why." He skillfully watched the faces of
the jury seated before him, determining who related to him
immediately, and who didn't. Then, he spoke directly to Juror
Four, a slightly built woman, her greying hair resembling
vegetable sprouts in a spring garden.

"Over the next weeks, you'll understand what I mean—
Harry Fenamore had no reason to commit such a crime,
and I'll prove beyond doubt there are others who wanted
the Beeman ranch heirs dead . . ." He waited, Juror Four's
eyes focused directly on him. "But," he continued, "they were

never considered." Brief eye contact. "At the conclusion of this trial, recall my words as I stand before you now—Harry Fenamore is not guilty!" Again, he waited.

"Yes, Bobby and Max Beeman were taken from us too early—two young men who had the best life has to offer. Yet, as I stand before you, I will prove beyond doubt Harry Fenamore had nothing to do with their murders. I will prove local police stymied *themselves* when they refused to investigate anyone other than Harry Fenamore!" He allowed the jury time to think during a few moments' silence. "But, why? Why would they let anyone slip through their fingers if it meant ferreting out the truth?" A pause. "I'll tell you why—they had their reasons. Reasons reaching far beyond the scope of this trial . . ."

Evelyn watched as Hastings fed the jury tidbits of information he knew would stick in their minds as the trial proceeded. It was brilliant, really—after watching him for only a few minutes, she understood his well-deserved reputation. It was then she knew Harry was in capable hands and, if anyone could prove his innocence, it would be Jeremiah Hastings. Throw Colbie and Brian into the mix? *How can he lose*, she thought, intently watching the jurors' faces.

Hastings took another long look at Harry, then back at the jury. "Beware of liars, Ladies and Gentlemen. Beware of ulterior motives. Beware of people whose lives are affected by this unspeakable tragedy."

With that he walked back to the defense table, turned, and cast a glance at Juror Four. "You'll see . . ."

Then, he sat.

Jeremiah Hastings was ready for battle.

\*\*\*\*

Brian checked the clock on his phone, glancing at Colbie who had her nose stuck in a file. Their time at the library was more productive than the courthouse and, by the time late afternoon rolled around, they had a few interesting items for Hastings. "Are you going to call him tonight to let him know what we found?"

She looked up, then looked at her watch. "I think I should, don't you? I definitely want him to know about what we found regarding Harry's and the Beeman's ranches . . ."

"Do you really think it's going to make a difference in the case?"

"Who knows? Hastings will have to decide about that—all we can do is put it in front of him." Colbie closed the file, then grabbed her messenger bag from the back of her chair. "I have what we need, I think, but I have to make copies . . ."

Brian followed her lead. "It's only five o'clock—how about if we pick up a couple of burgers, then hit the road for home? We can be there by nine . . ."

Colbie smiled, and patted his hand. "Getting homesick already?"

"Very funny—no, I'm thinking if we get home tonight, we can sit in on the trial tomorrow. I'd like to get a feel for Marshall Sage . . ."

"A 'feel' for Marshall Sage?" She couldn't help but laugh. "Why?"

Brian grinned. "It's weird to hear me say that, isn't it?"

"Honestly? Yes . . . I'm not sure I'll ever get used to it!"

Brian was quiet for a moment as he recalled the first time he attempted connecting with his intuitive abilities. Unsure of what he was seeing or what to do, he allowed his senses to take over, providing him with information that turned out to be important during the Remington case.

"So . . ." Colbie prompted.

"What am I feeling about Marshall Sage? I don't know exactly, but the one thing I'm sure about is I don't trust him as far as I can throw him . . ."

Colbie shook her head. "Neither do I . . ."

\*\*\*\*

Evelyn clicked off—Colbie and Brian were on their way home, and she still had to get supper on the table. It was important, she thought, to make sure Harry had a proper meal—somehow, it made their lives a little more normal. And, if she could give her husband a feeling of confidence and security? Well, it couldn't hurt.

That evening, she prepared his favorite—meatloaf and potatoes. It was the meal his grammy made for him until he left for college, and Harry never ate one bite without a smile on his face. Evelyn would never forget when he found out his grammy passed—it was a dark day, indeed. So, carrying on the meatloaf tradition was the least she could do, especially considering the circumstances.

As she mashed the potatoes, her thoughts turned to the trial. Both attorney's made an impression on the jury, but, if she had to guess, Jeremiah Hastings took the day. There was an arrogance about the prosecuting attorney she didn't like, and it was a good bet if she recognized it, so did members of the jury. Hastings, however, exuded experience and confidence, an approach the jury seemed to appreciate.

But, there was something else bugging her about Marshall Sage . . . *He's out of place,* she thought as she added the milk. *He dresses like he stepped out of the pages of Vogue.* His slick, city look was a blatant contrast to that of Hastings, cowboy boots and all. Evelyn had been in Wyoming for years and, if she had to bet, she'd take the hometown boy any day.

So would members of the jury.

Then, she recalled sitting in the courtroom. Alone. The young man with the scarf. Was he really there, or was it a vision of someone from decades past? She just wasn't sure— the strange thing was she could feel the soft cotton of the scarf. She could smell the young man's scent—one of sweat and hard work.

She could feel his soul.

\*\*\*\*

It was close to nine o'clock when headlights appeared in the windows of the ranch house. Evelyn greeted Colbie and Brian at the front door, apologizing for Harry—he was in bed, exhausted after the second day of his trial.

"It's best he gets some rest—it will probably get easier as the trial goes on. It's only been two days—the first days, I think have to be the worst . . ." Colbie gave her aunt a kiss on the cheek as she stepped across the threshold.

"That's what I think—he ate his dinner, then disappeared for a shower. I haven't seen him since . . ."

"If he's lucky, he's out like a light!"

Brian agreed as he appeared at the front door, luggage in tow. "I'm going to be out like a light in about five minutes— I'm exhausted!"

Evelyn grinned, holding out her hand for his jacket. "Do you have time for a nightcap, or is your date with sleep too important?"

Brian glanced at the grandfather clock in the entryway. "Okay—twist my arm!"

A few minutes later, the three of them relaxed in the great room, their nightcap being hot chocolate instead of a glass of wine.

"So, fill us in—how did things go in court?" Colbie sat across from her aunt, and she couldn't help but notice the dark circles under her eyes.

Evelyn took a sip, coupled with a slight sigh. "You were right—Sage is a pit viper . . ."

"I knew he would be—how was his opening statement?"

Another sigh. "He's out to nail Harry, that's for sure.

Oh, I know he's going to be tough, but there was something about him I don't like . . ."

"Such as?"

"His arrogance! I think, though, it may play against him."

That got Colbie's attention! "I haven't met him, but I certainly have the same thought—why do you think his arrogance will be in your favor?"

"Well, I don't know it will, but, folks around here? They don't cotton much to people who are full of themselves—they'll respond better to someone who is more like them."

Colbie smiled at her aunt's western vernacular. "That makes sense . . ."

Evelyn put her cup down, focusing her attention on her niece. "There's something else . . ."

Colbie noticed the change in her aunt's voice from concern to uncertainty. "Go on . . ."

"It was weird—I was sitting in the courtroom during the lunch recess trying to tap into Harry." She chuckled at Colbie's arched eyebrows. "I know—I just figured I'd give it a try!"

"What happened?"

"Well, like I said, it was really weird—I was sitting with my eyes closed, and suddenly I heard a voice . . ."

"What kind of voice?"

"It was a young man's—he held out a white scarf, asking me if it were mine. I said it was, and I thanked him. I started to ask where he found it, but, when I turned to him . . . there was no one there!"

"What about the scarf?"

Evelyn hesitated a moment. "There wasn't one—and, I don't know why I said it was mine. I don't own a white scarf."

Of course, Colbie knew of such manifestations, and she experienced one herself, but not to the same extent. Evelyn was clearly disturbed by it, but it didn't frighten her—Colbie, however, regarded it as a positive sign.

For the next hour, they picked apart Evelyn's visions—including the red-haired girl and the empty bed—and, by the time they were ready to hit the sack, Colbie's aunt had a better understanding of her ability to see spirit manifestations, as well as how to handle them. Colbie understood Evelyn's reluctance to admit she had a gift similar to hers—perhaps stronger—and, again, she wondered if their abilities were a genealogical trait.

*It's possible*, she thought as she and Brian said their goodnights to their hostess. It was then she realized the red-haired girl was someone in her family from years ago . . . the question was what did she have to do with the Beemans?

That's what didn't make sense.

\*\*\*\*

"Do you think it's too late to call Hastings?"

Brian glanced at the clock on his nightstand. "Yep—it's after ten . . ." He arranged his slippers just so in case he needed to get out of bed during the night.

Colbie nodded. "Maybe I should leave him a message that I need to meet with him as soon as possible . . ."

"If you're going to call him, do it now—it isn't going to get any earlier!"

"You're right—let's get to the courthouse early in case we can meet with him then. I'll send him a text to let him know we'll be there . . ." She glanced at Brian.

He didn't hear a word . . .

\*\*\*\*

Hastings returned Colbie's message first thing the following morning, suggesting they meet at eight-thirty. She figured he couldn't give her a lot of time, but some was better than nothing, so she rousted Brian out at seven o'clock.

"What time is it?" He looked at her through one open eye.

"Seven—I heard from Hastings, and he's going to meet

us at the courthouse at eight-thirty." She focused on him—
clearly, he needed a little more sleep. "Why don't you stay
here. I'll meet Hastings . . ."

"Are you sure?"

Colbie laughed, and pulled the blanket over his head.
"Of course, I'm sure!"

Thirty minutes later, she stood at the car, checking her
bag to make sure she had everything. Suddenly, standing
next to her, was the young man in coveralls Evelyn saw at
the courthouse. At least, that's who she assumed it was—he
was holding a white cotton scarf, smiling. She looked at him
for a moment, then held out her hand. He smiled, held out
the scarf, then dissipated into the morning light.

She glanced down at her hand.

Nothing.

****

Amanda Beeman sat at the farm table her grandfather
crafted, papers strewn in front of her. Randy, however, was
nowhere to be seen. *Good—maybe he's finally going to take
care of business* . . . Again, she thought of their most recent
row, and she began to wonder if sticking it out with Randy
were worth it. Granted, they worked hard to get the ranch
operating at peak efficiency, and the truth was they expected
to be rewarded handsomely for their efforts.

She took a quick drag on a cigarette, then an impatient gulp of coffee. To her thinking, Randy was disrespectful and impudent when speaking to her lately, and she didn't like it one bit. In fact, one of the reasons she agreed to marry him was her certainty she could manipulate him to suit her needs in just about every situation. Lately, though? He snapped back, effectively putting her on notice the old Randy was a thing of the past. *That's what he thinks,* she thought as she flipped through the papers in front of her.

*That old bat had a will—I know she did!* Amanda sat back, thinking about Hattie Pearl. If anyone knew anything about hiding a buck, it was her grandmother, and she didn't trust her for a second. And, even though she tried everything to patronize or placate her after her grandfather passed nearly a year prior, there was always a part of Amanda that knew her grandmother was capable of anything—including cutting her out of the will. Cutting her out of what was rightfully hers.

What she worked so hard to achieve.

Of course, she would never admit it to anyone but herself, but Amanda Beeman didn't give a rat's ass about her husband—and, she never would. The reason—and, only reason—she kept him around was his uncanny ability to be a dutiful scapegoat. If Hattie Pearl chastised her granddaughter for any reason, Randy was always handy for taking the blame. *Maybe this time,* she thought, *I pushed him too far . . .* But, after considering that possibility for a second or two, she immediately dismissed it as preposterous. Ultimately, she knew Randy had no backbone, and he would return to her, compliant as always.

Too bad she didn't know—for Randy?

All bets were off.

\*\*\*\*

"Are you sure?"

Colbie shook her head. "No—but, it does give us an idea of why there's such contention between the Beemans and Harry . . ."

Jeremiah Hastings leafed through the copies, trying to commit them to memory. "Who's Hedwin?"

"As far as I can tell, there are two . . ."

"Two Hedwins?"

"Yes—Hedwin Moore and Hedwin Beeman."

"So?"

Colbie cocked an eyebrow. "Don't you think it's a little strange there are two Hedwins within such close proximity?"

"Maybe 'Hedwin' was a popular name back then . . ."

Colbie knew Harry's attorney was playing devil's advocate. It wouldn't be prudent to consider any shred of possible evidence without having the information investigated and verified. "Maybe, but, I doubt it." Colbie paused, thinking about the two Hedwins. "The weird thing is my great-grandfather's name was Hedwin Moore, and Evelyn's maiden name was Moore. My mom's, too . . ."

"That may be true, but what difference does that make? What does Hedwin Moore—your family—have to do with this case?"

"That's the thing . . . I'm not really sure. Maybe there's

bad blood between Evelyn's and Amanda's families. My gut tells me there's a lot more to their history than we know, but does that get us any closer to who really killed the Beeman boys?" She leveled her most serious look at Harry's attorney.

"I think it does . . ."

# CHAPTER TWELVE

Evelyn snagged her seat in the first row, eagerly awaiting Colbie's report about her conversation with Hastings. Without seeming too obvious, she took mental notes of who was there as well as who was missing from the previous day. Linda Callahan—a wannabe political power of the Sundance city government—sat three rows back on the opposite side, stealing an occasional glance at her. She ran for Mayor once, but wound up slaughtered by Lincoln Mages and, when the vote tally was finally confirmed, it was the worst rout in the history of Sundance. *What the hell is she doing here*, Evelyn wondered, catching one of Linda's scathing glances, mid-shot.

"Hey! Sorry it took me so long!" Colbie slid in beside her aunt, careful not to arouse undue suspicion from the likes of Linda Callahan. "Did I miss anything?"

"Nope—they're late getting started . . ."

"That's not unusual," Colbie confirmed as she scanned the courtroom. "It happens all the time . . ."

Evelyn scooted a little closer. "Well?"

"Well—we didn't have time to talk about much, but I did show him the land transfer documents I copied at the Cheyenne main library, plus some other stuff. Neither one of us is sure they'll help, but, it was interesting—I pointed out how weird it was two men, a century ago, were named 'Hedwin,' and, they lived only a few counties apart."

"You mean Hedwin Moore? Buzz?"

Colbie nodded. "Exactly . . ."

"Who was the other Hedwin?"

"Hedwin Beeman . . ."

Evelyn pulled back a bit to get a better look at Colbie. Was she kidding? "Wait—what? Do you think they knew each other?"

As Colbie opened her mouth to answer, the bailiff stepped forward. "All rise!"

Robes flowing lightly around his feet, the judge entered, approaching the bench. Moments later, he was ready to conduct court. "Ladies and Gentlemen," he began, addressing the jury. "Again, I thank you for your service, and I remind you your instructions are no different than yesterday's. Discuss this case with no one, don't watch the news on television or the Internet, and stay away from newspapers or magazines." He paused for a sip of water. "Mr. Sage, call your witness . . ."

Marshall Sage stood, his full attention on the bench. "The prosecution calls Manny Sanderson . . ."

Evelyn turned slightly for a better view of the courtroom entrance. "I've never heard of him," she whispered to Colbie, a slightly alarmed look on her face as the heavy doors opened.

Colbie's eyes met hers as she placed her finger to her lips. "Let's listen . . ."

They watched as Manny Sanderson approached the witness stand, took his oath to tell the truth, then sat in the designated chair. He had the look of a ranch hand, his young face already weathered beyond his years.

"Mr. Sanderson, please tell the court how you know—or, knew—Bobby and Max Beeman."

Sanderson shifted slightly, leaning forward so his mouth was directly in front of the microphone. "I worked for them."

"Where?"

"At the Beeman ranch . . ."

"How long were you employed there?"

"Almost three years."

"Year round?" Sage inched closer to the witness box.

"Yes, Sir."

"Were you working at the ranch when Bobby and Maximilian Beeman were found, murdered?" Sage stopped walking, leaving a good ten feet between him and the witness.

Sanderson nodded. "Yes, Sir . . ."

And, so it went for the next three hours, Marshall Sage grilling his witness as he somehow seemed to forget Sanderson was on his side—a little too forceful. As spectators filed out for the noon recess, Evelyn and Colbie made sure everyone was out the door before saying anything. "Do you see what I mean about the arrogance," Evelyn whispered as the last person allowed the door to close quietly behind her.

Colbie nodded. "He does seem rather dramatic . . ."

"Dramatic? Well, I watched the jurors when he was talking, and I got the feeling they don't like him very much."

"Maybe—but, it doesn't make any difference if they like him or not. They're bound by law to make a finding based on the evidence. Not feelings . . ." Colbie noticed Evelyn's shoulders sag under the weight of her niece's words. Of course, Colbie knew how difficult Harry's situation was, but she didn't want her aunt to start reading something positive into something that wasn't there.

Time to steer the conversation in another direction. "I didn't get a chance to tell you before the trial started—I was standing at my car this morning, and I felt someone standing beside me . . ."

"What? Who? One of the hands?"

Colbie took a long breath. "The guy you saw in the courtroom yesterday . . ."

"Are you kidding?"

"Nope—I'm pretty sure that's who it was."

"Did he have the scarf?" Evelyn had a hard enough time believing she saw the young man, but, Colbie, too?

"He did . . ."

"He handed it to you?"

Colbie nodded. "Yes—but, as soon as I took it, he

vanished into the morning sun."

"What about the scarf?"

"Gone . . ."

Both women sat quietly for several moments, neither needing to speak. Finally, Colbie broke the silence. "Let's get out of here—I'm hungry!"

****

By midafternoon, Hastings took his shot at Sanderson and, finally, Marshall Sage wrapped up his recross, moving on to another hand who also had the misfortune to work for the Beeman's. Colbie, however, didn't believe a word that came out of his mouth. She tapped into him as Sage's questions resembled those he asked of Sanderson, tweaking them slightly so their testimonies didn't sound as if they were rehearsed. To hear the witness tell it, the Beemans were the best employers on the planet, and he couldn't think of anyone who would want the Beeman boys dead.

By five o'clock, the third witness—a cook for Amanda Beeman—was just ramping up before the judge called the evening recess.

"Have you ever seen her around town," Colbie asked as they headed for the car.

"The cook? No—but, her name sounds familiar."

Colbie clicked the key fob, the lights on the SUV flicking on, then off. "Keep in mind, Sage is setting the scene for the jury to believe the Beemans walk on water—it's going to be up to Hastings to show another side of them. A side that isn't flattering . . ."

"I know . . ." Evelyn turned to her niece. "Dinner? I don't feel like cooking tonight."

Colbie could feel her aunt's anguish as she struggled to wrap her head around the whole damned mess. "What about Harry?"

"I told him this morning there were leftovers in the fridge—just in case we decided to dine out!"

"Ah—planning a girls' night, huh?" Colbie grinned, and pulled her cell from her bag. "Let me call Brian . . ."

By five-thirty, they sat in a booth by the window, menus in hand, both eyeing the prime rib. Neither could resist, and by five-forty-five, they were eagerly awaiting queen cuts with baked potato and rosemary glazed carrots. "I always get prime rib," Colbie joked as she savored her first bite.

"Me, too!" Evelyn tipped her long-neck beer at Colbie, while Colbie sipped what she described as a 'mellow merlot.' "Now—what's this about two Hedwins?"

"Ah, yes—the Hedwins. I asked Hastings if he thought it were weird there would be two men, living in reasonably close proximity, with the same first name of Hedwin . . ."

"And? What did he say?"

"He wasn't buying it—according to him, it could be a complete coincidence."

Evelyn placed her beer on the pressed cardboard coaster, then patted her lips with her napkin, "He might be right . . ."

Colbie didn't say anything for a moment, recalling her conversation with Harry's lawyer. "You're right—but, I have the feeling there's something about the Beemans we don't know."

"Like what?" Evelyn picked up the thread of their courtroom conversation. "Do you think the two Hedwins knew each other?"

"I do—although I have no proof of it."

"And, what about the young man who appeared at your side this morning? The guy from the courtroom—do you know who he is?"

Colbie shook her head. "No—but there's something about him that seems familiar. When I thought about it on the drive in this morning, I realized he looked a little like Bobby Beeman."

"But, it wasn't Bobby—I knew Bobby, and that wasn't him . . ."

"I figured that, but I'll bet it's someone on the Beeman side of the family."

Evelyn shrugged. "Maybe—but, what about the cotton scarf? What does that mean?"

"That—blows my mind! I haven't had an experience like it, and I could have sworn I had that scarf in my hand—although, to be honest, I knew it wouldn't be there."

"Lucky you—I had no idea it wouldn't be!"

Colbie leaned back, and looked at her aunt. "What

about you, Evelyn? I know this is difficult on you, and I feel as though I'm not giving you enough support . . ."

"Oh, good heavens! You have enough to do! Forget about me, Colbie—just find something that will prove Harry didn't murder those boys. I know he didn't!"

For the next hour, both women nursed their drinks, fully aware they would be driving back to Sundance. Evelyn opened up, finally admitting she was scared to death she was going to lose her husband. Colbie tried to allay her fears, but, in reality, that's the way things could turn out. As many times as she testified in court throughout her career, she knew the odds weren't in Harry's favor.

Upon Colbie's prodding, Evelyn filled her in on what she knew about their ancestry—which wasn't much. Between the two of them, they covered only a fraction of their family members—most they knew by names on Christmas cards, leading them to believe the two Hedwins probably didn't know each other, and Jeremiah Hastings was right.

Coincidence.

By seven-thirty, they were back on the road, Evelyn at the wheel while Colbie reviewed her notes from the trial. As the sun fell to the western horizon, she suddenly picked up on what had been bothering her for weeks. "Have you noticed," she asked, turning her attention to Evelyn, "how many people there are with red hair in these parts?"

Evelyn laughed. "These parts? Now you're starting to sound like a Wyoming cowboy!"

"I'm blaming that directly on you! You're the one with the cowpoke euphemisms!"

Evelyn laughed, feeling a particular closeness to her niece. "Now that you mention it, yes—it does seem a little odd."

"I think it's more than a little odd—while you're in court tomorrow, I'm going to talk to some of the ranchers around Sundance . . ."

"That's *if* they're willing to talk to you—and, that's a big 'if.' Most folks around here stick to themselves . . ."

"I understand that—but, I'm willing to bet no one talked to them other than the sheriff. I can't imagine Hastings didn't have his people on it—but, even if he did, I'd rather hear their stories for myself . . ."

Evelyn pulled through the ranch gate, slowly making her way up the long lane. "Go for it—I'll keep you posted about what's happening at the trial."

"Text me when you have a break—but, don't call unless you know I'm not in an interview . . ."

Evelyn agreed, flicked off the headlights, and cut the engine. "Got it . . ." She looked at her niece. "I don't know what I'd do without you—knowing you're here keeps me going . . ."

Colbie leaned over, giving her aunt a loving hug. "Well, I'm not going anywhere . . ."

"It's too bad you're not a western gal—I wouldn't mind having you around more often!"

\*\*\*\*

Randy didn't care to be around people much, but, when
he got a call referencing the Beeman boys' murder, he chose
a meeting place far from prying eyes. The Stagecoach was
one of the oldest taverns in Sundance, its now owners direct
descendants of the town's first mayor. Dreary, desperate,
and dank, the tavern seldom had more than two or three
down-on-their-luck patrons nursing beers at the gouged and
dinged pinewood bar.

"Good! You're here—I don't have much time. My shift
starts at three . . ."

Randy nodded. "How long we're here depends on you.
What's up?" He watched as the man took a seat across from
him. "Drink?"

"Nah—I can't."

"Then let's get to it—what do you have for me?"

"Right—I assume you know of the guest staying at
Harry's place . . ."

Randy didn't admit or deny.

"Colbie Colleen—her boyfriend's name is Brian."

"Go on . . ."

"She was at the trial yesterday."

"So? That doesn't mean shit—give me something I can
use . . ."

The man shot him an impatient look. "Then, how about
using this—she met with Jeremiah Hastings before the trial
started yesterday. It seems she's working on Harry's case . . ."

Randy took a drag from his cigarette, contemplating
just how much of a thorn Colbie Colleen was going to be in

his life. "What did they talk about?"

"Well, they didn't meet for long, but she gave him copies of documents—land transfers."

"Anything else?" As much as he wanted to know who his source's mole was, he figured it prudent not to mention it. Colbie Colleen was already on his radar—thanks to the lovely Amanda—so that info wasn't news.

Giving copies of land transfers to Hastings?

Big news.

# CHAPTER THIRTEEN

Colbie sat at a tiny kitchen table in a tiny log cabin barely suitable for more than one. Across from her was Abbott, an old timer well into his eighties—maybe nineties—his face grizzled by years of bone-stiffening work. She glanced around the cabin as he poured two mugs of coffee, and it was easy to see the place never blossomed by a woman's touch. "I appreciate your seeing me on such short notice, Abbott. I promise I won't take up much of your time!"

He grinned, displaying tobacco-stained teeth in need of a serious cleaning, as well as black, empty spaces where teeth used to be. "It ain't like I have anything else to do. My days of runnin' cattle are long gone . . ." He watched as Colbie lifted the enameled mug to her lips. "Careful—it's hot. Now—what can I do for you?"

Colbie blew gently before taking a sip. "This is the

famous cowboy coffee?"

"Yep—nothin' fancy."

"How long have you been in Wyoming?"

"Seventy-seven years . . ."

"Wow! That's a long time!"

Abbott chuckled. "Yep—from what I hear, young people don't stay in one spot much anymore. They'd probably call me an old stick-in-the-mud!"

Colbie grinned. "Well, I'm afraid they'd call me the same thing!" She thought for a second before continuing. "Having been around these parts for so long, I'm guessing you know Harry Fenamore . . ."

"Harry? Hell, yes! One of the finest men in Wyomin'!" He eyed her carefully. "What trouble has he got hisself into now?"

"You don't know?"

Abbott shook his head. "Nope—know what?"

"So—no one talked to you about Harry within the last several months?"

"Not a one. And, as you can see, I ain't got no television. Don't read no newspapers, neither . . ." He waited for Colbie to continue—he wasn't one to ask questions.

"I can tell you have a lot of respect for Harry, so I'm sorry to be the bearer of bad news . . . Harry is accused of murdering the Beeman boys back in the fall."

"Murder?" He hesitated, as if contemplating the possibility of Harry's being caught up in something so heinous. "The Beeman boys? There ain't no way!"

"That's what I think! Tell me what you know about the them—the Beeman boys, I mean."

Abbott took a tentative sip of coffee, steam still rising from the mug. "Mind you, I didn't know them too good—but, I knew their granddaddy like the back of my hand. Both of us was from around here, so it's natural we got to know one another."

"Tell me . . ."

"We was friends since . . ."

"You and the Beeman boys' great-grandfather?" Colbie knew the answer to her question, but she wanted to be certain she and Abbott were talking about the same person. "What was his name?"

"Larson—Richard Larson."

"What was he like?"

Abbott chuckled as he recalled the good old days. "Oh, he was a troublemaker, and it wasn't until he met Hattie Pearl Beeman he straightened hisself out! Or, I should say, she straightened him out . . ."

"What do you mean?"

"Well, Hattie Pearl was the heir to the Circle B ranch—somewheres around seventeen thousand acres, if I recall."

"I don't understand—what does the Beeman ranch have to do with Richard Larson?"

He eyed Colbie, a sliver of doubt creeping into their conversation. "Why did you . . ."

Colbie picked up on his hesitation, instantly recognizing she had to gain his trust before he said another word. "Good heavens," she interrupted. "It just occurred to me I never told you why I'm here!" She sat back in her chair. "I'm working with Harry's attorney, Jeremiah Hastings—I'm Evelyn's niece, and I think Harry's being framed . . ."

"Of murder? Why, I can tell you that!"

It was then she knew Abbott could tell her what she needed to know. But, would he testify on Harry's behalf?

That was a whole different story.

\*\*\*\*

Randy watched the car's tail lights disappear over the horizon before he took a final drag on his cigarette, grinding the butt into the ground with his boot. Things were beginning to unravel, and he didn't like it.

*Over my dead body,* he thought as he climbed into his truck. *All the work I did to get to this point? I didn't put up with Amanda for nothing, and I sure as hell am going to get everything I'm due . . .* First piece of business?

Taking care of Colbie Colleen.

\*\*\*\*

"So, if I have the lineage correct, Richard Larson married Hattie Pearl Beeman. Right?"

"Yep—and, Richard knew he was marrying into money. But, that wasn't important to him. He saw the Beeman ranch as his road to success, making it on his own. All he cared about was the land—with enough land, he could build the cattle business into something the Beeman's never imagined. It was always about power."

"Then why do I always hear Hattie Pearl Beeman ruled the ranch?"

Abbott laughed. "Well, if you believe what I just told you about Richard, you'd think he'd be the boss!" Again, he chuckled, a look of fondness settling on his face. "But, that wasn't the way it was . . ."

Colbie didn't take her eyes from the old man. "Why?"

"I can't rightly say, but there was something about Hattie Pearl Beeman that wasn't quite right . . ."

Colbie's eyebrows arched briefly. "Not quite right how? Do you mean she was mentally unstable?"

"I can't speak to that, but what I can tell you is her granddaughter is thought to carry the same streak of mean. There wasn't anything Hattie Pearl wouldn't do for an extra dollar—and, anybody who got in her way?" He picked up his cup, tilting it to get every last drop. "God help 'em . . ."

"You know Hattie Pearl passed away?"

"I heard . . ."

Colbie followed his lead, draining her coffee mug. For the last thirty minutes, Abbott spoke willingly, but Colbie sensed she was about to smack into a brick wall. If she pushed him too hard, there was no doubt he'd clam up—then, he'd kick her out the door. "I haven't seen Amanda since her grandmother passed—but, to be honest, she doesn't want to see me, anyway . . ."

A flicker of interest. "Why?"

"Well, she's the one who instituted the trial—she wanted Harry charged for her son's deaths and, because she knows by now I'm working in Harry's interest, I have no doubt she researched me on the Internet. If I were in her shoes, I know I would . . ."

Abbott snorted. "It's a damned good reason to not have the Internet—too much invasion of privacy, if you ask me."

"Agreed—but, in my line of business, I need it—I use it every day." Immediately, she regretted her comment.

"And, just what exactly *is* your line of business?"

Anyone meeting Abbott might think he was just a worn out old cowhand, but, that, Colbie knew, would be an erroneous assumption. His eyes sparkled with intelligence and wisdom, and he didn't miss a thing. His question was one Colbie hoped wouldn't come up, thinking her explanation about working with Hastings would be enough.

No such luck.

"Well—like I said, I'm doing some work for Jeremiah Hastings. Investigative work . . ."

"I gathered that—but, that ain't all."

Colbie sat quietly for a minute. There was no getting around it—she had to answer his question. She looked at him, grinning. "You're probably going to think I'm nuts—so, if you want to kick me out, just know I'll go quietly!"

It worked. Old Abbott busted out a gut laugh bigger than the cabin. "Try me—I seen just about everything, so whatever you tell can't be that much of a shock!"

"Okay—please remember you said that!" She paused, wondering for a second if she should sugarcoat her intuitive abilities, but, she also sensed the old man sitting across from her would know. "My investigative work," she began, "is quite a bit different than a private investigator—I use my intuitive ability to solve what are sometimes considered impossible cases."

Abbott eyed her. "Intuitive ability . . . what's that?"

Colbie drew a deep breath. "I'm psychic, and I work with private clients—as well as the authorities—to solve cases that might otherwise go cold." She hesitated. "I'm a psychic, behavioral profiler . . ."

Even though Colbie had been there less than an hour, she wondered if the cabin had ever been so silent. Finally, Abbott shifted in his chair, then tugged on his beard. "Well, I'm not sure what all of that means, but that sure sounds a lot like Hattie Pearl—rumor had it she knew things she wasn't supposed to know. Folks didn't appreciate it much . . ."

"You mean Hattie Pearl had the same abilities I have?"

Abbott nodded. "Yep—visions, she called 'em. Everyone in the county knew she was different, and no one dared cross her because of it. Richard used to tell me about them—her visions—and, accordin' to him, she was one scary woman."

"What about Amanda? You said she has Hattie Pearl's

streak of mean—does she have Hattie Pearl's abilities, too? Colbie had a feeling she was about to hear what could be a significant break in Harry's favor. But, was she getting enough information to instill doubt in a jury of twelve?

Maybe.

Her radar at full strength, she thought about the Beemans. According to Abbott, it was possible Hattie Pearl and Amanda fell victim to an ancestral bad seed. But, what she was about to hear next, knocked the breath clean out of her.

"You kinda look like her . . ."

Colbie sat up straighter, her full attention on the weathered cowboy. "Who? Who do I look like?"

"Why, Hattie Pearl, when she was younger—and, you also favor her daughter, Amanda's mother—you got the same red hair. Same as Amanda's, too . . ."

At that moment, Colbie knew what she was suspected was true.

Hedwin Moore and Hedwin Beeman?

Oh, they knew each other, alright . . .

****

"They got copies of Circle B land transfers . . ."

Amanda threw a partially peeled potato in the sink and whirled around, her voice quivering with controlled exasperation and anger. "Colbie Colleen?"

Randy nodded. "I don't know how she got them . . ."

"Because they're public record, you moron! How do you think she got them?" Picking up the potato, she furiously began to peel. "I specifically asked Rory to slip those transfers under the rug . . ."

"How could he do that? And, why? What reason could he possibly have? Besides, what difference does it make? The only time the land changes hands is when one of us dies. And, just because Hattie Pearl died, nothing changes—we get everything. Everything transfers to us . . ."

Amanda ignored that last part. "How the hell should I know? All I know is he was supposed to do his job, and apparently that didn't happen!" She launched a scathing look at him as she realized the consequences of their family attorney's inability to follow orders. "I don't mind telling you, this really pisses me off . . ."

"Everything pisses you off . . ."

"That's right, Randy—and, do you know why?" Amanda didn't consider waiting for an answer, and the potato was quickly becoming the size of a peanut. "Because nobody listens to a damned thing I say! Do you realize what can happen because Rory didn't do his job like I told him to? Do you, Randy?"

Her husband smirked as his wife's temper swelled to the verge of exploding—something that pissed her off even more. "Oh, c'mon—what can possibly happen because Colbie Colleen has public documents?"

Amanda didn't care to answer his question—although, sooner or later, she knew she'd have to. At the time—and, she stood by her decision—her arrangement with the family attorney was private, and she saw no reason Randy had to know about it. After all, land transfers were common, and Hattie Pearl made it perfectly clear that, upon her death, Amanda was to inherit Beeman's Circle B—all seventeen thousand acres. And, as long as Randy remained her dutiful husband, he would be standing in tall cotton. If he didn't? Well . . .

Unfortunately, he was of the mind he would be the legal owner of a parcel of land closest to Harry's ranch, having no idea his loving wife decided to make an underhanded deal with Hattie Pearl on her own—coerced, of course—but a deal, nonetheless. Eventually, Hattie Pearl agreed with her granddaughter, and she changed her will and signed documents to transfer all land to Amanda upon her death— Rory was to make certain the necessary papers were filed. According to Amanda, it was the only way—but, it was, most likely, something Randy wouldn't take lightly.

"Never mind," she screeched, slamming the peeler on the counter. "I'm calling Rory right now! If he thinks he can get away with this, he's sorely mistaken!"

Randy watched his wife storm through the swinging kitchen door, her fury mounting with each step. "Don't let the door hit you in the ass," he muttered, his mind leaping to conclusions he didn't like. He knew his wife better than anyone, and she was definitely keeping something from him.

"I heard that!" Her voice trailed, muffled by stomping.

Thankfully alone, Randy wondered what it was about the land transfers that pissed her off the second she heard of it. Instinctively, he considered his wife's reaction a warning—something he should look into.

On the QT, of course.

****

"One more?" Abbott held out his hand for Colbie's coffee mug. "I think it's still hot . . ."

"Thanks—I'd like that!" She handed him the mug, then steered the conversation in another direction. "Did you ever work on the Beeman's ranch," she asked, watching him carefully pour the stout brew.

"Hell, yes! Close to thirty-seven years! Richard Larson made sure he paid his hands more than any other rancher— it was a good way to keep his help."

"Was that your last position before  . . ."

"Before takin' off my ranchin' boots for good?"

She nodded, quickly assessing his age as he placed the two mugs in the middle of the table—mid-eighties, if she had to guess.

"Careful—don't burn yourself!" He made himself comfortable, then took a tentative sip. "Yep—I decided enough was enough. It was time . . ."

Colbie was silent for a moment as she wondered about

the Beeman's land. It certainly seemed to be at the crux of family disputes and, with Hattie Pearl's fierce allegiance to the Beeman history, Colbie couldn't help questioning the importance of the land transfers.

"I know this goes back a long way, but, if I remember correctly, land around here was considered as valuable as gold . . ."

"Well, now, I don't know about that—but, a lot of killin' went on tryin' to take control of it. Ever heard of Tom Horn?"

Colbie shook her head. "No, not really . . . tell me."

Abbott tugged on his beard, and sat back. "Tom Horn was way before my time, but, to this day he's regarded as one of the most important characters in Wyomin's history . . ."

"How so?"

"My granddad told stories of how land was rich in this state, and Tom Horn was a man to be feared . . ."

Colbie leaned back in her chair. "Why?"

"Well, now, keep in mind what I know is strictly comin' from family . . ."

"Don't keep me in suspense!"

Abbott grinned, then stroked his beard as if in deep thought. "Somewheres around 1894, Tom Horn was in Wyomin' working as a cattle detective for local beef barons, charging five hundred dollars for each rustler shot. In them days, that was considered a lot of money . . ."

"How old was he in 1894?"

"Somewheres around thirty-three—if I recall, he was born around eighteen sixty. Anyways, Horn used a buffalo gun, and his trademark was to leave a rock under the dead man's head. By the time he was strung up in the early nineteen hundreds, folk said he murdered as many as seventeen men."

"I guess I must be thick, but I don't get what this has to do with land . . ."

"Hold your horses—I'm getting to it!" Clearly, Abbott was enjoying the company of a fine looking woman who would listen to his stories.

"I think it was in 1901—maybe 1902 . . . I don't recall—he was accused of ambushing and killing a fourteen-year-old boy."

"Fourteen! Why?"

"Because the father of the boy was trying to introduce sheep onto the Wyoming cattle ranges. Horn had been hired to kill the father, but mistook the son for his father and killed him with two shots from long range."

"Just because the father wanted to raise sheep instead of cattle?"

"Yep—in them days, raising cattle was how ranchers made their money, and bringing in sheep wasn't the way things was done."

"Did they prove he did it?"

"Yep—he opened his yap about the killin' when he was drunk. Not too long after, he was hanged for the death of that young boy."

Colbie was quiet for a minute. "But, what does that have to do with the land around Sundance?"

"Rumor had it a man with fire-red hair roamed these parts Tom Horn style, taking ownership of land however he could get it, legal or not. Folks say even though the thirties weren't as wild and woolly as Horn's days, they referred to the red-haired man as just as ruthless. Somehow, he staked claims on thousands of acres, taking down anyone in his way and, to this day, all of his land is a workin' cattle ranch." Abbott leaned forward in his chair, his withering hands wrapped around the warm coffee mug. "Sound like anyone you know?"

"The Beemans?"

Again, he bellowed a crusty laugh. "Yep—Hedwin Beeman hisself took Wyomin' by storm in them days, takin' care of anybody who went against him. Took over homesteads without a second thought, layin' claim to what's now the Beeman's Circle B Ranch.

"It's been in the family that long? No wonder Hattie Pearl was so protective of it! Although, it sounds as if Hedwin Beeman was as crazy as they come . . ."

Abbott nodded. "That he was . . . and, Hattie Pearl and Amanda aren't far behind him. Both of them women—as far as I can see—aren't any saner than old Buzz."

Suddenly, Colbie realized something smack dab in front of her since she and Brian arrived in Gillette. *But, that's impossible,* she thought as she rose to thank Abbott for his hospitality.

Minutes later, she pulled through the rickety gate on her way back to Sundance, the conversation with the old cowhand playing in her mind. *It can't be,* she thought as miles of road disappeared over the horizon.

*It just can't be!*

# CHAPTER FOURTEEN

66 I'm on my way to Harrelson's Gap," she told Brian as she turned onto the first intersecting road heading west. "I want to get a feel for it . . ."

"Check—what time do you think you're going to head back?"

"I won't stay long—I'll be back by five. I texted Evelyn a little earlier to let her know I'm not going to make it to the courthouse. It's too late . . ." Even though she wanted to meet her aunt, the conversation with Abbott lasted much longer than anticipated. But, it was still too early to call it a day with the investigation, so she opted for a quick trip to the place Maximilian Beeman was found with a bullet in his brain.

"Be careful!"

"Don't worry—I'll check in when I get there . . ."

As she drove the thirty minutes down what she considered the epitome of a lonely country road, hesitation began to creep in the closer she got to the narrow bridge where Max was found. Harrelson's Gap, it turned out, was nothing more than a few buildings, it's population of just under four figures displayed proudly on a hand-crafted sign. *How can anyone live here,* Colbie wondered as she pulled over on the side of the road.

She checked the map kept in the glove box to be certain she was in the right place, but she already knew from the way she felt something happened close by—her gut was telling her to stay alert, a warning she didn't take lightly. *Always good to be sure,* she thought as she double checked the location, then tucked the map into the console between the seats.

Colbie sat for a moment, calling on her intuitive mind to tune into what happened that day—the exact time when Max's life ended. Within seconds, images raced toward her, barely giving her enough time to get a good look at them— although, that was usual when she was investigating a case. But, even though they sped past her conscious mind, she managed to latch onto one which was particularly strong— one telling her Maximilian Beeman wasn't alone the day he drew his last breath.

An opaque form appeared and receded in front of her, but Colbie couldn't tell who it was—someone close to Max's height it seemed, but, from the back, she couldn't tell if the person were male or female. Facial features didn't favor either gender, nor did the dark, hooded sweatshirt provide clues about hair—how long it was, or whether it were light or dark. The vision provided little to go on, really, and the only thing Colbie knew as the image faded was the person who murdered Maximilian Beeman that day in early fall was someone he knew.

Someone he knew well.

As soon as she stepped from the SUV, a heaviness stifled the air as she started down a gentle embankment. She remembered reading on the Internet Maximilian Beeman was found close to a large boulder, his head partially submerged in shallow, cold water of a trickling creek—and, from the top of the tiny trail, she could smell and feel the freshness of the stream. But, when she reached the spot where he died? She realized the heaviness in the air didn't come from Max, or his murder. It was coming from something—or, someone—else, and rising hair on the back of her neck signaled something wasn't right.

Cop senses in full force, she scanned the area inconspicuously, but nothing seemed as if it didn't belong. The water in the creek barely exhibited interest in making it downstream, and the boulder? Well, it yielded nothing— until Colbie spied something white pressed beneath its oddly-formed ledge. *What is that?* Quickly, she snatched it from beneath the rock, dropping it into her jacket pocket as her intuition was telling her to get the hell out of there.

Then, the resounding crack of a long-distance rifle.

\*\*\*\*

Evelyn checked the time on her phone as spectators left the courtroom—not quite five o'clock. Colbie texted her shortly after four, suggesting they meet back at the ranch to go over the day's events, but Evelyn couldn't help feeling something was amiss. *I'll shoot her a text to let her know I'm on my way home*, she thought as the last person left. But, by the time she reached her truck, Colbie hadn't responded—something in direct violation of their agreed-upon procedure.

She dialed. "Brian? It's Evelyn—have you heard from Colbie?"

"Yep—about an hour ago. She said she was headed to Harrelson's Gap . . ."

"Harrelson's Gap? What on earth . . . why is she going there?"

Brian laughed as he thought of his headstrong better half. "You know her—she gets an idea in her head, and she's going to follow it through . . ."

"But, what's at Harrelson's Gap? Other than being the place where Max Beeman bought it, I mean. It's a backwater town where no one wants to go . . ."

Brian smiled at Colbie's aunt's lack of tact. "She mentioned she wanted to get a feel for the area—and, from that, I think she wants to tune in on the murder."

Evelyn chewed lightly on her lip, her own intuition telling her Colbie was in danger. "I don't know, Brian—something doesn't seem right. If you hear from her, will you ask her to text me, please?"

"I will—but, I've been here before, and Colbie always shows up, usually no worse for the wear."

"Usually?" She paused. "Well—okay. But, will you text

me, anyway?"

He assured her he would as his own concern began to mount. *Maybe she's right*, he thought as he hung up, then tapped a quick text message. *She'll get back with me if everything's okay . . .*

\*\*\*\*

Colbie dropped to a prone position, instantly trying to determine the location of the gunshot, her body protected by an overgrown bush by the side of the trail.

She barely breathed.

Slowly, she reached for her pistol, fully aware her assailant could be a thousand yards away—or, across the creek—either way, the rifle's sight was, most likely, trained on her from the time she arrived. *That doesn't make sense, though—no one knew I was coming here . . .* After a second to think it through, it was clear—someone followed her.

Intent? That was clear, too.

The thought of being in Wyoming didn't make her feel any better—gunshots were a common occurrence, and hearing one around dinnertime wouldn't arouse anyone's suspicions. *Hell*, she thought—*someone could be shooting just for the hell of it!* That thought opened the possibility of an errant shot, one not meant to harm her.

She waited, measuring her breathing so she could react quickly and with precision, if needed. But, as she lay obscured by that scraggly bush at the side of the trail, her intuition told her the threat was over. Nonetheless, she crawled military style to the SUV, managing to open the driver's door without exposing herself to another bullet.

Quickly, she pressed the ignition button, then swerved onto the road, flipped a uey, and sped toward Sundance, the past several minutes consuming each thought. *How could I have not noticed someone tailing me,* she wondered as her speed clocked past seventy. But, the more she considered it, the more she realized she wouldn't have recognized the surveillance—everyone drove a truck in Wyoming, and the trucks looked similar.

So, who wanted her dead?

That was a matter of opinion.

****

Her conversation with the family attorney didn't go particularly well and, by the time Rory ended the call with a curt goodbye, Amanda was no closer to knowing who funneled the land transfer information to Colbie Colleen.

To most people, the documents were just that—documents. Boring. But, to Colbie? Amanda figured it would be only a matter of time before she figured out Hattie Pearl signed everything over to her shortly before her death. That fact was certain to cause interest, especially to a behavioral investigator. Throw the psychic bit into the equation?

Not good.

Amanda did, however, have a few things in her favor. When Hattie Pearl passed, no one thought twice about anything—her grandmother was in her nineties for God's sake! And, since her grandfather's death, it was perfectly normal for Hattie Pearl to figure she was at the end of her life, as well.

Except, that wasn't the way it was.

Hattie Pearl had no intention of going anywhere, and she told Amanda so shortly after Richard died. She also had no intention of handing the ranch over to her granddaughter, knowing she would sell it before anyone could spit. No, that wasn't what the matriarch of the family wanted—as long as there was a breath in her body, Hattie Pearl would run the Circle B as she saw fit, and Amanda knew it.

In a moment of weakness, Amanda confided concern to her husband they wouldn't become rightful heirs of Hattie Pearl's estate. The old bat, she told him, wasn't playing with a full deck, and Hattie Pearl may well leave everything to a charity if she had a mind to. That left them, she also said, in a precarious position. Years of cow-towing would be for nothing, and she wasn't about to have any of that.

Her husband, of course, thought she was being dramatic, but, after giving the situation careful and serious consideration, he concluded his wife had a point. Her concerns certainly warranted further discussion and, after

a few rowdy conversations, he, too, knew something must
be done.

There was one thing wrong, however, with any plan to
resolve the problem—Hattie Pearl wasn't batty. She hadn't
lost her marbles. In fact, she had complete control of her
senses and intellect—all she had to do was listen, and marvel
at the stupidity of her granddaughter and her henpecked
husband. Although Amanda fancied herself a woman who
got what she wanted no matter what, the truth was she
couldn't begin to match Hattie Pearl.

It was during those problematic times Amanda and
Randy solidified the best, least obvious, manner of speeding
up her grandmother's eventual passing. Hattie Pearl wasn't
frail, but she wasn't in the best of shape, either. Decades of
life chipped away at her body, and many in town considered
it 'only a matter of time' before they were planning a funeral.
If Amanda and Randy played it right, no one would be the
wiser and, perhaps most important, the Circle B would
transfer to them. At least, that's what Randy thought.

Amanda had other plans.

****

She pulled into the ranch just before six-thirty, the
day warning of the coming dusk as the sun lowered to the

western horizon. On the way back, she constantly checked the rear view mirror, but she couldn't imagine anyone would be stupid enough to tail her again. *Then again,* she thought as she cut the engine, *they were stupid enough to try taking me out in the first place* . . .

Before she could get the door open, Brian showed up, obviously relieved. "Where the hell have you been? Evelyn and I were worried!"

"I know, I know! I'm sorry I couldn't text—I just needed to get out of there . . ."

He helped her out of the car, then closed the door behind her. "What does that mean?"

Colbie waved to Evelyn who was standing on the front porch, then looked up at him.

"Someone tried to kill me . . ."

\*\*\*\*

Within the hour, Brian and Evelyn knew the whole story, including her conversation with Abbott. Evelyn said she remembered meeting the old man once, but, that was years ago—she couldn't believe he was still alive! "The thing I remember about him," Evelyn told them as they finished dinner, "was his love for Hattie Pearl. Back then, everybody knew about it, but he chose not to interfere with the relationship between Richard and her . . ."

"What? We talked for quite a while, but he never mentioned Hattie Pearl being the love of his life . . ." Colbie paused, rehashing her conversation with the old man. "In fact, it was just the opposite—he told me Hattie Pearl had a mean streak in her, and Amanda was just like her. Both of them nuttier than fruitcakes!"

"Well, that's true—but, you can't blame the guy for not wanting to talk about it."

"The main thing," Brian interjected, "is to figure out who used you for target practice—are you going to report it?"

Colbie shook her head. "I thought about it, but there's something fishy going on in this town—with Harry's trial happening, I don't want to take focus away from him. And, you know the press would have a field day with this . . ."

"I get that, but next time you may not be so lucky . . ."

"I know—but, I have a feeling we're making a few people nervous, and I don't want to give up that position right now."

"But . . ."

"I also think we don't know all the players. Yes, Amanda is in the thick of it, but it makes me wonder how she manages to always slip under the radar . . ."

Evelyn glanced at Brian, then at Colbie. "Are you sure the shot was directed at you?" She noticed Colbie's eyebrows arch quickly, then relax. "I mean, it could have been someone with really bad aim . . ."

"Maybe . . ."

"And, remember—no one tailed you after it happened."

Colbie nodded. "True—I tried to rationalize what happened all the way back, but I keep coming back to the same thing."

"Which is?

"Someone tried to take me out, and they missed. No, I didn't hear a bullet whizzing past my ear, but I know as sure as I'm sitting here, I was the target . . ."

They sat quietly for a minute or two, until Brian broke the silence. "That leaves us, then, with one question—who wants you dead?"

"I can only think of one person . . ."

Evelyn and Brian glanced at each other, then focused on Colbie. "Amanda?"

She nodded. "Amanda . . ."

# CHAPTER FIFTEEN

"Randy! Good to see you!" Rory slapped the rancher on the back, a greeting as old as Wyoming. "C'mon in— have a seat!" He gestured to a comfortable chair in front of his desk. "You going to the barbecue on Saturday?"

Randy returned the greeting with a grin and a handshake. "Maybe—Amanda and I haven't decided yet."

"Well, you know there's going to be some of the best Wyomin' beef on the grill—I wouldn't miss that if I were you!" He paused, situating himself behind his desk. "Now— what can I do for you?"

"Well, I have a favor to ask . . ."

"And, what's that? Amanda made it perfectly clear she doesn't want me to handle any of the ranch's business anymore . . ."

"So I heard—but, you know Amanda! She gets pissed off, then a few days later she's over it . . ."

Well, that was a bald-faced lie—anyone who knew Amanda Beeman knew she was capable of carrying a lifelong grudge if the situation warranted it.

"Bullshit, Randy—you and I both know your wife means exactly what she says . . ." By his voice, he was clearly annoyed. Rory Gallagher wasn't thrilled by Randy's dropping by unannounced—over the years, he grew to distrust nearly everyone in the Beeman family, including Hattie Pearl, at times. Randy was no different.

"Well, now, that's probably true—but, you and I always got on well, didn't we?"

"That we did . . ."

Time to get to it. "So," Randy began, "what's up with those land transfers?"

Rory sat back, focusing on the man across from him. "I'm not sure I know what you mean—what about them?"

"I mean what got Amanda so upset when she learned Harry's niece got her hands on those transfers? Last I heard, Hattie Pearl passed everything to us right before she died."

"That's correct."

"Then what has Amanda cursing your name every time I mention it?"

"I have no idea—as I recall, the transfer was a fairly standard procedure. We did it when Richard died, as well."

"What about the boys?"

"You mean did their murders have any consequences

when it came to the land?"

Randy nodded, watching the attorney carefully.

"No, because the boys didn't have a stake in any of the property until you and Amanda die, or you can no longer run the ranch efficiently."

"Do you have copies of the transfers?"

"Here? Probably, but Mary's out for a couple of weeks—her son's wife had their first child—and, I don't have a clue where anything is. She runs this place!"

Randy thought it strange Rory couldn't put his hands on the most recent land transfers—but, he could also understand how the esteemed attorney wouldn't want to be bothered with such trivialities. "When does she get back?"

"Two weeks—she only left yesterday."

"Well, then—I'll just have to come back!" Randy rose, extending his hand. "Thanks for seeing me, Rory—I hope I haven't taken up too much of your time . . ."

Rory got up, accepted the handshake, and walked his former client to the door. "Not at all! Maybe Susan and I will see you at the barbecue!"

Conversation over.

Randy left with no more information than when he walked in the door, and his only course of action was to pay a visit to the county offices to get copies of the transfers. If he couldn't find what he needed on a local level, he'd have to make the drive to Cheyenne. It was a pain in the ass, but, if he wanted to get to the bottom of why Amanda told Rory to sweep the transfers under the rug, he'd have to do a little digging himself.

Rory stood at his office window facing the street, watching the once Circle B heir climb into his truck, then ease out of the parking space. *You poor bastard,* he thought. *You don't have a clue . . .*

The line he gave Randy about his assistant being on vacation was a line of crap—Rory didn't have an assistant, and hadn't had one for over a year. He decided it was much more prudent to have his wife take up slack when it came to legal paperwork, so he had no need for anyone else on his payroll except for him.

After a moment, he returned to his desk, deciding a call was in order . . .

He dialed, waiting only seconds before he heard a voice on the other end. "Rory? Is that you? It's a bad connection!"

"Yes, Velma—it's me. Do you have a sec?"

****

Harry's trial proceeded, each day a warm up for the possibility he would take the stand. Ultimately, the decision was his, but Jeremiah Hastings was against it for obvious reasons—one screw up, and the long time Wyoming rancher could be spending the rest of his life as a guest of the state.

Harry, however, saw it otherwise.

Perhaps too proud for his own good, Harry Fenamore was a man who lived his life according to honor. Time in the military as a young man taught him respect for the truth, and he wanted the jury to hear it from his own lips. It was a position Hastings understood and partially admired, but he continued to advise against it and, by the second week of the trial, the conflict remained unresolved.

Evelyn agreed with Hastings, but was on the fence about everything else. As much as she stood by her husband's side, she dwelled on things going against him to the point of his possible incarceration consuming every thought. But, no matter what Colbie and Brian said to assuage her greatest fear, nothing seemed to work, and Evelyn sank deeper into a depression that concerned everyone around her.

"This is starting to take a turn I didn't anticipate," Colbie confided to Brian as they took an evening walk in the pasture closest to the ranch house. "I'm not sure what we can do . . ."

"About Evelyn?"

She nodded, then stopped to look at him. "I know she could use some professional counseling to help her deal with everything—but, I'm afraid if I mention it, she'll misinterpret my intent . . ."

"Unfortunately, you may be right—I vote for ignoring it, and letting her deal with her emotions on her own. She's strong and obstinate . . ." He shot her an engaging grin. "Just like every other woman in your family . . ."

"Are you saying I'm stubborn?"

"Stubborn? No!"

Both laughed, then continued their walk down the fence line behind the barn. "But," Brian continued, "as always, it's you I'm worried about . . ." He didn't look at her as they sidestepped a petrified cow pie.

"Me? Why?"

"Seriously?" He paused, and leaned against a fence post. "You really have to ask?"

"Well—I assume you're talking about my close call at Harrelson's Gap . . ."

"Exactly—what are you going to do?"

"I don't know—but, I can tell you what I'm not going to do, and that's report it. I've had a feeling since we got here Uncle Harry's trial is guided by someone we have yet to surface."

"Like who?"

Colbie shook her head. "Well, if I knew that, we probably wouldn't be standing here wondering what we're going to do next!" She landed a playful punch on his arm. "What do you think? Who haven't we discovered?"

Brian plucked a stalk of timothy grass, then chewed on its stem as if he were born into a long line of cowpokes. "Good question . . . what I keep coming back to is the land transfers. Do you remember when we first looked at them, you commented on how easily the clerk located exactly what we were looking for?"

"Yes—I thought that was odd."

"Precisely—maybe someone gave her the heads up to have the documents ready in case someone came calling . . ."

"Like us?"

"Yep. If that's the case, who would have the knowledge about the system, and how it works?"

"And," Colbie added, "who has that kind of clout?" She thought for a moment, then looked at Brian. "It's obvious—an attorney."

"Whose attorney?"

"What was the name of the Beeman family attorney? We haven't really had any interaction with him, but I'm assuming they have someone in the background taking care of the legal end of things . . ."

"Good point. Rory . . . Rory . . . Gallagher! I think that's it—I remember seeing his name on the land transfers as the attorney of record."

Colbie nodded. "You're right!"

As they headed back to the ranch house, Colbie realized there was much about the Beeman's former attorney they needed to know. Aware her intuition was nudging her in the right direction, she vowed silently to make an appointment with him as soon as she got back to the house.

Neither spoke as they approached the gate separating the pasture from the ranch-house yard. Brian always found it best to allow her time and space to think things through, but, as they approached the front porch, he couldn't stand it any longer. "I know you're thinking something—care to clue me in?"

She grabbed his hand, and gave it a soft kiss. "You know me too well . . ."

"True—so don't keep me in suspense!"

"Okay, okay! Well—you know my suspicions about Amanda. I think she's directly responsible for her sons' murders, and we're finally beginning to unravel the details. First? I'm going to talk to Rory Gallagher. I know in my gut he's the missing link—and, if there's some kind of rift between him and Amanda? Well, then—maybe he's willing to share."

"What makes you think there's a rift between them?"

"I don't know that for sure, but when I envision the two of them together, there's a high-board fence between them, blocking one from the other."

"Weird." He gave her a quick smooch as he opened the massive front door. "Now—let's eat! Evelyn said she made brownies . . ."

"Award- winning brownies from what she tells me!"

"Even better!"

\*\*\*\*

By midmorning the following day, they sat in front of the lawyer's stately desk, Colbie trying to interpret the nondescript expression on Rory Gallagher's face. Brian was trying to figure out where he heard the attorney's name before, then realized it was the same name as an Irish blues guitar player.

"I appreciate your seeing me on such short notice," Colbie began, watching the lawyer's body language carefully—a slight flinch, the index finger on his right hand tapping the soft leather of his chair. "As you may or may not know, we're working with Jeremiah Hastings on Harry Fenamore's case."

"In what capacity?"

"As investigators . . ."

"Private?"

Colbie shook her head, and smiled. "No—I'm an intuitive behavioral profiler." She waited for a response, but the attorney gave little away about his understanding or feelings about such a thing. "I know—it sounds weird, but feel free to check my credentials . . ." She rattled off her website address.

"I already have, Ms. Colleen . . ."

*Is he trying to be intimidating,* Colbie wondered as she assessed the man in front of her. "Excellent! Then you understand how seriously I take my clients' needs and situations . . ."

"Indeed—now, how can I help you?"

Colbie concisely recounted their trip to the Cheyenne courthouse, turning the attention of their conversation to the land transfer documents. "And," she admitted, "it didn't come to my attention until recently those documents may or may not represent the most current information."

Rory Gallagher recognized fishing when he saw it. The lovely woman in front of him was acting on a hunch and, he suspected within the first minutes of their conversation, the unspoken question would be if he would side with Harry Fenamore.

Colbie knew if he decided to reveal the content of the documents, the case shifted successfully to Harry's side.

However, if Gallagher decided to keep the salient points of
the land transfers to himself, Colbie was no further along
than when she walked in his door. Her conversation with the
attorney would achieve nothing, but a waste of time.

Time she couldn't afford.

"So, Mr. Gallagher, if you have information that can
help Harry, I'll appreciate your letting us in on it. Harry
Fenamore isn't guilty!"

Gallagher didn't respond for a solid ten seconds. Then,
a sigh. "I know he isn't, Ms. Colleen . . ."

Colbie wasn't sure if she heard him correctly. "So . . . you
think someone else murdered the Beeman boys?"

"I do."

"Are you willing to share?"

He didn't take his eyes from hers. "I'm sure you're aware
of attorney-client privilege—and, I'm certain you'll agree it
would be foolish to discuss my clients' private business."

With a swift motion, he reached into his desk drawer,
and took out a small key, placing it within Colbie's reach.
Then he rose, and crossed to the door. "Please excuse me—
too much coffee this morning . . ."

He closed the door quietly behind him.

There was no denying Gallagher's intent—if Colbie
Collen needed to know something,  it wouldn't be from his
lips. *She's a smart woman*, he thought as he stood outside his
office door. *She'll do what she has to . . .*

He was right.

Colbie snatched the key from the desk, scanning the

room. "We don't have too many choices," she commented as she tried the key in the top drawer of the file cabinet closest to her. "Nope . . ." She tried two more, finally hitting pay dirt on the third try.

"Bingo!" Brian grinned as she slid the drawer open, flipped through the files, then plucked one from the back. She took a moment to leaf through it's contents, allowing her memory to record everything she needed to know.

"What about pics," Brian asked. "Do you have your phone?"

She nodded, but didn't take his suggestion. "Gallagher just did us a huge favor . . . I don't want to take advantage."

"Isn't that what he invited you to do by leaving the key on his desk?"

"Yes—but, I can learn all I need to know without photographs, and I don't want to put him in a precarious position."

"Well, you know what you're doing . . ."

"Geez, I hope so! Mom always said I had an almost photographic memory—now's a good time to put it to use." Colbie rifled through the documents, making mental notes of when Beeman land was transferred, and to whom. But, it wasn't until right before Gallagher returned, she discovered what she needed.

"Bingo, indeed!" She returned the file folder to the drawer, making certain nothing was out of place. "Let's get out of here . . ."

\*\*\*\*

Saturday turned out to be a picture-perfect day with cornflower blue skies, and barbecue smoke wafting into the air. According to Evelyn, the turnout was better than previous years. Of course, everyone looked forward to the midsummer barbecue, but it seemed more people gathered to discuss local events, as well as gossip about the biggest news in town. Would Harry Fenamore spend the rest of his life in prison? Many thought so for they were privy to Harry's dislike of the Beeman boys, as well as their plans for the ranch. Others? There was no way Harry did it, and the sheriff should look at those closer to home.

The community divide was obvious.

By six o'clock, the fire pit and several wood-burning grills were operating at full throttle. "I can't believe you managed to finagle an invitation for Brian and me," Colbie commented as she noticed small groups forming just far away enough from each other to keep conversations private.

"John and Helen always invite us . . ." Evelyn glanced at Harry who was talking to dual owners of Wyoming's largest working ranches. "Look at how much weight he's lost—I don't know how much more of this he can take."

Colbie nodded. "It's rough—there's no getting around that."

By seven-thirty, bellies were full as charcoal and hardwood embers in the grills served their purpose, finally fading to a warm, red glow. Throughout the evening, Colbie and Brian introduced themselves to everyone, and most were welcoming, offering to refill their cocktails when they noticed glasses were low. Others held them in reserve, the gossiping spearheaded by Linda Callahan. Colbie recognized her from court, recalling Evelyn's story about the Wyoming socialite's run for office a few years back. Every now and then, Callahan glanced at Evelyn and Colbie, then pointedly turned her attention to her adoring minions—both of them.

But, what captured Colbie's interest was what was happening by the backyard gate. Amanda's husband and the sheriff were talking quietly, both occasionally scanning the crowd for anyone who may be paying them a little too much attention.

"Check out Randy and the sheriff," she whispered to Evelyn as both made themselves comfortable in comfy patio chairs. From their vantage point, Colbie could keep an eye on everyone while Brian inserted himself into a few of the mens' conversations.

"I noticed—they seem to be pretty buddy-buddy . . ."

"It's also interesting Amanda didn't show up . . ."

"No surprise there—over the last ten years of these shindigs, she showed up twice. Three times, maybe . . ."

"Interesting—I wonder why?"

"Probably because there are a bunch of people in this town who hate her guts."

Colbie continued to watch the two men by the gate. "Randy looks pissed—oh, to be a fly on the wall . . ."

"A fly on the fencepost, you mean . . ."

Colbie glanced at her aunt, grinning. "Okay—fencepost." Just then, she caught Brian's eye, inconspicuously motioning for him to work his way toward the backyard gate. It was a

communication system they used in Zurich and, on a couple
of occasions, they ferreted out information they wouldn't
have otherwise obtained.

He nodded slightly, and she watched him make his way
toward a small group of ranchers closest to the gate. *That boy
has such a gift of gab*, she thought as he effortlessly inserted
himself into the conversation. His easy smile played well
for him and, before long, he was laughing with some of the
richest men in the state.

Again, Colbie noticed how relaxed he was, and she
couldn't help thinking he was in his element. During their
stay in Wyoming, she saw a side of him she never thought
possible. Cowboy life agreed with him, and he mentioned
more than once 'he could get used to this . . .' *Not in my
lifetime*, Colbie thought as she watched him skillfully
maneuver the group closer to the gate.

She wondered if he could get close enough to overhear
the sheriff's and Randy's conversation without looking
obvious. By then, everyone knew who she was, what she
did for a living, and why she was in town—and, they knew
Brian played a major role in her career. Chances of snagging
previously unknown information were slim, at best. Colbie
knew it was a good bet conversations would be held to social
pleasantries with, perhaps, conflicting opinions of Wyoming
politics thrown in as they straddled the political fault line.

Then, she noticed Brian slipping his hand into his right
pants pocket, no one the wiser he was activating the recorder
on his cell phone. It was a move he practiced, but never had
the chance to use.

Until then.

\*\*\*\*

"How the hell should I know?" The sheriff's voice was louder than he intended, but he appeared unconcerned as his face burned with a florid flush.

Randy stood to his side, beer in one hand, cigarette in the other. "How should you know?" He took a swig, then faced the man next to him. "You should know, Roy, because you're the one driving this whole damned mess!"

It was true, too. Yes, Amanda somehow managed to convince the sheriff Harry Fenamore was the one directly responsible for the death of her two sons—but, it was the sheriff who guided the investigation in a specific direction from the beginning. Few questioned his good sense, and he made sure certain investigation particulars remained undisclosed.

To anyone.

The sheriff pulled back as Randy hissed spit through the slight gap in his teeth. "Is there a problem, Roy? Is there something I should know?"

"I don't know what she does—the only thing I hear about is her attendance at court. Other than that? Nothing."

Amanda's husband thought for a moment, grinding his cigarette butt into the ground with his boot. "Then, it appears to me you're not doing your job. Don't forget the reasons, Roy." He took another swig as he walked away. "Don't forget the reasons . . ."

\*\*\*\*

By nine-thirty, everyone was ready to call it a night. Main players in Gillette politics were the first to leave, followed by Sundance ranchers who should have been in bed by eight. "I seem to have lost a button," Colbie advised her host. "Do you mind if I look for it in the backyard?"

"Not at all—would you like help? A flashlight?"

Colbie smiled. "No, no—I'm pretty sure I know where it popped off . . ." With that, she stepped onto the patio through the sliding glass doors, acting as if she were looking for the button. As she approached the backyard gate, she positioned her body with her back to the patio doors, then discreetly retrieved the cigarette butt, quickly tucking it into her jacket pocket.

A few minutes later, Evelyn, Brian, and Colbie bid their hosts goodbye, relief flooding through them as they climbed into their SUV. "Did you get it," Brian asked as he pulled onto the dirt road leading to Sundance.

"Yep!"

Evelyn leaned forward from the back seat. "Now what?"

"Now, I call in a few favors back in Seattle. I know we can have the results within a few days . . ."

"I hope so . . ."

Colbie nodded. "We will—I'll tell them time is running out . . ."

# CHAPTER SIXTEEN

Two weeks into the trial, the prosecution rested, the defense welcoming the opportunity to present its case. Harry was holding up well, keeping faint hope alive as he realized the prosecution really didn't have jack shit. Marshall Sage proved himself a master of manipulation, but, as of the time he rested, there was little evidentiary substance. There was no doubt Jeremiah Hastings would take advantage of such a weakness, and Harry's family was beginning to believe he might come out on top. Things needed to fall into place, of course, but, throughout the trial to date, Hastings lived up to his reputation as a master trial chess player, never revealing his strategy for the win. It was a ploy that served his clients well, and he won more often than not.

"Who's slated to be on the stand today?" Colbie took off

her jacket, laying it carefully beside her.

Evelyn did the same, making herself as comfortable as possible on the hard, church-pew-like seats. "I don't know—Harry was late getting out the door, and I forgot to ask . . ."

"Well, we'll find out soon enough . . ." Colbie pointed to bailiff who readied himself for the daily announcement as the judge entered from his chambers. "All rise!"

Spectators stood and, for all the days Evelyn was in the courtroom, she never got an inkling—intuitive, or otherwise—of the judge's feelings about the case. He reminded her of the freshman Latin teacher in her high school—everyone called her 'stoneface,' and Evelyn couldn't remember her ever cracking a smile. "Did your mom ever talk about 'stoneface,'" she whispered to Colbie as the judge took his seat at the bench.

As they sat, Colbie looked at her as though she were nuts just as the proceedings began.

"Never mind . . ." Evelyn grinned at her niece, then settled in.

As he did every day of the trial, the judge reminded jurors of their civic duty, as well as warned them about discussing the case with anyone—same old mantra. "Call your witness, Mr. Hastings . . ."

Hastings stood. "The defense calls Abbott Wilson . . ."

Heads turned toward the doors leading into the courtroom, expectant looks on the faces of some. The door creaked slightly as it opened, allowing a grizzled cowboy to make his way to the front. After being sworn in, he glanced around the courtroom, his eyes signaling recognition as he noticed Colbie.

"Abbott!" Evelyn's voice was barely a whisper as she watched the old man take his seat. It was years since she saw him, and her eyes filled with tears, noticing his difficulty as he tried to get comfortable in the witness box.

"I wasn't sure he'd testify . . ."

Evelyn glanced at her. "What will he testify about? He hasn't been in Harry's or my life for years!"

"I don't know for sure—we talked about a lot of stuff. If I had to guess, though, I think Hattie Pearl will come into the conversation . . ."

The courtroom was silent as Jeremiah Hastings buttoned his suit coat, approaching the witness. "First, Mr. Wilson, thank you for your testimony today . . ."

Abbott nodded.

"How long have you lived in the Sundance area, Mr. Wilson?"

"Somewheres around seventy-seven years." He reached forward to adjust the microphone—it was directly in front of his face, and he didn't like it.

"Seventy-seven years! I imagine you've met many people throughout those years. Is that correct?"

"Yes, Sir—that's correct."

"Before these court proceedings, Mr. Wilson, did you have the opportunity to meet Harry Fenamore?"

"Yes, Sir, I did . . ."

"When was that?"

"When did I meet him?"

Hastings nodded. "Yes—how long ago did you meet Harry Fenamore?"

Abbott's forehead wrinkled as he tried to pinpoint the year. "I don't know exactly, but I reckon we've known each other for thirty—maybe forty—years . . ."

Hastings was off and running.

Guided by adroit questioning, Abbott Wilson recounted how he met Harry, then silenced the courtroom as he explained how he knew the Beemans. He recounted how Hattie Pearl Beeman was known to have a screw loose even in her younger years, and her daughter and granddaughter weren't much better. He told of her being labeled a witch as she claimed her place in ranching society and, from what he could see, that was pretty close to the truth even with differing definitions of the word. Then, as Hastings tiptoed around Abbott's unrequited love for Hattie Pearl, spectators didn't miss the inference.

There was something sad about the old cowboy's story, and, if his testimony about Harry and the Beemans were true—well, it changed things considerably. Introducing the Beemans as possible suspects in the boys' murders required a tricky line of questioning. Hastings walked the line when it came to hearsay, but, somehow, either Marshall Sage missed the opening for an objection, or he didn't recognize the possibility.

Either one was an egregious mistake.

"That was impressive!" Colbie grabbed her jacket as she and Evelyn headed for the door. "Hastings was respectful to Abbott, and I think everyone in the courtroom appreciated it—except, of course, those who believe Harry is guilty."

"Well, if you ask me, I think more people are beginning

to see Harry didn't have anything to do with the Beeman boys—outside of their known disagreements, I mean."

"Is that something you know, or something you feel?"

"A bit of both, I think—but, since you've been here these past months, I'm much more secure about what I know intuitively . . ."

Colbie stopped, turning to her aunt. "It's weird, but this place is growing on me. When you think about it, Brian and I will only be here for another couple of weeks . . ."

"I know—I was thinking about that last night. Once Harry is cleared, there's no reason for you to stay—it's back to your comfortable life in Seattle!"

"I know. I talked to Tammy—she's my assistant—and, she's ready for us to get back to the office. She says she's lonely!"

Evelyn laughed, linking arms with her niece. "I get the feeling Brian would jump at the chance to be a real-life cowboy . . . any chance you'll stay?"

"Well, Brian dropped hints for the past couple of weeks about getting a place in Gillette. 'Vacation purposes only,' he said."

It was something Colbie never considered and, she knew herself well enough to know she could never think about hanging her hat in a state she thought of as wild—and, in come cases, slightly uncivilized. "No," she replied. "As much as Brian would love to have a life here, I think we're better suited to the city. We tried the rural thing when we were on the East Coast, and it didn't work out too well . . ."

"The East Coast? Holy cow! Are you kidding? That's nothing like Wyoming!"

"I know—but, I have to think about my work. The city is where my work is . . ." Immediately, Colbie recognized her comment as a lame excuse. The truth was she could do her work anywhere—but, she wondered if she had what it took to live like Harry and Evelyn. There was an alluring simplicity to their lifestyles and, if Colbie admitted it, she willingly entertained a speck of jealousy. "How about this? I'll think about it . . ."

"Really?"

"Maybe . . ."

\*\*\*\*

By the time court adjourned for the day, there was speculation Harry Fenamore might not be as guilty as previously thought. It wasn't anything anyone said—Colbie found it simple to tap into individuals as they watched the proceedings, and paying attention to body language offered information most fail to recognize. No longer was there a heaviness in the air, something she attributed to the collective energy of spectators.

Abbott Wilson concluded his testimony by late afternoon, and there wasn't a soul in the courtroom who questioned his veracity. "I kind of got the feeling people felt sorry for him," Evelyn noted as they headed for Sundance. "I bet there's going to be a lot of dinner conversation and pillow talk tonight about Harry's defense . . ."

"You're right about that! For the first time, the jury is getting a picture that someone else is possibly responsible for the murders . . ."

"Namely, Amanda Beeman." Evelyn paused. "Did you get the results back from Seattle?"

"Not yet—I expected them today . . ."

Evelyn glanced at her watch. "Well, Seattle is an hour behind us, so there's still time."

Colbie nodded. "If not today, then tomorrow for sure!"

"How do you think it's going to turn out?"

"Let me put it this way—if the results come back like I think they're going to, Hastings's job just got that much easier . . ."

"I still don't see what a cigarette butt is going to do for Harry—we know Randy smoked it at the barbecue."

Colbie sighed, knowing she had to reveal something she chose to keep private until the right moment. As much as she wanted to tell Evelyn she might have evidence solid enough to exonerate Harry, she couldn't take the chance of disappointing her. *I have to know for sure*, she thought as she focused on her aunt.

*Maybe I can wait until tomorrow . . .*

\*\*\*\*

DNA results arrived in Colbie's email inbox the following day, her suspicions corroborated, and it was time to tell Evelyn she found a cigarette butt near the rock where Maximilian Beeman drew his last breath. Instantly, Evelyn picked up on the connection. "Randy?"

Colbie nodded. "Yep—so, why is a cigarette butt smoked by Amanda's husband inches away from where Max was found?"

"Because he was there! Oh, Colbie—this definitely puts a damper on the prosecution's case! At the very least, it raises reasonable doubt!" Evelyn hugged her niece as relief raced through her.

"It certainly looks that way—but, we can't rush to conclusions. I'll call Hastings in the morning to let him know—and, I think you should be the one to tell Harry . . ."

"Now?"

Colbie laughed, enjoying the delight on her aunt's face. "Yes, now!"

Evelyn gave her another quick hug, then headed for the barn. Harry was preparing to inoculate calves the next day, enjoying the fact he didn't have to be in court for another two days. Sunday was always a day of rest on the ranch, and he looked forward to a hearty midday meal, then a long nap. Colbie would have loved to be a fly on the wall, but she also knew it was a moment to be shared only by them.

She pulled her cell from her pocket, tapping a quick text message to Hastings.

*I have news . . . I'll call tomorrow.*

\*\*\*\*

"You know the news about Randy's being at the scene of Max's murder is the death knell for the prosecution." Brian focused his attention on Colbie, putting his laptop aside on the bed.

"I know—Hastings couldn't believe it when I told him, and he agreed it's the type of information that makes and breaks cases. But, he also cautioned it's circumstantial . . ."

"You'd think the DNA match would be enough . . ."

"Yes, and no—Randy could've dropped that cigarette butt at any time. Just because it's there doesn't mean he was there the day Max Beeman was murdered."

"Did Hastings give you any sort of hint about how he'll use the info?"

"Not really, but I figure he'll put Randy on the stand. If Hastings asks him about the last time he was at Harrelson's Gap, and Randy lies . . ."

"Ahhh—the noose tightens!"

"It does, indeed. And, don't forget, this is the week when Amanda and Randy will probably take the stand. Armed with the DNA info, Hastings can make mincemeat out of Randy. Amanda, however, will be another story . . ."

"She's one tough woman, that's for sure . . ."

Colbie hopped on the bed, then sat cross-legged, facing him. "That's an understatement—I think Hastings will have his hands full."

"Randy, on the other hand, will be a pushover. A total moron can see who wears the pants in that family . . ."

"That's what I meant when I said Hastings will make mincemeat out of him." She paused, picturing Randy on the witness stand. "The question is will Amanda's husband throw her under the bus . . ."

Brian's eyebrows arched. "So . . . you think Randy knows about Amanda's murdering her boys?"

"Yep—Hattie Pearl and her husband, too."

Brian adjusted his long legs to a more comfortable position. "You're talking four murders . . ."

"I know . . ."

Both were silent for a few moments—the ramifications of Randy's testimony were staggering! "If, after Hastings's searing questioning," Colbie continued, "Randy figures out he's implicated in at least one murder, he'll have a decision to make—save himself, and throw his wife to the wolves, or fall on the sword for her . . ."

"Do you really think he'll take all the blame so Amanda can get off without so much as a slap on the wrist?"

Colbie shook her head. "Well, if he does, I don't think it will matter . . ."

"What do you mean?"

"I don't think there's any way Amanda will skate . . ."

"Why?"

"Think about the land transfers—because of our visit with Rory Gallagher, we now know Randy has been cut out altogether. Hastings knows it, too—but, does Randy know?"

"You think Amanda had Rory Gallagher draft new documents indicating Hattie Pearl transferred all of Circle B Ranch to her granddaughter?"

Colbie nodded, wincing slightly as she shifted position. "My leg's asleep!" She wiggled her toes. "That's exactly what I think . . ."

Brian grinned, moving his legs to the side of the bed so she could stretch out. "I hate it when that happens!" He waited until she was comfortable. "I get it—you're saying if Hastings hurls the bombshell that Randy's been eighty-sixed from the land, he's going to be pissed!"

"Royally! I have the feeling he's at his breaking point with his wife, and it makes me wonder if the only reason he's staying with her is because of the ranch land . . ."

"Maybe—if nothing else, it's going to be an interesting week at the old courthouse!"

"I see the trial lasting through the end of this week, or a teeny bit longer. Not much, though . . ."

"That means we'll be out of here by the middle of next week?"

Colbie took off her glasses, and rubbed her eyes. "Well, maybe . . ."

"Maybe?"

She nodded, fluffing the pillow next to her. "What do you think about staying a few extra weeks? I called Tammy to be sure she could hold the fort without us, and she assured me she was doing just fine . . ."

"I don't get it—I thought you couldn't wait to get out of here!"

"That's partially true—I admit ranch life is starting to grow on me—but, there's another reason I'd like to hang out for a while after Harry's trial."

"And, that is?"

"Well, the more I talk to Evelyn, the more I realize I don't know anything about my family—neither does she, really. Mom knows some stuff, but, after digging into the Beeman's lives, I'd like to learn about my own family."

Brian propped himself up on his elbow, busting a grin. "Seriously?"

"Seriously . . ."

"You know I love it here—there's something about the wide open spaces that makes me feel alive . . ."

Colbie laughed. "You sound like a Wyoming Chamber of Commerce ad!"

They were quiet for a moment, each realizing something in their lives was shifting. The life she craved for so many years was beginning to fade, and she wondered what it would be like to live a ranching lifestyle. *It seems to agree with Evelyn and Harry just fine,* she thought as she watched Brian consider staying so she could research her family. *Maybe there is something to living a simpler life . . .*

"I'm all for it . . . how long do you want to stay?"

"A few weeks—Evelyn's okay with our staying as long as we want."

"I bet she is—this is the first time she's had family around in years."

Colbie agreed. "It's interesting—I never really cared

much about learning my family's history. But, as I get older, I realize it's a huge part of who I am—I feel as if I need to pay ancestral homage to those who walked these prairies before me."

There was a sadness in her voice Brian rarely heard. The only other time he could remember was when he told her he wanted to end their relationship when she was in Cape Town. "I know what you mean—my family is never around, and I miss that. My sister is a flake, and my parents are always trying to improve their lives by finding themselves—I don't know where they are half the time! 'Finding themselves'—I don't even know what that means!"

Colbie was quiet for a moment before laying out a plan for the rest of their time in Wyoming. Of course, she'd see the trial to fruition, but she knew in her gut it was coming to an end. Harry would be exonerated and, with the information she uncovered about the Beemans, as well as the DNA results, it was certain Amanda and Randy would be on the hot seat. Whether they would be arrested immediately, Colbie wasn't sure. What she did know was their lives would change dramatically within the coming months. "Let's plan on traveling to different parts of the state if we need to—I don't even know if my family was in these parts . . ."

Brian laughed, placing his laptop on the chair close to their bed. "And, you say I sound like a cowpoke!"

Colbie crawled under the covers with a delighted chuckle. "I can't believe it—maybe ranch life is beginning to agree with me more than I thought!"

Two gentle kisses later, Brian switched off his nightstand light. "Can you feel it," he asked Colbie in the dark.

"Feel what?"

He didn't answer immediately, thinking she may think he's nuts. Finally, he explained. "Something's changing . . ."

Silence.

"I know . . ."

# CHAPTER SEVENTEEN

Wednesday. Hump day. The day Randy, the supposed Beeman co-heir, would take the stand. During passing weeks, the trial lost few spectators, and many more waited to score a seat in the courtroom. *Good luck*, Colbie thought as she and Evelyn walked past those standing in line.

"How long do you think Randy will be on the stand," Evelyn asked as she opened the courtroom door. "I wonder what everyone is thinking . . ."

"About . . ."

"Harry. I know a bunch of these people, but there are many I don't know. I wonder if they think he's innocent—or, guilty . . ."

"Hard to say—I imagine you'll find out who stands with Harry when the judge announces the verdict." Colbie scanned the courtroom as she and Evelyn took their seats.

"You're right . . ."

Moments later, court proceedings ramped up, a tangible excitement lacing the air. The usual preamble out of the way, the judge leaned forward, pointing his pen at Jeremiah Hastings. "Call your witness, Mr. Hastings . . ."

Hastings stood, his commanding tone more solemn—different than previous trial days. Everyone in the courtroom understood the seriousness of the day's testimony, knowing it could tilt the trial definitively in one direction. "Defense calls Randy Howard . . ."

For someone who didn't give a rat's ass about the trial a few months prior, the look on Randy's face as he approached the witness stand was one of someone who cared—a lot. Colbie never thought of him as a masculine man and, as he sat in the witness box, his eyes darted around the room like a scared cat. Based on that? Hastings already had him cornered, and he methodically crafted his questions to rattle the witness. Several times throughout the morning session, the seasoned lawyer raised his voice to a dramatic pitch, then took advantage of a purposeful, well-orchestrated silence.

Finally, the question. "Mr. Howard, when was the last time you were at Harrelson's Gap?"

Colbie watched him carefully, noticing Randy squirm almost imperceptibly in the witness chair.

"Harrelson's Gap?"

"Yes, Mr. Howard. When was the last time you were at Harrelson's Gap?"

Randy swallowed, then leaned toward the mic. "I've never been to Harrelson's Gap . . ."

Jeremiah Hastings allowed just the right amount of time for Randy's words to sink in. "How long have you lived in Sundance, Mr. Howard?"

"Over thirty years."

"Do you know where Harrelson's Gap is located, Mr. Howard?"

"Yes."

"But, you've never been there?"

"Not that I can remember . . ."

*Not remembering is very different than saying you've never been there . . .* Colbie glanced at Evelyn, wondering if she noticed Randy's back pedaling. Her aunt, however, couldn't take her eyes off the man in the witness box—a man who suddenly realized his testimony wasn't going as planned.

"Okay—not that you can remember. So, you *may* have been at Harrelson's Gap at sometime in your life, but you just don't recall. Is that correct, Mr. Howard?"

Randy hesitated as if he were trying to figure out what to say. He knew Hastings's reputation, and he had no doubt the attorney would attempt to corner him in a lie. "Yes—that's correct."

Colbie heard Evelyn sigh as she leaned back in her seat. Both women hoped he would admit to being at Harrelson's Gap, but Colbie wasn't surprised when he managed to worm his way out of it. Still, Randy didn't know anything about the cigarette butt and, if needed, an expert scientist could determine approximately how long it was exposed to the elements. When Colbie picked it up, it was clear the cigarette butt was barely degraded due to its being shoved under the shelf of the large boulder. *That, Randy Howard,* she thought as she watched Hastings cross directly in front of the witness, *will be your undoing . . .*

\*\*\*\*

Anyone could tell by looking at him, Harry Fenamore was showing the rigors and stress of the trial. He, too, hoped Randy would admit to being at Harrelson's Gap and, when he didn't, his disappointment was obvious. "Most of Randy's testimony was a lie," Hastings assured his client. "But, that doesn't matter—it was just as I expected . . ."

To Jeremiah, Randy Howard wasn't the most important witness of the trial—he suspected from the beginning Randy was nothing more than his wife's lackey, ready to do her bidding with the hope of becoming part owner of a successful Wyoming ranch. He considered such a man infinitely pathetic, regarding him with a certain amount of private disdain.

An opinion he chose to keep to himself.

At dinner that evening, Harry excused himself so he could get a good night's rest. Even with the trial consuming every moment of his day, he tried to maintain ranch operations as if nothing changed. Evelyn took up much of the slack, but he knew she couldn't keep it up much longer. And, it was in those times of solitude he thought of how his big mouth was affecting everyone in his family, including Colbie. Although he didn't know her well, he admired her for putting her life on hold to help him—it was something he would never forget.

After Harry's exit, Colbie and Brian followed his lead, bidding an early goodnight. Once Colbie closed their bedroom door, she teared up at the thought of her aunt. "I know she's exhausted," Colbie commented as she stepped onto the small deck off of their room. "Time to herself will do her good . . ."

Brian nodded as he joined her, a bottle of merlot and two glasses in hand. "It also gives her time to spend with Harry without having to worry about us—even though we're family, there's always some stress when someone else is around . . ."

"Oh, I know—I know exactly what you mean. And . . ." She hesitated, wondering if Brian would agree with what she was about to say. "Speaking of family . . ." She leaned against the deck railing, watching the late summer sun drift toward sunset. "I think I'll head to the library before going to the courthouse—I'll meet Evelyn for the afternoon session."

"To research your family?"

Colbie took a sip, then focused on him. "Well, I don't think there's any more we can do for Harry, and Evelyn can keep me posted on what's going with the trial." She paused. "I may as well make the best use of the time we have left in Wyoming . . ."

"What do you hope to learn?"

She shook her head, fully aware she had no idea of what she might find. "I don't know—I guess that's kind of the point!"

He looked at her, his eyes narrowing slightly. "I know that look—what's bugging you?"

She laughed, holding out her glass for a pour. "Just a little, please . . ."

Brian bowed. "Don't try to get out of answering my question," he teased. "I know you have something—or, someone—in mind!"

Colbie settled into one of two deck chairs, perfectly placed so they could see the sunset. "I've been thinking about the vision I had of Hedwin Beeman . . ."

"Which one?"

"The one where he splits in two—I'm not sure what it means. I have a strange feeling about it . . ."

"Don't forget you also had a vision of Hedwin—or, at least you thought it was him—with the red-haired girl when she was young. They were on a country lane—or, something like that . . ."

Colbie sat up a little straighter. "That's right! LaRee—or, at least, we think it's Amanda's mother's sister. I forgot about her! I've seen her a couple of times when she was young, and then once when she was older."

He glanced at her just as the sun became a glow on the western horizon. "You never told me about that . . . "

"I didn't tell anyone . . . it was definitely the same person, though, except she had long, curly hair."

"How old was she?"

Colbie thought about Brian's question for a moment before answering. "It's hard to tell—late teens, I think. Maybe early twenties. I'm not sure if she's Amanda Beeman's mother's sister, or someone else."

"Someone else? Who?"

She took a last sip of merlot, a soft expression in her eyes. "Me . . ."

\*\*\*\*

Testimony resumed the following day, Jeremiah Hastings requesting a recess shortly after court was in session. The judge wasn't wild about the idea, and everyone in the courtroom had the feeling he was ready to call the trial a wrap. "Explain," he commanded, his patience already at a low ebb.

"New information, Your Honor—information that may impact the outcome of this trial."

That little bombshell was enough to evoke a collective, soft gasp among trial spectators, and the courtroom would have been eerily quiet had it not been for Linda Callahan's sneeze, followed by an unladylike snort.

"How long?"

"Until tomorrow morning, Your Honor . . ."

The judge remained silent as he quickly considered the defending attorney's request, then focused his attention on the young prosecutor. "Mr. Sage?"

Marshall Sage stood. "We have no objection, Your Honor." Although it wasn't the best scenario for the prosecution, Sage figured it was best to be somewhat compliant.

No sense in pissing off the judge.

The judge reached for his gavel, giving the obligatory signal court was in recess for the rest of the day. "Granted. We'll resume at nine tomorrow morning . . ."

With that, everyone in the courtroom suddenly had extra time on their hands, so Evelyn snatched her sweater and purse, eager to text Colbie about the turn of events. Linda Callahan shot her a look as she hurried out the door, but she didn't notice.

As soon as she was situated in her car, she tapped out a brief message to her niece. *Recess until tomorrow morning— call when you can.* Seconds later, her cell phone chirped. "Colbie?"

Evelyn filled her in on the details of the trial, thinking Hastings must have something he's not sharing with anyone. "If he has new information, what do you think it is?"

Colbie hesitated before answering, hearing the hope in her aunt's voice. "Well, I don't know—it may be something, or nothing."

"Sage didn't offer any argument—that was strange, I thought."

"Not necessarily—don't forget, if there's a new witness,

or a new anything, Hastings has to divulge the information to the prosecution. My guess is Sage doesn't have any idea of what it is and, if he's smart, he'll want to find out as quickly as possible."

"I never thought of that . . ."

"All we can do is wait—have you talked to Harry? He'll know . . ."

"Not yet—I wanted to get in touch with you before you buried yourself in ancestral paperwork!"

"Well, enjoy your evening together—I haven't talked to Brian about it yet, but I'm thinking we'll spend the night in Gillette. That way, we can start again in the morning without wasting time on a drive into town . . ."

Evelyn hoped Colbie didn't hear her small sigh of relief. Of course, she loved her niece, and appreciated everything she was doing for her and her husband. But, the truth? She was ready to get back to her life with Harry—it was simpler. Comforting. "Good idea—I'll be in the courtroom first thing—I'll text you once I hear."

They rang off, agreeing to keep in touch throughout the following day. "I think she's glad to have time with Harry," Colbie commented to Brian as she accessed a hotel website on her phone. "Where do you want to stay?"

"Makes no difference to me . . ."

Minutes later, reservations made, they started their search on the library's microfilm. "This is weird," Brian commented. "You'd think with all the technology we have today, this system would be obsolete . . ."

"I know . . ." Her eyes focused on the screen as she slowly began to scroll through archived newspaper documents, articles, and whatever else she could find. "I'm going to start with Hedwin Moore—from the little I know, he was known throughout several counties in Minnesota . . ."

"What you told me about Hedwin when we started this case wasn't much—do you know anything, at all?"

"Not really . . ." She squinted as she tried to focus on the article in front of her. "All I know is Hedwin Moore was my great-great grandfather, and he lived in Minnesota—and, as far as I can tell, he didn't live in Wyoming . . ."

"Well, let's keep digging—there's bound to be something to put us on the right track."

Colbie agreed, raising her Starbuck's paper cup for a mock toast. "Here's to a productive day!"

Five minutes later, both were engrossed in archived files, saying little. It wasn't until three hours passed when Colbie sat back in her chair, an incredulous look on her face.

Brian noticed immediately. "What's up? Did you find something?"

She nodded, the look of disbelief refusing to fade. "The vision . . ."

"Which one?"

"Of Hedwin dividing in two . . ."

"What about it?"

She spoke to Brian, but couldn't take her eyes from the microfiche screen. "I'm not sure if this can possibly be right—but, from what I gather, Hedwin Moore and Hedwin Beeman were the same man!"

"The same man? But, how can that be?" He thought for

a moment, registering his own look of disbelief. "Are you sure?"

Colbie paused. "Pretty sure—you know what this means, don't you?"

"Yes—but, why don't you tell me."

"Think about it—if Hedwin Moore and Hedwin Beeman are the same man, that means I'm related to the Beeman family—so is Evelyn! That's why I can't find any record of Hedwin Moore living in Wyoming—it was the other side of the family that headed west!"

At that moment, both realized the ramifications of Colbie's theory. The two Hedwins the same man? It was an astonishing revelation, and something she never considered. She was certain no one on her side of the family had any idea the roving and randy Hedwin Moore of the last century kept a secret life from everyone. The more she thought about it, however, the more it made sense—in fact, he dropped off the planet at just about the time his bastard son beelined it to Wyoming, using the only name he knew—Hedwin Benjamin Beeman. The difference between his father and him?

Their middle names.

# CHAPTER EIGHTEEN

Amanda Beeman sat at the kitchen table, drink in one hand, a smoke in the other. Both were filthy habits according to Hattie Pearl, but Amanda refused to honor any requests to quit. *It was none of her damned business*, she thought as she took a long drag, then blew smoke rings into filtered, kitchen light.

For the previous couple of weeks, she didn't like the way Marshall Sage was conducting the trial. Of course, she didn't attend, but there were those deeply embedded within the legal system keeping her in the know. Witnesses weren't supposed to be privy to previous testimony, so shelling out a few bucks seemed the only logical answer when it came to finding out the latest news. All were individuals she could trust, and having more than one mole came in handy when it came to verifying information.

Randy wasn't any help—in fact, he barely spoke to her since the first day of his testimony, refusing to tell her anything at all about the trial. *He picked a hell of a time to get pissy*, she thought as she took another drag. Normally, she could care less if he spoke to her, but during the trial? Such childish actions were beneath her, and she wasn't about to have any of it.

As she pondered a life unencumbered—what she truly wanted—she couldn't help smiling. With her family all but gone, she was once again—or, would be—free to live as she chose. And, she chose to live life by herself. If everything worked out, her adoring husband would wind up in the slammer, taking the rap for murder times four. At least, that was the plan.

The crapshoot was Randy.

She hadn't yet heard from her sources regarding what he said on the stand, so she had no clue which road to choose when she testified at the end of the week. Still, she figured there was little reason for concern.

After all, she had an incredible eye for details.

# CHAPTER NINETEEN

E velyn never saw anything like it! A hundred people—
or, more—lined up at the courthouse entrance, hoping
to snag a seat for what many considered the best part
of the trial.

She watched as those at the front of the line were scanned
and admitted, apparently giving little thought to the fact
someone's life was on trial. *What a bunch of hypocrites*, she
thought as she made her way to the door, nodding to friends
who showed up to support Harry and her. Others looked at
her as though she carried the plague, their minds made up
her husband was a killer.

Of course, there was rampant speculation about why
Jeremiah Hastings requested a twenty-four-hour recess.
Rumors and innuendo trickled into households the evening

before, reporters from local television stations doing their part to keep the masses informed. Unintentionally, the recess sparked a communal desire to be present for the following day's testimony, and lookie-loos showed up from Cheyenne, as well as Gillette and Sundance.

At nine o'clock sharp, the judge entered, taking his place at the bench, signaling the beginning of testimony. "Call your witness . . ."

Jeremiah didn't stand even though the judge directed him to begin—he thought it more powerful to remain seated when Randy Howard walked down the aisle to the witness stand. Such an act left no doubt he had no respect for the supposed Beeman heir. *What a day it will be, Mr. Howard— what a day, indeed!*

"Defense recalls Randy Howard, Your Honor . . ."

Moments later, a police officer held the door open as Randy Johnson Howard entered. Everyone's eyes turned toward him as he made the long walk to the front of the courtroom, many noticing something strange. There was something about him that was . . . well, they didn't know what it was, but he looked different. Stronger. Confident.

Like a man who made up his mind . . .

\*\*\*\*

"Evelyn texted me about the giant line around the courthouse this morning—she said she had a hard time making it through the front door!"

Brian shot her a dubious look, then took a sip of coffee. "In Gillette? Somehow, I can't quite picture it . . ."

Colbie laughed, then grabbed a few files from her messenger bag. "I know, right? Who would've thought Gillette, Wyoming, would host a sensational murder trial?"

"Sensational? I don't know—that may be going a little too far . . ."

She handed him the daily copy of a leading national paper, the trial garnering a short article. "Page two . . ."

Brian quickly scanned it, then gave it back to her. "I can't believe it—nice you got a mention, though."

"Oh, I don't think I had much to do with it—don't forget Evelyn told us the Beeman boys' murder made national news, so I'm guessing it's a customary follow-up . . ."

"Don't kid yourself—you had a lot to do with turning the trial to Harry's favor by finding that cigarette at Harrelson's Gap."

"Maybe—but, as long as Harry is exonerated, it doesn't matter who did what. His freedom is what's important . . ."

"Agreed." Brian fired up the microfiche, turning his attention to what he and Colbie had to accomplish. They planned on leaving Gillette by four o'clock, so they agreed to work until then. Both stashed a few snack bars to get them through, figuring they could splurge on a nice late afternoon dinner when they finished their research.

What Colbie hoped to learn, she wasn't sure. Researching

Hedwin Moore seemed the logical place to start, so it made sense to pick up where she left off the previous day. She knew it would take targeted digging to unravel what seemed to be a well-kept secret. If Hedwin Moore and Hedwin Beeman were the same man—and, she was sure that was the case— could there be anyone in her family who knew? Her mother? Is that why she suggested Colbie help Harry? *Maybe it was her way to put me on the trail of my family,* she thought as she scrolled through the first page of a long-defunct newspaper.

But, as she stared at the microfiche screen, her intuitive mind merged with her conscious mind, suddenly in overdrive with vision after vision. A window into decades past opened, images appearing as portraits flickering in and out. She didn't recognize any of them, until the vision of a country lane.

It was then Colbie locked onto the red-haired girl.

Considerably older, she smiled at Colbie with a familiarity touching Colbie's soul. *It can't be LaRee,* Colbie thought. *She died in a tragic accident when she was a child* . . . No, the gentle face was like staring in the mirror, encouraging Colbie to accept what she already knew to be true—she was the red-haired girl from a time she'd never known.

The young woman in the vintage, white dress, and long, burnished, curly hair held out her hand much as she did when she visited Colbie for the first time as a young girl— when Colbie thought she was LaRee.

In her mind, Colbie took her hand, feeling the cool touch of the young women's fingers, images of Hedwin flooding her mind.

And, Hattie Pearl.

The Beeman matriarch held a piece of paper—a

document—holding it out to Colbie. But, as soon as Colbie reached toward the old woman, it disappeared, the image fading to nothing.

Then? Amanda.

Within her intuitive mind, she watched a black truck pull off the road, rolling to a stop in front of a trailhead sign pointing to a tiny, narrow trail. *I know that place!* Her focus fully on the vision, Colbie watched as a darkly-clad individual got out, the figure's face contorted with anger. *Amanda Beeman!* The Circle B heir pointed down the trail, then flicked a cigarette into the bushes.

Moments later, the movie in her mind vanished, leaving Colbie with knowledge no one else knew—Amanda Beeman had a history with Harrelson's Gap.

****

The second day of Randy's testimony turned out to be explosive compared to the previous day's. Emotions and expectations were high, and the collective energy of spectators seemed to fuel his personal fire. In fact, as soon as he faced the courtroom, Evelyn, too, noticed something was different from the man she watched and listened to only one day earlier.

Jeremiah Hastings stood, leveling a serious eye on the witness. "Yesterday, Mr. Howard, we established you have never been to Harrelson's Gap. Is that correct?"

Randy didn't bother to lean forward so the courtroom could hear better. "Yes."

Hastings walked toward him, strategically stopping where no one's view would be blocked—it was one of those subliminal tricks he learned as a young attorney, and he never ignored its importance. "Where are you employed, Mr. Howard?"

Randy looked at him as though he were nuts. "Circle B Ranch."

"In what capacity?"

"Ranch foreman."

"How long have you been employed by the Circle B?"

"Thirty-five years."

"Who hired you thirty-five years ago?"

Again, Randy looked confused, privately wondering what difference it made who hired him. "Richard Larson."

"Who is Richard Larson?"

"My wife's grandfather . . ."

"And, who is your wife, Mr. Howard?"

"Amanda Beeman."

Hastings paused, then walked slowly back to the defendant's table. "How long have you been married to Amanda Beeman," he asked as he turned, once again, to face the witness.

"Thirty-five years."

"So, you became ranch foreman at the same time you married Amanda Beeman?"

"Yes."

"How big is the Circle B, Mr. Howard?"

"Seventeen thousand acres . . ."

"And, it's a working cattle ranch, is that correct?"

Randy was starting to get perturbed with Hastings's questions—what did that have to do with Harry Fenamore killing his stepsons?

"Yes."

"It's a profitable ranch, is it not?"

"Yes."

Hastings paused again, taking only a few steps from the defendant's table. "Do you have any stake in the Circle B Ranch, Mr. Howard?"

Randy fidgeted slightly in his seat. "What do you mean?"

"I mean, Mr. Howard, do you have any financial stake in the Circle B Ranch?"

"You mean, do I own any of it?"

Evelyn thought she noticed Randy's bravado shrivel as Hastings expertly directed the testimony.

"Yes, Mr. Howard. Do you own any part of the Circle B Ranch?"

The witness looked down at his feet for a second, then back at Jeremiah Hastings. "No."

Hastings feigned a thoughtful, rather confused look. "So, you don't own any of it?"

"No, Sir."

"Will you ever?"

"Do you mean will I ever own part of the Circle B?"

"Yes, Mr. Howard. Will you ever own any portion, or all, of the Circle B Ranch in Sundance, Wyoming?"

It was a question Randy didn't anticipate and, for a moment, he considered more than a monosyllabic answer. He decided, however, not to give the defense anything other than a yes or no. "Yes."

"Are you provided for in any documents such as a will?"

"Yes, Sir."

Hastings stopped, looked at Harry, then back at the witness. "What kind of document?"

Randy's slight fidget morphed into a full-fledged squirm. "Land transfers . . ."

"Land transfers—please explain."

"When Hattie Pearl Beeman passed away—she was the owner of the ranch—she transferred all of the Circle B land to her granddaughter."

"Who's her granddaughter?"

"Amanda Beeman."

"If Hattie Pearl Beeman transferred the land to Amanda

Beeman, how is it you're going to get any of it?"

"Amanda made arrangements to have five thousand acres put in my name . . ."

"Made arrangements—with whom?"

Randy hesitated, realizing at that moment he was about to be bushwhacked, but there was nothing he could do about it. "The Beeman family attorney . . ."

"And, who is the Beeman family attorney?"

"At that time, it was Rory Gallagher."

"I'm not sure I understand, Mr. Howard. Are you saying Rory Gallagher is no longer the family attorney?"

"Yes."

That was all Hastings needed. "Do you recognize this document, Mr. Howard?" The defense attorney approached the witness, handing him what appeared to be two-pages of legal-sized paper.

Randy briefly looked at both pages. "No, Sir."

"No? It's a land transfer document, is it not?"

"Yes."

"On the last page, Mr. Howard, who is named as the attorney of record?"

Randy flipped to the second page, skimming the content. "Rory Gallagher."

"Now, Mr. Howard, I ask you look at the document carefully. Is there anything pertaining to five thousand acres of the Circle B ranch being transferred to you upon the death of Hattie Pearl Beeman?"

That was the moment.

Randy's face turned scarlet as he realized his wife lied to him. As well as he knew her and after reviewing the document, he was certain she had no intention of transferring land to him—ever. *That bitch played me for a fool,* he thought as he struggled to regain his composure.

He concentrated on the document, not hearing or noticing the Sundance sheriff standing by the courtroom doors, arms across his chest, jaw set—to anyone looking, the sheriff looked as if he were about to blow a gasket.

"Shall I repeat the question, Mr. Howard?"

"No . . ."

Hastings waited. Everyone in the courtroom watched as Randy Johnson Howard struggled with what had to be a personally devastating bombshell. All those years as Amanda Beeman's doormat? They were for nothing.

*Not worth a damned thing . . .*

\*\*\*\*

Brian kept a careful eye on Colbie, recognizing instantly she was deeply engaged with her intuitive mind. Ever since his own experience with visions in Zurich when they were on the Remington case, he had an understanding and appreciation for what she could do. Eyes closed, her eyelids flickered, moving rapidly as if she were watching a movie—it was something he dare not interrupt.

It didn't last long—two or three minutes—and, it turned out Brian didn't have to worry about disturbing her. Her cell phone vibrated just as she was approaching the present, jarring her to complete awareness. "This is Colbie . . ."

"Colbie? It's Jess—from Seattle."

His was a voice she didn't expect. "Jess! Hold on a minute—I'm at a library, so I'm going to step outside . . ." Colbie glanced at Brian, then got up and headed for the main doors. "Okay—now, what's up?"

"Remember the cigarette butt?"

"Oh, yes . . ."

"It turns out there were two DNA profiles on it . . ."

"Two? Are you sure?"

"Positive—we dropped the ball on our end, and I apologize. You didn't get a copy of the second profile . . ."

Colbie couldn't believe what she was hearing! "Do you have any idea who it is?"

"Not specifically—all I know is the profile is a Caucasian female. I didn't get a hit when I put it through the system . . ."

Colbie wasn't sure what to say—but, what she did know was having two profiles on one cigarette butt meant only one thing—it was shared. *Were both people smoking it at the same time, passing the cigarette to each other?* "Thanks, Jess—I might need you to do another analysis, same as last time—as quickly as you can."

"We're the ones who screwed up—we're here if you need us."

After a quick goodbye, Colbie tapped out a text to Jeremiah Hastings.

*I have news. Pls call.*

\*\*\*\*

Hastings listened as Colbie relayed her conversation with the DNA analyst, knowing it was what he needed to free Harry by a full acquittal. Reasonable doubt?

Handy, but not needed.

"I can only think of one situation," Colbie offered, "when there are two profiles on one cigarette—it was shared. Now, who would typically share something like that?" She didn't wait for Hastings to answer. "A girlfriend and boyfriend." She paused, knowing what she was about to say would break the Beeman boys' murder case wide open. "Or," she continued, "a husband and wife."

Hastings kept his voice low. "Randy and Amanda . . ."

"Yep . . ."

"Do you know if Amanda's in the DNA system?"

"My contact says no—but, I've been thinking about that. I would be willing to bet the sheriff has DNA from the Beeman boys' belongings—bloody clothes, or something. If he does, my contact can compare their DNA to the second profile on the cigarette butt. It won't be an exact match, but I think it will be enough to put the proverbial nail in the coffin. I'm pretty sure it's Amanda's . . ."

"Of course, that doesn't prove either one of them killed the two boys—in fact, the prosecution could argue they didn't have to be together at the same time. Amanda could have smoked part of it, then Randy was the one to finish it off."

"You're right—but, that scenario doesn't make logical sense. Could it happen that way? Yes—but, I think they were there together. She briefly filled him in on her recent vision that included Amanda Beeman's being at Harrelson's Gap.

"Are you sure it was her?"

"Positive—she was pointing to the trailhead sign, which makes me think someone was with her. And, I think that person was Randy—if nothing else, it confirms my suspicion Amanda is, at the least, familiar with the location where Maximilian was killed. Don't you think that will make a juror think twice?"

Hastings was quiet for a moment, thinking through how he could use Colbie's latest information. "Perhaps . . ." he finally commented "At least evidence is mounting in Harry's favor instead of against him . . ."

A few moments later, they clicked off, and Colbie headed back inside, taking her seat in front of the microfiche monitor.

"Well? What did he say?" Brian sat back in his chair, taking off his glasses.

"He agrees—he didn't discuss how he'll use the information, but, just from the way he was talking, I think he knows that cigarette butt puts Randy and Amanda in the crosshairs . . ."

"Have you talked to Evelyn?"

"No—unless something goes haywire, I probably won't talk to her until we get home . . ."

Brian smiled, looking at her for a long moment. "You ready to get back to work?"

"Yep!" She checked her watch. "It's only ten-thirty—we still have enough time to make the best use of the lovely Gillette library!"

# CHAPTER TWENTY

Evelyn put dinner on the table just as they pulled up in front of the ranch house. When Brian learned she was preparing elk steaks, he was quick to bag the idea of a leisurely dinner on the way out of Gillette.

"I'm so glad you're here!" Evelyn smiled as Colbie's better half enjoyed the fragrance of freshly baked bread. "Sit down! Harry's in the vet barn—one of the calves got caught in fencing on the back forty, so he's busy stitching her up."

"Did he get a chance to eat? It's not every day we have elk!"

"You sound like such a flatlander!" She laughed as she handed Brian a tall, cool, iced tea.

"There's a reason for that," he commented as he took a drink. "It's because I am a flatlander!"

They barely had time to get situated before her aunt had full plates in front of them. "Now—it's perfectly okay to talk with your mouths full! What did you find out at the library?"

Between bites, Colbie filled her in on the call from Seattle, her talk with Hastings, and her suspicion Amanda was at Harrelson's Gap with Randy the day Max Beeman was murdered. "Of course, it doesn't prove anything, but Brian and I think the jury will see the sense in believing they were together at Harrelson's Gap . . ."

"What does Hastings say?"

"He agrees—tomorrow will be interesting. He did mention Sage will redirect in the morning. After that? I'm not sure. What happened in court today?"

Evelyn gave her a blow-by-blow, watching her niece's face as she described the moment when Randy learned Amanda didn't keep her promise of deeding five thousand acres to him. "I swear, Colbie, you could see the steam coming out of his ears! He was beyond pissed . . ."

"I can imagine! Did Hastings tell you who's on deck for tomorrow?"

"No, but I'm pretty sure Amanda has to make an appearance if Hastings is going to wrap up within a day, or so.

Over blackberry cobbler with vanilla ice cream, they discussed possibilities, none of which were a given. Then, as Evelyn poured second cups of coffee, the conversation turned to Colbie's research. "So, what did you find out?"

"Well, I was beginning to think the trip was going to be a bust, but, early this afternoon I hit pay dirt . . ."

Evelyn made sure her guests had what they needed,

then made herself comfortable. "Tell me!"

"Okay—get ready for a good story!"

Colbie glanced at Brian, then launched into Evelyn's and her family history. "The story picks up about 1921— there wasn't anything of interest before that, other than he was a young man trying to make a living. It turns out Hedwin Moore worked at various times as a grain buyer in Minnesota."

"Winter wheat, I would imagine . . ."

"I don't know what it was . . . but, the 1921 census indicated Hedwin was working as a barber, living in a three-room, rented house."

"A barber? What happened to buying grain?" Evelyn grinned at Colbie, then tugged on her hair. "Too bad hair styling talent doesn't run in the family!"

"I know!" Colbie paused, as if trying to fine tune something in her mind. "Remember the vision I had months ago of the red-haired girl, and I thought she was LaRee?"

Evelyn nodded. "What about it?"

"I saw the girl again—but, she was older. Probably in her late teens or early twenties—long, curly hair."

"Well, I do know about curly hair in our family, but it's not a prominent trait—a couple of cousins, I think, and us. Do you still think she's LaRee?"

"At first—but, something about that didn't feel right."

Evelyn noticed a peculiar expression in Colbie's eyes. "So . . . if she's not LaRee, then who?"

"Me—or, I was her. Not sure which . . ."

Evelyn wasn't sure what to say. When Colbie arrived in Wyoming, she brought a new way of thinking with her—for cowboy country, at least. Now? The concept of previous lives was one she hadn't previously considered, but, with all that happened over the previous months, it was something she couldn't discount. "Interesting—that raises a whole bunch of questions in my mind!"

"Me, too—but, for now, let's concentrate on the family. The two Hedwins . . ."

"Right . . ."

"So, I discovered a marriage certificate, and he married in 1915. So, that probably puts him in his early twenties. The same census shows he and his wife—Rose, I think—had a baby girl, and they named her Joan Vivian."

"I don't remember hearing those names . . ."

Colbie shook her head. "Neither do I. According to records, in April of 1926, Hedwin's family was still living in Minnesota—Joan would have been five—and, it was around that time they moved to Brainard."

"Was he still a barber?"

"Yep—he worked for two different barber shops. And—the family lived in two different homes."

"Two different homes? Why? How did you get all of this information?"

Colbie grinned at her aunt. "Thank God for the Internet! Some of it, though—the Wyoming information—was on the microfiche at the library."

"Oh—so, was he still a barber?"

"I don't know—I also discovered it was around that

time he had a girlfriend, who had a baby. A boy they named Hedwin Benjamin Beeman."

Evelyn motioned for Colbie and Brian to join her in front of the fireplace. Evenings were becoming cool, and it wouldn't be long before early fall turned fickle, bringing the season's first whiskey snow. "It kind of sounds like gossip to me . . ."

Colbie laughed, and cozied up in her favorite chair. "You're right about that! The real stroke of luck was the librarian happened to have family in Wyoming back then, and she put me in touch with her grandmother. It turned out Hedwin's shenanigans were the favorite subjects of the town busybodies . . ."

"Wait 'til you hear the rest of it," Brian interjected. "It's amazing what you can learn from old-time gossip!"

Evelyn laughed. "I don't know if I want to—this is our family!" She checked her watch. "It's getting late—how about if we pick this up tomorrow?"

"Good idea—there's quite a bit more to tell, but we're tired, too." Colbie turned to Brian, her face weary from the last two days in Gillette. "Okay with you?"

It was.

\*\*\*\*

Late August was more of an early fall rather than late summer. Ranchers were already baling hay which was a portend of an early winter, and Harry's trial was growing to a close with only Amanda's testimony left. Hastings confided to Colbie he knew the prosecuting attorney didn't want to call Amanda Beeman as a witness, but she insisted. Yes, it was a huge mistake, but one Marshall Sage couldn't circumvent. Randy's testimony didn't go as planned, leaving everyone in the courtroom with the idea someone else was guilty of the Beeman boys' murders. Who, they weren't sure, but everything pointed to there being something rotten when it came to Randy—and, Amanda.

As newspaper and television reporters predicted, Amanda's testimony garnered more attention than her husband's. As before, lines formed in front of the courthouse long before the witness was scheduled to begin and, those not lucky enough to be granted entrance, were turned away half an hour before court was underway.

Finally, the courtroom doors closed. "Call your witness, Mr. Hastings . . ." The judge didn't look at him as he issued his directive.

"The defense calls Amanda Beeman . . ."

Every head in the courtroom turned as the only living Beeman heir approached the witness box—for a woman who cared how she looked, it was clear the last two years took their toll. But, in all fairness, how could they not? Losing four family members within twenty-four months, including her own two boys, was surely enough stress to cause a few grey hairs.

Dressed conservatively, she strode down the aisle with a certain confidence and elegance befitting a millionaire ranch owner, not making eye contact with anyone. There was always an air of arrogance about her, but, Colbie and

Evelyn noticed a fleeting look of fear as Amanda was sworn to tell the truth. *Fat chance of that,* Colbie thought as she watched the witness take her seat.

Hastings stood, his presence always intimidating. Maybe it was his stellar, winning record that put the fear of God in witnesses—or, maybe there was something about him that subliminally let them know they should tell the truth. To do otherwise, would be reckless disregard for his ability to annihilate their testimony.

"State your name, please."

"Amanda Beeman."

"Are you the sole owner of the Circle B Ranch, located in Sundance, Wyoming?"

"Yes."

"What is your relationship with Maximilian and Bobby Beeman?"

"They're my sons . . ."

They were off and running. During the morning testimony, Hastings carefully laid groundwork for the afternoon session, asking questions to which everyone in the courtroom wanted answers. Methodically, he recounted the days and weeks before and after the Beeman boys' murders, allowing the judge and jury to think privately about what Amanda had to gain by her sons' untimely demise.

Then, the hammer.

"When was the last time you were at Harrelson's Gap, Ms. Beeman?"

Amanda's eyes focused on the defense attorney who now stood closer to the witness stand than he had any other witness in the trial. "I've never been to Harrelson's Gap . . ."

"Really? During all of your years in Wyoming, you've never been there?"

"Not really—I drove through it a couple of times, but that's it."

"When was the last time you 'drove through' Harrelson's Gap, Ms. Beeman?"

Amanda offered her most condescending smile. "Years ago—maybe twenty."

"You're right—twenty years is a long time," Hastings agreed as he returned to the defense table, then picked up what spectators assumed was a photograph.

"Do you recognize anything in this picture, Ms. Beeman?" He handed her an eight by ten photo of a trailhead sign, gauging her response and reaction carefully.

Amanda studied the photo for several moments, then handed it back to him. "No."

"No? You've never seen this location before?"

"No, not that I know of—I imagine there are a lot of places in Wyoming that look like that . . ."

Before Marshall Sage could say a word, Hastings calmly crossed to the prosecutor, showing him the photograph. Then, he again approached the witness. "How, then, do you account for the fact a cigarette butt with your DNA on it was found tucked under a boulder mere steps away from the trailhead sign in the photograph?"

Amanda blinked, then swallowed. "I'm not sure I understand your question . . ."

"It's a simple one, Ms. Beeman—if you've never been to Harrelson's Gap, and you don't recognize the trailhead sign, how is it a cigarette butt with your DNA on it was found close to the trailhead sign in the photograph—the trailhead sign located at Harrelson's Gap, Wyoming. Please enlighten me, Ms. Beeman, because I don't understand . . ."

"Mr. Hastings," the judge intervened, "are you planning to enter the photograph as an exhibit?"

"Yes, Your Honor—defense exhibit seventeen." Hastings handed the photo to the judge.

"Mark it in," he ordered after studying it briefly.

Amanda's eyes darted from the defense attorney to the judge, trying to figure out how the hell one of her cigarettes was found in Harrelson's Gap. She could count on one hand the number of times she was there, but, at no time, did she have a smoke. A faulty memory? Perhaps.

"Well, Ms. Beeman?" He asked his question as he again stood no more than ten feet in front of her.

"I don't know . . ."

"Okay—where was Maximilian Beeman's body found in September of last year?"

"Harrelson's Gap."

"Did he go there often?" Hastings didn't take his eyes off of her, a glare daring her to lie.

"I don't know . . ."

And, so, the afternoon session progressed, Amanda digging herself in deeper, having no idea how to extricate herself from the lies she had to tell. Hastings, of course, didn't drop the bomb about Randy's DNA being on the cigarette butt, as well, and Colbie figured he was saving that little gem for Amanda's last day of testimony.

Colbie thought there was a point toward the end of the day's session, Amanda appeared confused—could it be she really wasn't at Harrelson's Gap? It was a possibility the defense had to consider, although they doubted that was the case. "Just because of my vision," Colbie mentioned as she and Evelyn headed to their car, "I have no doubt she's been there—but, did she murder Max? And, what about Bobby?"

Evelyn stopped as she dug the keys from her purse. "Are you saying Amanda might not be the murderer?"

"No—but, just from the way she looked on the stand, she seemed . . . blindsided."

The ride back to the ranch was filled with conversation about the trial, until it turned to Colbie's family research. "I think I left off at the point Hedwin had a girlfriend, and a new baby—a boy."

"Yep," Evelyn confirmed. "Then what happened?"

"Here's where it gets a little confusing—so, Hedwin suddenly had another family and, according to several articles, he had a significant problem with drinking, and he was always involved in shady deals."

"Sounds like the Beemans, to me . . ."

Colbie nodded. "I know—and, that's not all. One time, Hedwin walked home from work, professing to his wife he was in a car accident, telling her his passenger slit his throat on the shattered windshield."

"Of course, that wasn't the truth . . ."

"Probably not—but, it didn't make any difference. He

gave a bloody barbershop razor to his wife, swearing her to secrecy. And, although there was rampant speculation Hedwin murdered his passenger—a man—no one could prove it except his wife who refused to testify against him. Case closed . . ."

"No shit? Why did he murder him?"

"I don't think anyone knows that, but, when I tuned in to it, I think it's because Hedwin and the other guy were vying for the affections of a certain, young, single girl . . ."

"Seriously? You saw that?"

"Yep—it was like watching an old-time movie."

"Did the cops ever talk to him about it?"

"Yes, and that was the crux of the articles—I found three—but, as I said, there wasn't any proof."

"If his wife had any brains, she would have disposed of the razor the second he gave it to her . . ."

"Well, I imagine she did—unfortunately, that wasn't the only thing about Hedwin. I managed to locate a newspaper clipping telling of his trying to burn the house down with his wife and daughter in it!"

Evelyn glanced at Colbie as she signaled to turn onto the road leading to the ranch. "What was his wife's name?"

"Rose—his daughter was Joan."

"Oh, yeah—that's right. How could she even stay with such a man?"

"Who knows? I imagine it was the same as it is today—I have the feeling those aren't the only things he did . . ."

"You know . . . it seems like Hedwin Moore—the Hedwin Moore I heard about—wasn't anything like that!"

Colbie nodded. "Family secrets, I guess . . ."

\*\*\*\*

Amanda and Randy weren't speaking. Neither wanted much to do with the other for the previous week or so, both concentrating on the trial, consumed with trying to figure out what went wrong. Nothing went according to plan, and Randy's temper simmered as he constantly thought of his wife's betrayal, only comforted by the fact he made 'arrangements' in case such a thing happened.

And, that was the thing about Randy. Most people in town didn't care for him much, and the only person who occasionally met him for a drink or socialized with him at a barbecue was the Sundance sheriff. On the force for over thirty years, Sheriff Roy Dardon didn't see Randy as others did—a whipped man who didn't have the spine of a snake. No, he had a much different opinion of the middle-aged rancher—one he knew to be true.

Years back, when Amanda and Randy decided to tie the knot, Randy also decided to take his wife's name and, since that day, folks knew him as Randy Beeman. They adapted to his new name, not giving it a second thought as he settled into life on the ranch—to them, he seemed like a regular guy.

What Randy kept under wraps, however, was his above-average intellect—way above average. It was something he chose not to divulge, and Amanda was really the only one who knew of his intellectual capabilities. During the fledgling days of their relationship, she was slightly intimidated by it, but soon discovered an interesting dichotomy—he was completely malleable. With little effort, she could mold him into the person she needed in her life, and he would willingly acquiesce. To her, it was the perfect arrangement.

To Randy, everything was going according to plan.

\*\*\*\*

The last days of the trial packed the courtroom, an undercurrent of change coursing through spectators. According to gossip, Harry Fenamore was slipping off the hot seat, Randy and Amanda taking his place as favored targets. Amanda couldn't understand where she went wrong—never for a second did she consider she might attract attention as a viable suspect, especially since she was careful to keep the land transfer information to herself. Rory Gallagher was the only other person who knew of her duplicity and, since she paid him a tidy sum, there was no way he would sell her out.

Was there?

Duly sworn, Amanda sat in the witness box, ready to
do battle. Gone was the confused expression of the previous
day—sometime during the night, she managed to muster
an acceptable bravado, one readily accepted by those who
knew her. It was disquieting for some to see such a stalwart
woman teeter and topple from her societal high horse, the
subject of increasing conversations.

"Ms. Beeman," Hastings began, "yesterday you testified
to the fact you've never been to Harrelson's Gap—is that
correct?"

Amanda straightened her shoulders as if steeling herself
for an onslaught, her eyes refusing to meet his. "Yes—that's
right."

"Thank you—moving on. What brand of cigarettes do
you smoke, Ms. Beeman?"

"Marlboro."

"Regular or menthol?"

"Regular." Amanda didn't flinch. She anticipated the line
of questioning and, after considering every possible answer,
there was no way she could lie when pressed for specifics
such as her preferred brand.

"Much like this cigarette, Ms. Beeman?" Hastings
approached the witness, handing her an eight by ten,
magnified photo of a slightly weathered cigarette butt.
"Please pay particular attention to the brand of the cigarette
in the photo . . ."

Amanda studied it, knowing the questioning was about
to get very specific. "Yes—like this one, I suppose."

"What is the brand of cigarette?"

"Marlboro."

"Do you wear lipstick, Ms. Beeman?

"No."

Hastings shot her an unbelieving stare. "No lipstick? Lip gloss? Lip balm?"

Amanda's thoughts scrambled as she tried to figure out how he planned on trapping her. "I wear lip balm, but not lipstick."

"What brand of lip balm, Ms. Beeman?"

"Blistex."

Hastings walked quickly back to the defense table, picked up a sheet of paper, then returned to stand directly in front of the witness. "Please read paragraph two, line three—it's highlighted . . ."

Amanda read it, her jaw setting as the content of the text sank in.

"Please read it aloud, Ms. Beeman . . ."

"Trace evidence—Blistex Medicated Lip Balm."

The collective gasp of spectators said it all—in their minds, the trial was all but over. To the majority, Amanda Beeman was guilty of murdering her own two boys—especially Maximilian—her actions cold and calculated.

By the end of the day, Hastings rested the defense. All that was left were closing arguments, then the case was in the hands of the jury. He knew he didn't have to prove Amanda Beeman's guilt—all he had to do was plant reasonable doubt. In his professional opinion, there was no way Harry Fenamore would be found guilty.

Marshall Sage knew it, as well. His mind already turned to prosecuting Amanda—and, Randy—assessing it would be an uphill battle simply due to her standing in the ranching community. For a nanosecond he considered not pursuing a guilty verdict, but quickly discarded such a dreadful idea. Yes, he was going on record as losing the Fenamore case, but there was much more on the table when it came to the Beemans.

Compared to them, Harry's case was peanuts.

# CHAPTER TWENTY-ONE

For the first time—almost from the time Colbie and Brian arrived in Wyoming—Harry was all smiles as they gathered for dinner that evening. Closing arguments were scheduled for the next day and, according to Hastings, neither he nor Harry should be surprised by a swift verdict. If everything went smoothly, he'd be an exonerated man by the beginning of the weekend—and, Colbie and Brian would be gone shortly thereafter.

"So," he commented, focusing on his wife's niece, "what's the plan for the two of you? I imagine you can't wait to get out of here!"

Colbie reached across the table, then squeezed his hand. "I admit, Uncle Harry, I never thought for a second we'd be in Wyoming this long—but, when everything is said and done, it wasn't too bad!"

Harry squeezed her hand in return. "I never thought I'd be in such a position at any time during my life—I don't think I can properly thank you for everything you've done."

"We're just happy we could help . . ."

He glanced at Evelyn, then at Colbie and Brian. "I imagine you're looking forward to getting back to your city life . . ."

Colbie laughed. "Am I that transparent?"

Brian looked at her, eyebrows raised. "Really, Colbie? Yes—you're that transparent!" He leaned over, kissing her on the cheek. "But, I don't blame you—I know you're ready to head for home."

"What about you, Brian?" Harry had an inkling Brian would jump at the chance to stay. "You seem to enjoy the cowboy life—any chance you and Colbie will stay? You can live with us until we can get a proper ranch house built for you on the back forty . . ."

Colbie and Brian stared at him, not sure they were hearing him correctly. "What are you saying, Uncle Harry," Colbie asked, glancing at Evelyn.

"I'm saying we can build you a ranch house on the southwest corner—I'll transfer two hundred and fifty acres to you, to do with as you please." He watched their reactions. "With the exception of drilling, of course . . ."

Colbie sat back in her seat, stunned by her uncle's generous offer. "I don't know what to say . . ."

"Don't say anything—it's nothing you have to decide now. Go back to Seattle, and think about it—the offer will always stand."

She looked at Brian, noticing a faint expression of hope—he'd stay in a New York minute, not caring if he ever returned to the soggy northwest.

"It's a very generous offer, but . . ."

Evelyn cut her off. "But, nothing—think about it. Like Harry said, the offer is aways on the table." She got up, and headed for the pantry. "Who wants hot chocolate?"

Three hands shot up in the air like school kids knowing the answer to a question.

"Colbie—why don't you fill Harry in on what you learned about the Moore family? I haven't told him anything!"

At Harry's insistence, Colbie brought him up to speed, ending with their great-grandfather Hedwin's trying to torch his own house with his wife and daughter in it—fortunately, they went out the window. "It was no secret Hedwin liked the ladies—he'd bring them home and, allegedly, Rose would make sandwiches for them . . ."

Evelyn stared at her in disbelief! "You've got to be kidding!"

"Nope—Rose actually admitted it when questioned by the authorities . . ."

"Sounds to me like he was the black sheep of the family," Harry commented. "

Colbie nodded. "I can well imagine he was—there was an arrest record from right before the Great Depression accusing Hedwin of stealing a woman's ring. He had it made into a stickpin so she wouldn't recognize it—that was when he had his own barbershop in a swanky hotel."

"Just to be certain I'm understanding you correctly, Hedwin Moore and Hedwin Beeman are the same man . . . right?

"Yes . . ."

"So, when does he come to Wyoming?"

Colbie sat back in her chair, getting more comfortable as she brought Harry up to speed. "Good question . . . I couldn't find much until the thirties when Rose filed for a legal separation. According to documents, Hedwin and his family were still living in Minnesota, and that's when Rose discovered she contracted a venereal disease—not once, but three times!" Colbie paused. "That was the basis for Rose's wanting the separation—her doctor testified for her, and the judge granted her request. Hedwin was ordered to pay spousal and child support—which he didn't—and, shortly after that, Minnesota reports dried up."

Harry glanced at Evelyn, then focused again on Colbie. "What happened to him?"

"Another good question—he was off the radar, and no one heard from him again, including his wife and daughter. That, however, was a good thing because Rose and Joan went into hiding—both believed if Hedwin returned, he'd kill both of them . . ."

"I'll bet," Evelyn suggested, "that was when he headed for Wyoming, wife and little Hedwin Benjamin Beeman in tow . . . And, that's probably when he decided to use the name Beeman instead of Moore . . . "

Colbie agreed. "I think you're right—and, the time frame fits."

"From what Evelyn told me," Harry interjected, "Hedwin was known throughout Wyoming as a roughneck . . ."

"You're right, Harry—and, no one trusted him. That's how he managed to acquire so much land. He blackmailed anyone he could, threatening them in such a way they willingly handed over all they had. At least, that's what Abbott told me when I visited him at his cabin . . ."

The four sat in silence, each one understanding the ramifications and consequences of Hedwin Moore's— Hedwin Beeman's—actions. "That makes you and Evelyn related to Amanda Beeman," Harry stated.

Another silence.

"That's something I never anticipated in a million years," Evelyn finally commented. "I'm not sure what to think . . ."

"I know . . ." Colbie reached for Brian's hand. "It's kind of a bitter pill to learn our ancestor was a murderer."

"Don't forget thief," her aunt added.

"Knowing the real story, however, it makes sense—it also explains the bad seeds in the Beeman clan. Hedwin's predilection for taking the illegal low road seems to have filtered down to his heirs . . ."

"By bad seeds, you mean Amanda?" Evelyn placed three steaming mugs of hot chocolate in the center of the table. "Go for it!"

Colbie pulled a mug toward her, wrapped her fingers around it, then took a sip before answering Evelyn's question. "Exactly—and, don't forget what Abbott told me about Hattie Pearl. According to him, she was of the same crop . . ."

"And, he said Hattie Pearl had visions—maybe that's where you get it!"

Harry listened intently as Colbie and Evelyn discussed

their ancestry. "There's no doubt Amanda isn't playing with a full deck," he added. "All she knows is money and power—and, apparently, she'll go to any end to get them."

By the time they finished their hot chocolate, everyone was ready to call it a night. Colbie and Brian headed for their room, while Evelyn and Harry decided to sit on the back porch for a while before turning in. Evelyn loved the chill of the coming autumn, welcoming the crisp, cool air.

"Well—what are you thinking," Colbie asked as she slipped into her bathrobe. "When do you want to head out?"

"You mean to Seattle?" Brian flipped his right shoe toward the closet.

"Yep—our work here is done . . ." She looked at him, noticing his disappointment.

"I have to admit, I was stunned by Harry's offer to build another ranch house for us . . ."

"Not to mention two hundred and fifty acres!" Part of her wished she could seriously consider making a move, but the bigger part suspected she would feel isolated, and it was time to level with Brian. "I'm a city girl," she confessed. "I don't know if I have what it takes to live so far from a metropolis of some sort. The only country life I really know is when my parents took my brother and me camping . . ."

"I get it—it would be a monumental change for us, and the last thing I want is for you to feel as if you're not in the right place. I know what that's like . . ."

Colbie wasn't certain if he were making a general statement, or referencing something in their past. "You mean the East Coast?"

He shook his head. "No—not really. Although, to be

completely honest, I never felt at home there . . ."

She looked at him, her expression serious. "What do you want to do? I mean, what do you *really* want to do . . ."

Brian thought for a moment. "The truth is I want to spend the rest of my life with you. I don't really care where it is . . ."

Colbie eyes brimmed with tears. "I feel the same . . ."

Ten minutes later, it was lights out, but, sleep? It didn't come easily.

It didn't show up for quite some time.

\*\*\*\*

By two o'clock the following day, the jury received the case. Harry's stomach was in his throat as they filed from the courtroom, their faces reflecting the seriousness of their task. Many spectators hung around, thinking the verdict would be swift and decisive—at least, that's what the Linda Callahan camp hoped. Even though the trial tipped in Harry's favor a few weeks prior, the clique refused to believe he was innocent—something that would undoubtedly pick at them for the rest of their born days, no one hesitating to voice their dissatisfaction.

Brian suggested getting a bite to eat while the jury deliberated, but Evelyn declined—she preferred to remain close in case there were news. She did, however, insist they get something to eat. "Go! I'll text you if the verdict comes in . . ."

Had Brian not skipped lunch, he probably would have opted to stay with Evelyn—or, get take out. But, as it turned out, Colbie said she wasn't hungry, feeling her duty was to remain with her aunt. "I'll be gone thirty minutes," he promised. Are you sure you don't want anything?"

Colbie glanced at Evelyn, and both shook their heads. "We're too nervous to eat . . ."

With that, Brian trotted down the sidewalk to the nearest restaurant, leaving Colbie to the task of assuaging her aunt's fears. Nearly half an hour later, his cell vibrated. "Gotta go," he explained to the young man behind the counter as he flipped him a ten dollar bill. "Keep the change!"

****

It was standing room only. Spectators who didn't attend a single day of the trial figured the last day was the best. After all, why waste all that time when they could catch up on the news?

Verdict day, however, was different.

Several of Evelyn's friends nodded in her direction, an unspoken 'good luck' on their lips. Some averted their eyes if they happened to catch her glancing their direction. Did they think Harry was guilty? She didn't know. Having a verdict returned in less than an hour was as troubling as it was exciting. As much as Evelyn wanted to believe and hope her husband would be walking out of the courthouse for the last time, it was almost more than she could bear.

As the three of them sat in the first row, Colbie paid particular attention to the jury as they filed in shortly after the judge called the court to order. None gave away their verdict as they sat down, none looking in Harry's direction. *That's not good*, Colbie thought as she listened to the judge ask the jury if they arrived at a verdict.

"Yes, Your Honor."

"And, that verdict is, Mr. Foreman?"

"We, the jury, find the defendant—not guilty."

Despite warnings from the judge prior to reading the verdict, the courtroom erupted in cheers! Evelyn was up like a shot, ready to make her way to Harry, tears streaming, while Colbie hugged Brian. "Thank God," she mumbled into his chest.

Moments later, the foreman handed a piece of folded paper to the bailiff, who handed it to the judge.

The courtroom was silent.

"In the case of the State of Wyoming versus Harry Michael Fenamore, the jury finds the defendant not guilty."

Spectators settled down as the judge thanked the jury for their service, then ended the proceedings with a drop of the gavel.

Finally, it was over! Brian glanced at Harry and Evelyn, both grinning from ear to ear. "Are they riding with us?"

Colbie nodded as she watched the judge leave the courtroom. "Yep—but, it might take Harry a little longer to get out of here!"

She was right.

Press waited by the front doors, reporters vying for the first interview. Hastings instructed Harry to keep his comments short and sweet, and it wasn't until the crowd started to disperse they could think of going home.

Finally, in the privacy of their SUV, Harry's emotions spilled as he grappled with the memories and struggles of the last year. "If it weren't for you," he said to Colbie through his tears, "I'm not sure I'd be here right now . . ."

"You're welcome, Uncle Harry. You're welcome . . ."

# CHAPTER TWENTY-TWO

As they emerged from the depths of the airport just before Thanksgiving, Seattle's humid, frigid air was like a stinging smack in the face. "I can't believe we were gone so long! It was around last Thanksgiving when we stepped off the plane in Wyoming!" Colbie took a deep breath, loving the salty fragrance of Puget Sound.

"I know!" Brian grinned as a familiar car pulled up next to the curb, honking the horn. "Hey, you two!" Tammy bolted from the driver's side, giving each a huge hug. "I was beginning to think you weren't ever coming home!"

"I know! Me, too!" Colbie returned the hug, then held her assistant at arm's length. "You look fabulous!"

Tammy twirled, ending with a slightly clumsy curtsy. "Thank you, thank you—I lost fifteen pounds, and I feel wonderful!"

"Well, it shows!" Colbie gave her another quick hug, then checked to make certain they had everything as Brian loaded the trunk with their luggage. "I think I came back with more than when I left!"

"You were gone almost a year, you know—I'm surprised you don't have more than that! Shopping in Wyoming must have been an experience!"

Within minutes, they were on their way home, and Colbie couldn't wait to walk in the front door of their cottage by the water. The second she stepped across the airport threshold, she was struck by how much she missed the city—even sounds of emergency vehicles streaking down the highway were comforting.

Tammy glanced at Brian in the rear view mirror, then at Colbie sitting next to her in the passenger's seat. "So . . . how was it?"

Colbie didn't take her eyes from the passing cityscape. "Interesting. Very interesting . . ."

"Have you ever been to Wyoming," Brian asked from the back seat.

Tammy chuckled, then exited the highway to head toward the Sound. "Good grief, no! Wyoming? Never in a million years!"

Brian scooted forward as much as the seat belt would allow. "Why do you say that? It's pretty incredible!"

That was a surprise! Granted, she didn't know Brian as well as she knew Colbie, but she never would have figured him for the cowboy life. "Seriously? What on earth is in Wyoming?"

He thought about it for a moment, then sat back in his seat. For all the time he was there, he found it interesting no one ever asked him that question. "Peace. Quiet. Spectacular sunsets . . ."

No one said anything. Colbie sensed Brian was already regretting their decision to return to the West Coast. It weren't as if she talked him into it, but, in her heart, she knew their time in the western state awakened something in his soul. Hers, too . . .

She just didn't want to admit it.

\*\*\*\*

Harry's trial didn't affect the residents of Sundance and Gillette for long. A week or two after it ended, folks went back to life as usual, few thinking about the Beemans. And, virtually no one remembered the red-headed gal from Seattle who, with Jeremiah Hastings, managed to get Harry acquitted.

So, the never-ending question—if Harry didn't murder the Beeman boys, who did? It was what everyone wanted to know. Hastings left no doubt in many minds Amanda Beeman was guilty as sin for offing her two sons—the kicker was no one really suspected Amanda or Randy would stand trial for the murder of her boys. Was there enough evidence?

Maybe. But, what about the deaths of her grandparents, Richard, and Hattie Pearl?

No one knew.

In the end, the upper crust of Sundance and surrounding area regarded the Beemans as one of them—after all, they were pillars of the community, and how dare anyone impugn their integrity?

\*\*\*\*

Rory Gallagher sat in his office, leafing through newspaper articles chronicling the last few weeks of the trial, thinking about what must be done. Harry's acquittal was big news for about five days after it ended, but, after that, headlines dwindled—maybe a small reminder tucked away where no one cared, but, that was about it. Still, he flipped through articles, reading each carefully in case there were something he didn't know.

In case there were something he needed to know.

Gallagher chose not to attend the trial, but, from newspaper and television reports, he knew of secrets still buried, embedded in false truth. He knew more than anyone about the inner workings of the Beeman clan and, if people had any idea about the real story? Well—things might move a little quicker.

And, justice would be swift.


\*\*\*\*


Randy raised his glass in a toast. "To better days, Roy! To better days . . ."

The sheriff met the toast, took a sip, then wiped foam from his upper lip. "We need to talk business . . ."

"What business is that?" Of course, Randy knew perfectly well what business the sheriff was referring to, and it was a topic he chose to ignore. But, his misguided attempt at changing the subject didn't go unnoticed.

"You know exactly what I'm talking about . . ."

Randy nodded. "The land transfers . . . look, I had no idea that bitch wife of mine would jack me over just like everyone else in her life!"

"What are you going to do?"

"Do?" Randy's voice slightly resembled a screech owl. "What do you expect me to do?"

The sheriff stared at the man sitting across from him, then glanced toward the bar to make certain no one was listening. "I expect you to make good on your word."

"How, Roy? I can't just waltz up to Amanda and say, "You better give me my five thousand acres, or else!"

Roy Dardon stood, laying a five-dollar bill on the table. "Well, Randy . . ." He paused, as he lit a cigarette. "You better think of something . . . you have two weeks."

Without looking back, he strode out the door, his resolve solid and unyielding. Randy watched him, trying to ignore the beads of sweat collecting at his hairline as he considered the sheriff's words—a threat, really.

There was little doubt—things were going to get dicey.

\*\*\*\*

It was strange Colbie and Brian seldom discussed their time in Wyoming as they, once again, adjusted to city life and home. Maybe it was because neither wanted to broach the subject of Harry's offer to build a home, plus two hundred and fifty acres. That would call for a decision, and Colbie wanted to relax at least a few weeks before she had to decide anything—including her next case. She was in the process of speaking with prospective clients, but, there was one, in particular, who piqued her interest.

She hesitated mentioning it to Brian—he gave more than one indication he was ready to settle down a bit, remaining in one location for more than a few months. But, when she considered the pros and cons, she figured she could take a case on her own—she did it before, and she certainly could do it again. The question was did she want to . . .

Colbie was the first to admit there was a certain comfort knowing Brian was by her side for the case in Zurich, as well as Harry's in Wyoming. His being there made her job easier, and she definitely liked decompressing with him at the end of the day—a glass of wine was much more pleasant when there were two. So, it came as no surprise when, after their first week home, he mentioned living on their own ranch. But, when Colbie's receptors receded?

Time to clam up.

Evelyn, too, figured it was best to let Colbie and Brian decide what would work best for their lives, although she made it clear having family nearby would be a treat. Harry agreed, although his delight was a little more selfish—he enjoyed showing ranch life to a city boy. At least, that's what he told Colbie—the truth was he came to consider Brian the son he never had. Early in their marriage, he and Evelyn learned she couldn't have children, and adoption was something they considered, but didn't work out. But, when Brian expressed interest in learning from Harry, Colbie's uncle didn't hesitate to bring him into the cowboy fold.

Still . . . could they make a life there?

****

Throughout the following weeks, there was little to report when it came to Amanda and Randy Beeman. Evelyn kept Colbie apprised whenever the Beeman name cropped up in the news, but none of it related to the possibility of indictments for the Beeman boys' murders. Richard's and Hattie Pearl's deaths were most likely chalked up to old age and, if anyone did suspect, they kept it to themselves.

In fact, no one seemed to care.

The strange thing was Amanda and Randy were rarely seen together, and rumors of trouble in paradise snaked through the community. Whether it were true was of no consequence—bridge clubs bubbled with gossip while churchgoers appropriately kept their feelings to themselves— in public. Between bids, bridge ladies discussed everything wrong with the Beemans, yet few exhibited interest in believing they were innocent until proven guilty. Expressing such an opinion could possibly be regarded as duplicity, and card-playing mavens expected their types to stick together in politics, gossip, and otherwise.

It wasn't until things blew up at the Beeman ranch did they see the situation for what it truly was.

\*\*\*\*

Amanda wasn't expecting him to speak to her—after weeks of barely saying a word? Not likely. No—conversation wasn't on her list of things to do, nor Randy's. So, when he walked through the kitchen door with a gorgeous bouquet of flowers and a box of her favorite chocolates, she wasn't only stunned—she didn't trust him for a minute.

It was the reaction Randy expected.

From his years as her husband, he knew his best approach needed to be believable. "For you," he commented unceremoniously as he laid the flowers on the kitchen table.

She eyed the bouquet. "For me? For what?"

Randy took a deep breath, then took a seat across from her. "I don't know . . . all I know is I'm tired of fighting. I guess I don't have the stomach for it anymore . . ."

Amanda didn't say anything, watching him carefully for his usual tells of lying. "Explain . . ."

How typical—ordering him to respond. "Well, when you think about it, we've been together for a hell of a long time. Longer than most . . ."

"So?"

He looked at her, refusing to let her get the best of him. "So—it just seems to me we should be pleased at the way things turned out instead of being at each other's throats all the time . . ."

"A lot's happened . . ."

"I know."

Amanda didn't say anything—for the first time, perhaps ever, she felt a connection with him. "We hurt each other, " she finally responded. "I'm not sure we can get over that . . ."

Her husband nodded, careful not to show emotion other

than stoicism. "Can I ask you a question?"

She nodded.

"Why did you decide to rescind your offer to deed me the five thousand acres?" He could have said more, but he was a firm believer in understatement. If he took the accusatory route, Amanda would have her Irish up before he could spit, and the conversation would head south, never to be retrieved. Clearly, accusation wasn't the right way to go about getting what he wanted.

She took her time extracting a Marlboro from its pack, flicking the lighter a few times before it ignited. The truth was she wasn't accustomed to such candor from her husband. But, as she took a hard look at him, she noticed something different—perhaps it was the same, stolid confidence he had when he testified for the second day at Harry's trial.

"Well? I promise I'm not going to blow my stack . . ."

She took a long, deliberate drag. "Because I want everything for myself . . ."

It was the first bit of truth that passed between them in years. "What about me?"

"What about you?"

"Does your desire to own this ranch by yourself include me, at all?"

She shook her head. "Not really—you can stay if you want, but I really think I'm better off by myself." Her eyes grew cold as she looked him in the eye. "You know I'm right."

That was it. Decades of self-degradation down the drain. "Do you want me gone?"

Another drag. "Not necessarily. That's up to you—but,

as homage to our years together, you're welcome to stay." Before he could speak, she continued. "In the guest room."

Randy sat back in his chair. *No great loss there*, he thought as he watched her every expression. "Then, it's settled . . ."

"It was settled a long time ago . . ."

# CHAPTER TWENTY-THREE

"What do you think about archaeology?" Colbie took off her reading glasses, then dove in to homemade apple pie, savoring the first bite. "Forget archaeology—all of these years together, and you never made this pie for me? What's up with that?"

Brian laughed as he plopped a huge scoop of ice cream on his. "Shall I take your questions in order?"

"If you wish . . ." She grinned, then reached for a slice of cheddar.

"Okay—archaeology first. What do I think about it?" He paused, mid-bite. "I have to confess I'm woefully ignorant when it comes to the subject."

Colbie nodded. "Me, too . . . what about the pie?"

"Evelyn took the time to teach me when you spent that afternoon interviewing Abbott . . ."

"Seriously?"

"Scouts' honor . . ."

"This is up there with the pie at Nettie's—we'll never have to go out for dessert again!" Colbie discovered the small diner while working Brian's case several years prior. A little hole in the wall, Nettie Calhoun made the best homemade pies in Seattle, locals preferring to keep it a best-kept secret. Nothing fancy—just good old-fashioned goodies.

Both enjoyed their pie for several minutes before the subject came up again. "So—I'm considering taking a new case, but, I want to know what you think . . ."

Brian swallowed his last bite, sat back, and patted his stomach. "Dang, that was good!" He paused. "What are the particulars?"

"About the case? Well, I don't know a whole lot yet—I'm scheduled to talk to the guy at the end of this week. He contacted me by email, but, from what I understand, he thinks there's a curse on one of his digs . . ."

"You're kidding!"

Colbie, too, swallowed her last bite, then took a sip of coffee. "Nope—maybe I misunderstood, but, according to him, a few of his best workers have disappeared, and he fears the worst."

"The worst . . . that could mean a lot of things. What does that have to do with a curse?"

"I'm not sure. But, I definitely got the impression from his rather cryptic email there are secrets . . ."

"Ahhh . . . secrets. Sounds intriguing."

"That's what he said—obviously, I have a bunch of questions for him when we talk on Friday. But, back to archaeology—does it interest you?"

Knowing Colbie as well as he did, Brian knew she was getting at something. "Yes—I find it interesting. Now, tell me—where's the purported archaeological dig . . ."

"Mexico."

Brian's eyebrows arched. "We're going to Mexico?"

\*\*\*\*

Rory Gallagher sat in front of a warming fire, a gin and tonic helping him wash away the challenges of the day—it had been a long time since he felt the peace and quiet of his small ranch. Usually, he spent most of his time in Gillette or Cheyenne, depending on his case load. But, whenever he could, he drove the three hundred miles or so to a tiny sliver of land in the northwest corner of the state.

On that particular trip? He had a lot of thinking to do—and, it all boiled down to ethics. It would be easy to let life ride—after all, his comfort zone seldom pushed the limit of its constraints. But, was staying within that zone the right thing to do? Probably not—although, it would be the easiest.

Two drinks in, he stared at the envelope in front of him on the rustic, handcrafted coffee table he made when he was twenty-two. Guided by his grandfather's hand, what started out as a project because he needed a table turned into a love for woodworking. Without compromising his western design aesthetic, his wife threw in a touch of glam, a testament to her need for something pretty to create the perfect marriage of style, taste, and comfort.

He stared at the envelope, thinking about its possible contents. Hattie Pearl made a big to-do about his never opening it and, in the event of her passing, he was to deliver it to the recipient—seal intact—any time after six months from the date of her death. He suspected, of course, it had to do with Amanda, but, then again, what didn't? After she cut him loose as the family attorney, it never occurred to her Hattie Pearl covered her bases long before she called it a day—permanently.

Call it intuition or knowing her granddaughter better than anyone—either way, the matriarch wasn't about to go out without a fight. In her gut, she knew Amanda was a self-serving bitch, and it became prudent to make certain—as power heir of the Circle B Ranch—her interests were top priority. So, when Amanda severed the legal relationship between Rory Gallagher and the Circle B, Gallagher continued to represent Hattie Pearl's separate, private interests—none of which were any of Amanda's beeswax. Amanda may have cut him loose, but that was superseded by a private contract between Hattie Pearl and him.

He made sure of that.

\*\*\*\*

*Why in the hell did I agree to this*, she wondered as they headed toward Cody. *I ought to have my friggin' head examined* . . . Prairie landscape turned to gentle hills as they headed west, the sun slinking lower in the sky. Five hours in the truck with Randy wasn't a picnic, and they barely spoke except for obligatory conversation. For some reason, he got it in his head they should go to Cody to rekindle their relationship. "Maybe see if we can restart," he said as he tried to convince her they needed a few days to themselves.

"How far?" Amanda didn't look at him, keeping her attention focused on the road.

"We'll be there in about forty-five minutes—just in time for dinner. I'm getting hungry . . ."

"When are you not hungry?" The second the words left her mouth she regretted them—sort of.

Just as she was about to say something snide, the truck coughed, then lurched to a choking stop. "What the hell?" Randy glanced at Amanda, then the dashboard. "I just had this damned thing serviced!" His voice cracked a little as he realized there weren't services for miles around.

Amanda crushed her cigarette into the ashtray. "This is great—just great! We're in the middle of stinkin' nowhere!" She glared at him, her anger already at a boil. "Try your cell," she ordered.

As much as Randy hated to do what he was told, he snatched the phone from his pocket, then tapped on the screen. After several moments, it faded to black. "Nothing.

No service . . ."

"Are you kidding me?" Amanda opened the passenger
door and grabbed her cigarettes, screaming at Randy as her
feet hit the ground. "You better think of something because
I'm not staying here overnight . . ."

Then, something snapped.

Randy watched as Amanda crossed in front of the truck,
glaring at him as she flipped him the finger. "Fix it, Randy!
Fix it!" Her voice rose to a shrill shriek—luckily, he could
barely hear her with his window rolled up all the way.

Calmly, he climbed out of the driver's seat, scanning the
horizon. In the distance was a stand of trees slowly losing
form as the sun offered its final rays. *Perfect*, he thought as
he opened the tailgate, grabbing his holster complete with a
.357 Magnum.

"What do you need that for?" Amanda walked up from
behind, watching as he buckled the holster around his waist.

"Jesus! You scared the crap out of me!"

"Well, answer me—why are you taking your weapon?"

Randy pointed toward the stand of trees. "See those? I'll
bet money there's a house over that rise . . ." He glanced at
her, then locked the shell of the truck. "I don't know about
you, but I'm not going anywhere without a weapon. Stay
here, if you want."

"Over my dead body I'm staying here!" Abruptly, she set
off for the shaded trees two or three hundred yards to the
west, then turned to her husband. "Well? Are you coming?"

"Yeah, yeah . . ."

\*\*\*\*

After Colbie spoke to her prospective client at the end of the week, she was no closer to making a decision about taking a new case. For the previous three days, she interviewed clients via video chat as well as phone, all hoping to snag her expertise to solve some sort of mystery. Being in demand was one of the perks of success, but, now that she had time to decompress? She wasn't sure if taking another case was in their best interest.

She had to admit, taking time off felt pretty darned good, and she completely understood why Brian was content to hang around the house. It was where they were building their lives together, and neither was sure anything needed to change.

"Well—what do we know? You spent quite a bit of time with him on the phone . . ."

Colbie sank into the overstuffed club chair by the window, filtered sunlight illuminating her already lustrous red hair. "Over an hour, I think—I gotta say, it sounds interesting!"

"It's in Mexico, for sure?"

She nodded, then sat back in the chair, closing her eyes. "Yep." She hesitated before continuing. "I don't know, Brian—I feel as if I should take on another case, but I'm not sure if I want to . . ."

Brian watched her, stunned, her comment a concern. "I've never heard you say anything like that. What's wrong?"

"There's nothing 'wrong,' really—I just wonder if

jumping into another case is the right thing to do. Don't forget, you said you're ready to take it easy for a while. Maybe it's time for me to do the same thing . . ."

"So, if you don't take any of these cases, what are you going to do? I know you well enough to know you're not particularly good at doing nothing . . ."

"That's the problem . . ." She was quiet for a moment. "Maybe I'll write a book . . ."

Brian watched a smile play on her lips as she opened her eyes. "Or, not . . ."

****

Six months to the day of Hattie Pearl's passing, Rory Gallagher stood in the check-in line at Cheyenne Regional Airport, considering himself lucky because he scored the last available direct-flight ticket to Seattle. Traveling anywhere wasn't his idea of having a good time, and he dreaded the trip ever since he decided to take care of business face-to-face. Although he was uncertain about the contents of Hattie Pearl's letter, since the end of the trial, he had the nagging feeling he should deliver her letter personally.

It wasn't an easy decision, and he wrestled with whether to give Colbie and Brian a heads up about his impending arrival. He quickly decided against it, however, for doing so would open a conversation for which he was ill prepared. Since he didn't have any idea of the letter's contents, there was no need for questions to which he had no answers.

As he awaited the call for his flight, his thoughts turned to the Beemans, as well as his disappointment in the knowledge Amanda or Randy—maybe both—would never serve a day for their part in the Beeman boys' murders. But, there was nothing he could do or say to change that sorry state of affairs—besides, he had no proof to shore up his suspicions, so what would be the point? As an attorney, he knew conjecture would serve only to ignite matters and, without a shred of evidence to convince prosecutors or a grand jury of their suspected guilt? Well, it wasn't nearly enough to go on.

By the time he was seated, the plane ready for takeoff, he could think of nothing else but his last conversation with the matriarch of the Circle B. She arrived at his office unannounced, accompanied by a woman whose name he couldn't remember. "Rory," she commanded, "We need to have a chat . . ."

And, chat they did.

Hattie Pearl demanded he craft another will—to supersede the one executed a month previous—removing Amanda Beeman as not only the sole heir of the Circle B, but an heir of any kind. The short and sweet of it?

Amanda was out.

# CHAPTER TWENTY-FOUR

The stand of trees was much farther than Randy anticipated, and Amanda did nothing but bitch, moan, and complain the entire way. Once the sun set, the air turned to an unsettling chill, ramping up her displeasure to the point Randy would have liked nothing better than to put a bullet through her head. But, based on the events of the previous months, the last thing he wanted was involvement with the Wyoming legal system.

As they reached the crest of a small ridge and stood amid barren cottonwoods, it was apparent Randy miscalculated.

"Where's the house, Randy? You said there was a house here . . ." Amanda's tone was accusatory and impatient, her face contorted in simmering anger.

Her husband didn't say anything as he scanned the area.

From his vantage point, he had a clear view in all directions, and it was obvious there was nothing for miles. "How the hell should I know?"

"You said . . ."

Well—that was it. Randy snapped. Maybe it was Amanda's incessant berating—or, perhaps it was something as simple as the sound of her grating, irritating voice.

Whatever. It didn't matter.

Calmly, he reached underneath the back of his untucked shirt, his palm gently closing over the pistol grips of a silenced Sig Sauer nine mil. He drew. Aimed. Fired. Just as Amanda whirled around to emasculate him a little more, the bullet met its mark with perfect precision between her eyes.

She dropped like rock.

Quickly, Randy again scanned as far as he could see in all directions. Obscured by trees, autumn shadows seemed to forgive his deed and, with a quick glance at his dead wife, he turned and headed back to the truck.

But, only after total darkness fell.

# CHAPTER TWENTY-FIVE

Colbie stared at the man standing on her front porch, not quite believing her eyes. "Mr. Gallagher?" She didn't open the door all the way as Brian took station behind her.

He nodded. "I know this must be quite a surprise . . ."

"Indeed, it is . . ." She held the door open. "Please, come in . . ."

She gestured toward a chair in the living room as Brian headed for the kitchen. "Can I get you something to drink," he called as he opened the fridge. "I'm afraid all we have is iced tea and orange juice . . ."

"I'm fine, thank you—I'll try not to take up too much of your time . . ."

Instantly, Colbie's intuitive mind exploded with visions of Hattie Pearl, Amanda, and Randy Beeman. "Of course, it's a pleasure to see you," she commented, "but, I can't help thinking you're not here for a social visit . . ."

Gallagher nodded as he sat. "I apologize for showing up unannounced—but, considering the circumstances over the last several months . . ." He reached into his briefcase, then handed Colbie the letter from Hattie Pearl. "I have no idea as to its contents . . ."

Colbie glanced at Brian, then gently took the envelope. "I don't think I understand . . ."

"Before she died, Hattie Pearl came to my office, requesting I draw a new will for her. At that time, she gave me this letter with specific instructions I wasn't to deliver it until six months after her passing."

"I still don't see what I have to do with it—I met Hattie Pearl once."

"Well, I don't know anything about that—but, assuming that's the case, you must have made one hell of an impression." He watched as Colbie slit the top of the envelope with a letter opener she kept on her desk. "Would you like some privacy?"

She shook her head. "No, thank you . . ." As she opened the letter, Colbie's intuitive mind flashed, the red-haired girl appearing instantly. She smiled, but didn't hold out her hand as before—it were as if she were content, somehow.

While Brian and Gallagher sat quietly, Colbie read Hattie Pearl's words written with an unsteady hand.

*Dear Colbie,*

*I imagine receiving this letter is quite a shock. Hopefully, after reading it, you'll understand why I had to keep everything* from you until at least six months after my passing. Colbie glanced at Brian, then continued reading.

*From the first time I met you, I knew you were a Beeman— all I had to do was take one look at you to know that. But, there was also something different—I felt the gift I have is also within you.*

*It's no secret Amanda and Randy expect to be the rightful heirs to my Circle B Ranch, but, it's not what I want. My life's work should be respected, and that's why I'm writing this letter. I hereby bequeath the Circle B Ranch located in Sundance, Wyoming, to you, Colbie Beeman Colleen. Of course, it's not your rightful name, but it's how I think of you.*

*As for Amanda and Randy, you probably know I died at their evil hands. It was my granddaughter's dream to inherit the Circle B, and she would do anything to get it, including murdering me and my husband. And, that's why I had Rory Gallagher execute a new Will and Testament, cutting Amanda from her expected inheritance. It's why I'm asking him to wait six months before handing this letter over to you. If Amanda and Randy are not being held accountable for what they did, by now, they believe Amanda will inherit it all.*

*This letter changes everything, as does my new will.*

*Please—take care of my Circle B Ranch. I wish we could have known each other.*

*Hattie Pearl Beeman*

Stunned, Colbie sat down as she finished the letter, flipping the stationery over to make certain there was nothing else, then placed the letter on the table. "You said you have no idea, Mr. Gallagher, what's in this letter . . ."

He nodded. "That's true—but, I can make an educated guess, especially since Hattie Pearl had me draft a new will. With Amanda—and, Randy—out of the picture, it doesn't take a genius to figure out the letter's contents . . ."

Brian focused on Colbie. "I must be thick, but I don't get it . . ."

Her expression changed as she realized the enormity of Hattie Pearl's letter. "She left me everything . . ."

"What? What do you mean, 'everything?'"

"The Circle B—she left the ranch to me!"

Not usually speechless, Brian suddenly found himself with nothing to say. In fact, no one said anything. Gallagher felt it wasn't his place to comment, and Brian was shocked out of his socks.

But, that wasn't all. Rory Gallagher again reached into his briefcase, extracting a legal-sized document. "This is a copy of Hattie Pearl's most recent Last Will and Testament." He handed it to Colbie. "You'll see," he continued, "you're named as the sole heir of the Circle B Ranch, effective immediately . . ."

Colbie flipped through three pages of specific last requests. "I can't believe this . . ."

"Well, it's true—you're the proud owner of the Circle B Ranch in Sundance, Wyoming!" Gallagher stood. "I'll be going—I know this is a lot to digest." He headed for the door, then turned to Colbie. "I also know Hattie Pearl suspected Amanda and Randy for her death, and I'll be contacting the authorities."

"Sheriff Dardon?"

Gallagher shook his head. "No—in fact, I think our local sheriff's going to hate his life within short order . . ."

Colbie opted not to pry,  knowing he wouldn't divulge any information, anyway. "I understand . . ."

With that, Rory Gallagher stepped into a settling fog, Colbie watching him round the sidewalk until he disappeared. Moments later, a taxicab passed her house, its passenger looking straight ahead.

"I don't know about you, but I feel as though I've been hit by a tank!" Brian held out his hand. "Do you mind if I read the letter?"

"No . . ."

Neither said a word until he placed the letter on the end table. "Your life just changed . . ."

# CHAPTER TWENTY-SIX

Months passed. Evelyn and Harry couldn't believe the news when Colbie told them about her inheritance, everyone agreeing to keep things hush-hush for a while. Evelyn commented she hadn't seen 'hide nor hair' of Amanda over the past months, and she only saw Randy once—maybe twice.

"I don't know, Colbie—something doesn't feel right over there. Maybe you should check on the ranch—since you're the new owner, I mean . . ."

"Maybe I should—I have the same feeling. Still, if something happened to Amanda, surely we would have heard by now. When was the last time you saw her?"

Evelyn thought for a moment. "Last November—toward the end of the month. I remember because she and Randy flew past me in their truck just as I was turning into our lane."

"Six months ago?"

"I think so—I remember it was November for sure because we were coming back from shopping in Gillette for Thanksgiving."

Colbie tried to tune into Amanda Beeman as she listened to her aunt, but her frequencies felt blocked. "I agree with you, Aunt Evelyn—something doesn't feel right . . ."

"Why do you think that? Are you seeing something?"

"No, not really—but, when I tune in on Amanda, I feel nothing, but cold. Maybe it's nothing . . ." She paused, closing her eyes. "Then, again . . ."

"By 'cold' you mean she's dead?"

"I'm not sure—maybe . . ."

"Good heavens! Who killed her? Can you tell?"

Colbie didn't respond for a moment. "I don't know—but, all I feel is evil . . ."

"Holy shit!" Evelyn's voice dropped to a whisper. "What are you going to do?"

"There's nothing I can do . . ."

"But, your feelings might be important! Why won't you talk to the authorities about them?"

Colbie was quiet, then answered her aunt's question in an even, measured tone. "Because it's all coming to an end."

****

There's nothing quite like a spring thaw to get the blood pumping. Ranchers were busy with newborns, paying particular attention to fickle weather. With little effort by Mother Nature, young calves were at risk not only from predators, but also from rogue snowstorms waiting to take lives.

It was a time of year most ranchers welcomed—except Randy. Ever since Harry's acquittal, workers were hard to find, especially those who were seasonal. A good ranch hand is the backbone of any ranch operation and, as the Circle B's employee roster plummeted, he had to pitch in just to keep things running. It was a situation he didn't like, but, even so, he spent zero time considering the reasons for his current problems.

Everyone, of course, knew he was in trouble, and he seldom showed his face in town, always electing to send one of the few ranch hands he had left to run errands. Surely, townsfolk were talking about him—how could they not? Still, he seldom thought about them or their gossip—or, he simply didn't care. Although his attitude seemed cavalier to some, Randy considered himself safer by not subjecting himself to possible spontaneous conversation at the grocery store, or Stubbins Barbershop.

He would just . . . rather not.

****

Against her attorney's and Rory Gallagher's advice, Colbie didn't want anyone to know she was the sole heir of the Circle B—up until recently, ranch operations continued to produce a profit. During the last few months, however, profit and loss statements indicated a sharp decline, and she considered whether she should intercede. Doing so would mean a trip back to Wyoming—but, unlike her first visit, she wasn't obligated to stay.

"What do you think—should I go?"

Brian didn't answer for a moment as he concentrated on spreading strawberry jam on his toast. When it was covered from side-to-side, he grinned at Colbie, holding up the slice for her approval. "Perfect!"

She returned the smile. "Very nice. Now, what about my question—should we go to Wyoming?"

"Well—I think you need to find out why profits are declining, and you probably can't do that efficiently from here. If it were me, I'd want to see everything in person . . ."

Colbie's forehead creased slightly as she thought about it. "Maybe you're right—you game?"

"Yep! You don't think I'm going to let you go alone, do you?"

"I was hoping you'd say that!"

****

Little changed in Sundance since the last time they were there. As they drove toward Harry and Evelyn's, Colbie noticed wildflowers in the pastures waving slightly in the ever-present prairie breeze. *It really is beautiful here,* she thought as miles passed.

"So—Harry and Evelyn's place first?" Brian glanced at her as he turned onto the country road leading to both ranches.

"I don't think so—I'd like to drop in on Randy without his having any idea we're in town. If we wait, someone might get wind of us, and I don't want anyone telling Randy we're sniffing around . . ."

"You make it sound so clandestine—you own the property, after all! You have the right to 'sniff around!'"

"True—but, you know what I mean. If we arrive unannounced, we'll see things as they truly are. Not only what he wants us to see . . ."

"Do you think he has any idea you own the property?"

"No—he would have gone ballistic by now."

Both were quiet, thinking about Randy's possible reactions when they showed up without notice. "As we get closer," Colbie finally commented, "my intuition is really starting to act up." She paused. "Evelyn's right—something is very wrong here . . ."

****

The Circle B was exactly as she remembered it, although there didn't seem to be the usual hum of activity. When they arrived, Randy was nowhere to be found until one of the hands rounded him up stringing fence at the southwest corner of the ranch. When advised he had a visitor, he threw his gloves on the ground, disgusted someone had the audacity to show up unannounced.

He was really disgusted when he saw Colbie.

Reining in his immediate irritation, he extended a hand to both. "What brings you back to these parts?"

Colbie noticed his hands were clammy, as well as the few beads of sweat collecting on his brow—the warm weather? Or, was Randy nervous because they stood in front of him? That wasn't all—his looks changed considerably from a well-dressed man to a disheveled cowboy. Was he purposely avoiding his personal hygiene? Or, was his new look due to something more . . . sinister.

She accepted his handshake. "It's been a long time, that's for sure . . ."

As if reading her mind, he snatched a bandanna from his back pocket, swiping it across his forehead. "What can I do for you folks?"

Suddenly, they were about to have the conversation Colbie tried to avoid for so many months. From that moment forward, everything would change—not only for Randy, but for Brian and her, as well. "Is there a place where we can talk?"

Randy eyed her, his eyes narrowing. "We can talk right here, although I can't imagine what we could possibly have to talk about . . ."

"How about if we go inside? It's cooler . . ."

He didn't say anything as he stroked his scraggly, salt-and-pepper beard. Colbie noticed his shoulders sag slightly, and she knew he made his decision. "Follow me . . ."

Five minutes later, they were seated at a large farm table in the kitchen. "I'm sorry I don't have anything to offer you—I wasn't expecting company . . ."

Colbie took the lead. "No problem." She hesitated a moment. "Is Amanda here? She's going to want to be a part of our conversation . . ."

Randy didn't miss a beat. "She isn't here . . ." No explanation of where she was, or when she might return.

"Do you expect her soon?"

"Nope—now, why are you here? Let's get on with it . . ."

For the following thirty minutes, Colbie defended her position as the sole owner of the Circle B, bolstered by proper court documents, signed by Hattie Pearl Beeman. "There's no refuting it, Randy," she commented as she watched his anger nearly erupt. "What we have to do now is figure out what to do with the ranch—that's why I thought it would be a good idea for Amanda to be here."

In the momentary silence, Colbie's intuitive mind jumped to life, showing her a large field with a stand of trees in the distance. What it meant, Colbie didn't know, but she had no doubt it related to Amanda. "I think both of us know I'm going to make a change in operations due to declining profits over the last several months . . ."

Then, without warning, Colbie changed the course of the conversation. "Where is she, Randy?"

"Where's who?"

Colbie focused her full attention on him. "Amanda."

Randy's eyes met hers, his resolve evident. "She's not here—I told you that!"

Brian didn't say anything. He recognized the tells, and Colbie was functioning on a different level, although no one would know it to look at her. Something—or, someone—was guiding her in the direction she needed to go.

Suddenly, she stood up, motioning to Brian it was time to leave. "I know you have a lot to think about—I'll touch base with you in the morning . We can resume our conversation then . . ."

With that, they headed to their SUV, never looking back. Colbie could feel Randy watching them go, knowing she touched a nerve when she asked about Amanda.

"Amanda's dead . . ." She looked straight ahead as they followed the ranch lane to the main road.

"You're positive?"

"No question . . ."

Brian glanced at her. "So . . . now what?"

"Let's head to Gillette . . ."

\*\*\*\*

Rory Gallagher ushered them into his office, closing the door. "Now, then—what's so important?"

Colbie filled him in on her conversation with Randy, as well as her visions as she spoke to him about her being the new owner of the Circle B. She had no idea on which side of the fence Gallagher would fall when it came to believing in her abilities, but, she was convinced he would know how to approach her belief of Amanda's death. "And," she concluded, "not by natural causes . . ."

Gallagher tapped his desk with the end of a pencil. "And, you think Randy killed her . . ."

She nodded. "I'm certain of it. But, I don't know this area—in my vision, I saw a large field with a bunch of trees in the distance, but that's it. All I can tell you is I have a very strong, gut feeling . . ."

"A large field with trees in the distance doesn't exactly narrow down the location . . ."

"I know—it's definitely a needle in a haystack."

"That's it?"

"Well—I'm not sure why I saw this because it doesn't make any sense, but, as I was thinking about Amanda, I had a vision of my cousin Marsha's son . . ."

"How old is he?"

"In his early twenties, I think . . ."

"Name?"

"Cody—Cody Franklin."

Gallagher sat up a little straighter. "Cody? Are you sure?"

Colbie nodded. "Oh, yes—I've seen pictures of him many times, although I haven't met him in person."

The attorney didn't say anything as he attempted to rationalize what Colbie was telling him. Since she wasn't from the area, there wasn't much reason for her to know any of the towns or outlying areas in the state. But, Cody?

The implications were obvious.

"Then, I believe you should start your search in the northwest part of the state—in Cody, Wyoming."

She glanced at Brian, then focused again on Gallagher. "That makes perfect sense!"

"How far is it from here?" Brian's intuitive senses were kicking in, as well, and he had the feeling once they made their way to Cody, the mystery of Amanda's disappearance would be in the books.

"Somewhere between four and five hours—closer to five if you're doggin' it . . ."

Colbie stood, extending her hand across the desk. "Thank you, Rory—I know it was a lot to lay on you. We'll be in touch . . ."

Minutes later?

They were on their way.

\*\*\*\*

"Cody's about twenty-five miles from here . . ."

Brian scanned the road in front of them. "Where did it say that?"

"Back there—the sign was tiny, and handmade . . ."

"Well, from what you said about your vision, I don't think we're looking for anything in Cody—the actual town, I mean. We're probably better off sticking to the outskirts . . ."

"Agreed—let's slow down a little in case I can get something . . ."

For several hours they drove every country road outside of Cody, and then again to make sure they didn't miss anything. But, just before they were about to call it a day, Colbie sat straight up in her seat. "Right here!"

Brian checked his rear view mirror as he slowed to a stop, then scanned the entire area. "There's no one around here for miles," he commented as Colbie hopped out.

She stood by the side of the SUV, looking across a blossoming, spring prairie, at a stand of massive trees in the distance.

Brian joined her. "This is it?"

She nodded. "I think so—but, it looks very different than it did in my vision. The trees were bare, and it looked cold."

"Maybe Randy offed her in the winter . . ."

"I think you're right . . ."

"Well—let's go. It won't be long before the sun starts going down . . ."

It only took fifteen minutes until they stood under blooming trees, their wispy cotton barely hanging on as they awaited a gentle breeze to carry them. Nothing seemed out of place. Nothing revealed unspeakable violence.

Nothing betrayed Randy Howard Beeman.

That's until Brian tripped over something barely sticking out of the ground. As he righted himself, he noticed what he thought was a stick, but, upon closer inspection, he recognized it as part of a rib. "Hey! Check this out!"

He didn't touch it, but stood staring as Colbie joined him. Instantly, she knew—she felt—the magnitude of what Brian found.

"It could be anything, you know—it could belong to an animal." Brian stepped back gently in case there were more.

Colbie nodded. "It could . . . but, I don't think so. We need to contact the authorities immediately . . ."

# CHAPTER TWENTY-SEVEN

By the end of the week, there was no question the remains found on that lonely, country road were Amanda Beeman's. When the coroner announced the cause of death a homicide, there wasn't a soul in the county who didn't suspect her dutiful husband.

Shortly thereafter, Sheriff Dardon found Randy swinging from a rafter in the main barn. Naturally, folks yapped about it, many not trusting the good sheriff as far as they could throw him—something about blackmail, but no one could prove a thing. So, when he was the one to find Randy dangling from the rafter as blue as an iceberg, consensus was he had something to do with it, and his fate would be sealed during the next election.

To most of Sundance, it was unfortunate Amanda and Randy would never stand trial for the murders of her two boys. Rumor had it an arrest was in the making, but no one could figure out why the sheriff was dragging his feet. Maybe that's why he was at the Circle B the morning he found Randy—at least, that's what he said.

For the rest of the month, Colbie scrambled to find a temporary ranch manager, conducting interviews before they were to head back to Seattle. Finding the right person was more difficult than anticipated, but she decided on a skilled young man who was bright, motivated, and hungry for a better life.

Finally, it was time go home.

\*\*\*\*

"Now that we're neighbors," Evelyn commented as she watched baggage being loaded onto Colbie's and Brian's plane, "when do you think you'll be back?"

"I have no idea! I need to get back to work, that's for sure!"

"Any irons in the fire?"

"A few—I'm close to making a decision as to which case

I'll take next . . ."

"Give me a clue?"

Colbie laughed. "Okay—just one. Think about . . . archaeology!"

Evelyn's eyebrows shot up, but, before she could open her mouth to respond, the young man at the gate counter announced it was time to board. Once again, Colbie and Brian said their goodbyes, Evelyn tearing up, knowing she wouldn't see her niece again for quite a while—she could feel it. She also realized there really wasn't a life for them in Wyoming. "I know you'll never live here, but our wonderful state is a great place to visit. Don't be strangers!"

With that, she hugged them and was out the door.

Watching her go, Colbie felt a tiny pang of sorrow, thinking of all she learned about her family. When she first arrived in Wyoming—when Harry was in trouble— she barely knew anything about her ancestors. When she left? She had the real story about Hedwin Moore and his lineage—and, although stories of abuse and murder weren't what she expected or wanted to know about her family, it was something never to change. Privately, she vowed to keep learning about them—she still had questions.

"Ready?" She looked up at Brian, a tear slipping down her cheek.

He pretended not to notice. "Yep—ready when you are!"

PROFESSIONAL ACKNOWLEDGMENTS


**CHRYSALIS PUBLISHING AUTHOR SERVICES**
L.A. O'NEIL, Editor
chrysalispub@gmail.com
www.chrysalis-pub@gmail.com


**COVER DESIGN**

WYATT ILSLEY, Designer
hmdesign89@gmail.com
www.Highmountaindesign.com

Made in the USA
Middletown, DE
27 April 2018